Rick turned to look at the girl and saw her wide-eyed expression of horror.

"Sara, what is it?"

"He's come back," she whimpered. She raised an arm so slender it reminded him of photos he had seen of death camp survivors, and pointed to something behind him. "I remember now. He comes back here."

Rick looked at her, puzzled. "What are you talking about? Who comes back?"

Sara suddenly shrieked and buried her face in her hands, cringing against the stones of the fireplace. A latch rattled behind him and Rick whirled to see the French doors flung open. A snow-encrusted figure stood swaying in the open doorway, reflections of the dim kerosene lantern he carried glittering like burning coals in his bloodshot eyes. Rick recognized the cruel face instantly, a face he had last seen on the front page of a yellowing newspaper on the study's cluttered desk.

"Oh God!" Rick moaned as Harold Raynor's stony gaze settled upon the trembling girl by the fireplace.

Darkling

A NOVEL BY

MICHAEL
O'ROURKE

HarperPaperbacks
A Division of HarperCollinsPublishers

This is a work of fiction. The characters, incidents, and
dialogues are products of the author's imagination and
are not to be construed as real. Any resemblance to actual
events or persons, living or dead, is entirely coincidental.

HarperPaperbacks   *A Division of* HarperCollins*Publishers*
10 East 53rd Street, New York, N.Y. 10022

Cover illustration by Kirk Reinert

First printing: January 1994

Printed in the United States of America

HarperPaperbacks and colophon are trademarks of
HarperCollins*Publishers*

❖ 10 9 8 7 6 5 4 3 2 1

*To Sally and Betty and Dorothy
with love and appreciation*

Burn the great sphere thou mov'st in;
darkling stand
The varying shore o' the world.
                    —William Shakespeare

In visions of the dark night
I have dreamed of joy departed—
But a waking dream of life and light
Hath left me broken-hearted.

Ah! what is not a dream by day
To him whose eyes are cast
On things around him with a ray
Turned back upon the past?

That holy dream—that holy dream
While all the world were chiding,
Hath cheered me as a lovely beam
A lonely spirit guiding.
                    —Edgar Allan Poe

CANTO PURGATORIUM
(song for lost souls)

Ye shall walk the best loved corridors of the life ye last lived, seeing and hearing all the fleshly pleasures ye most desire, yet feeling and touching naught but the pain of thy loss.

Living souls may not look upon thee that their pity may assuage thy suffering, but only that thy brightest or basest lights may serve to free thee from these earthly wanderings, hence to pursue thine own eternal destiny.

Thou mayest not consort with thine fellow spirits lest they give solace from thy loneliness, thus distracting thee from the realization of thine own destiny.

Thy wanderings shall continue until thou hast shown thyself worthy of breathing the spirit of renewed life or been finally judged and found unworthy of salvation.

Thou shalt not consort with witches and demons and thou art charged with interceding against all such vile creatures as seek to contaminate the living.

—The Coptic Rituals: Conditional Damnation

Prologue

**Dubrovnik, Yugoslavia,
March 1992**

T H E horror show.

Rick Masterson stood on the steps of the four-teenth-century cathedral in the center of the besieged Croatian city, grinning. He scanned the wintry Adriatic sky for signs of more approaching aircraft, flinching involuntarily as a rattle of small-arms fire echoed from a nearby street. A flock of startled gray pigeons exploded into the air and wheeled above the plaza fronting the ancient church as a group of old women in black shawls and broken shoes, their empty net shopping bags flapping behind them like deflated party balloons, dashed toward the shelter of thick stone walls. He still couldn't believe his luck. An honest-to-God European war and he was here covering it.

Masterson raised the sleeve of his slate-colored

Eddie Bauer parka and glanced at the no-nonsense stainless Rolex on his wrist. It was nearly 3:30 in the afternoon. He cursed silently, mentally subtracting five hours from the local time: 10:30 in the morning in New York. His on-the-scene stand-up from the besieged city would have to be uplinked to the satellite within the next hour in order to make the noon broadcasts on the East Coast, and his camera crew was nowhere to be seen.

Digging into a side pocket of the parka, he extracted a small notebook and flipped it open to the page on which he had scribbled the location where Jimmy had said he was to meet the transmitter-equipped Range Rover he was sharing with the British news team. The note read, *old cathedral, west end—good shell damage.* Looking up at the undamaged facade of the church, he realized he must be at the wrong end of the sprawling structure. "Shit," he exclaimed, hurrying down the worn stone steps and heading toward a narrow side street he hoped would lead him directly to the opposite end of the locked cathedral.

Masterson walked briskly along the front of the church, a handsome dark-haired man in his midthirties, mumbling aloud to himself as he reviewed the opening lines of his report on the carnage being inflicted on the helpless civilians of the historic coastal city. Ships of the old Yugoslav navy had been indiscriminately shelling Dubrovnik for two days now. Since he had arrived aboard an Italian coaster early this morning, Masterson had visited a bombed-out maternity hospital, watched a phalanx of government tanks crush a crudely constructed barricade of shiny new Toyotas, and interviewed a weeping pensioner cradling the bodies of two precious goats that had been machine-gunned by government soldiers.

"What a fucking world," the BBC cameraman had remarked to Rick, stopping to press two five-pound notes into the old man's hand.

"Yeah," Rick had replied, shoving his own cameraman into position for a close-up shot of the pensioner's tear-streaked face. "Good old Freddy Krueger's got nothing on us news hounds, huh?"

"What?" The Brit's shocked expression was genuine. "What on earth are you talking about?"

"The horror show," Rick had said, pushing his cameraman's head aside to peer through the eyepiece, then tilting the lens up ever so slightly in order to include the smoldering remains of a bombed-out cottage in the background. He'd stepped back to let the camera guy get the shot and turned to the Brit with a sardonic grin. "Let's face it, we're all in the same business, old Freddy and you and me. Only difference is, our stuff's better than Freddy's 'cause it's real."

"Bit of a cynic, aren't you?" The Englishman had shot him a self-righteous look and hustled his crew down the street to a spot where there were rumored to be some bodies left over from the previous night's fighting.

"Yeah, sure. See ya later, asshole," Rick had called. He'd leaned over the old man with the dead goats and stuck a crisp new fifty in the tattered pocket of his shirt. "Here ya go, Pop. Buy yourself a new flock."

The horror show.

Rule one, never let it get to you.

* * *

Approaching the buttressed corner of the massive cathedral building, Rick looked up, surprised to see a number of other people heading for the same narrow side street. A tall blond girl with the leggy good looks of a fashion model swept past on high heels, her bright yellow rain slicker flapping around a Delta Airlines shoulder bag. "Pardon me, miss," he called. "Do you happen to speak English?"

She slowed but kept on walking, turning to look at him through eyes of an amazing blue shade. "Yes, a little bit." She smiled.

"Great." He pointed to the side street, noting that the crowd funneling into it from the plaza was composed mostly of young people. "Can I get to the west entrance of the cathedral down that way?"

She nodded. "It's just at the other end of the street, past the bus station. I can show you, if you wish."

"Thank you," he said, falling in beside her.

"You are an American journalist?"

Rick laughed. "Does it show that much?"

She nodded, pointing to his shoes. "I'm afraid the Nikes give you away. Very few Europeans would wear such shoes, fewer still of my people." A sly smile played at the corners of her full lips. "Also," she added, "our tourist trade has fallen off sharply in recent days, and you don't look Japanese anyway."

"Touché!" Rick smiled, turning on the charm that had gotten him into, and out of, a dozen international trouble spots, as well as any number of bedrooms. "Are all the beautiful young ladies of Dubrovnik so perceptive?"

"I wouldn't know about the others," she replied. "But I have taken a few courses at the university. Fashion design and marketing."

"Aha, then you must be one of those modern women I've heard so much about!" he teased. He was beginning to enjoy this, mentally working himself up to asking her to dinner—if there was still a place to have dinner here. Take it easy, he told himself. Don't scare her off.

They were almost at the end of the heavy stone wall that fronted the cathedral. The noisy throng of young people hurrying ahead of them was turning at the corner and disappearing down the narrow side street. "This crowd really surprises me," he said, pointing with his chin. "Where's everybody going?"

She shrugged prettily. "The bus station. The university has suspended classes until the war . . ." Her face fell and she glanced in the direction of the sea, where the gunboats that had been shelling the city still lay offshore. "People of my age have never known a war. No one is exactly sure what to do, so we go back to our homes."

Rick started to reply, casually taking her elbow to guide her around the corner, glancing at her face to watch her reaction to his touch. "Yes," he agreed solemnly, "the war is a terrible thing, but perhaps it won't last too—"

BLAM!!!

The flat, sharp concussion of high explosives down the narrow street blew a hot tornado of smoke and fire filled with flying debris a scant ten inches before their faces. Sheets of metal, scythes of glass, and lengths of splintered wood sliced through the crowd of young people just ahead of them.

Masterson and the girl stood frozen at the very end of the heavy stone wall. Another foot, he thought. Another fucking foot. A boy in a red ski jacket turned soundlessly to stare at them from the street, a glittering foot-long dagger of glass plate protruding from the center of his chest. The boy fell to the ground in a rapidly spreading pool of blood. Other people, dozens of them, were lying on the cobbles a hundred feet out from the entrance to the street, bright piles of rags upon the bloody stones.

Rick's mind raced as the sound of the explosion echoed off the walls of the buildings. Not artillery, he reasoned. You hear artillery coming. Not aerial ordnance either. Same reason; you always hear the bastards coming. He was still clutching the girl's arm, unconsciously tightening his grip on her. He looked up to see her tugging desperately at his hand. Trying to pull herself free.

"No!" he exclaimed as she tore loose and stumbled forward into the street. She stopped for a moment, looking at something beyond the range of his vision. A siren sounded somewhere in the distance and the moans and screams of the dying filled the air.

The girl looked back at him, her beautiful features contorted into a mask of agony. "Come, we must help them, please." Then she ran.

"No!" He screamed it this time, his voice drowned by the clanging of alarms and the shrieks of the wounded. He ran after her, following her into the mind-numbing carnage of the narrow street and feeling his feet splashing through warm liquid. He looked down to see the blood. Blood running inches deep in the gutters.

He caught up to her halfway down the block, jerking her cruelly away from the writhing form of a legless teenager on the sidewalk. "Look, it was a bomb," he yelled, pointing to the ruptured remains of the flaming bus angled across the street ahead. "A terrorist bomb."

She stared at him, not comprehending his combat journalist's sense of logic, the logic of one who had seen this particular aspect of the horror show before, in other times and other places.

"It's an old terrorist trick," he shouted, dragging her back toward the relative safety of a doorway he had spotted deeply etched into the stone wall at the side of the cathedral. "They call it the old one-two."

Firemen were flooding into the street now. Ambulances clanging to a stop, their medics running out to lean over the nearest casualties. Uninjured people from nearby streets were flowing into the horrible space, too, perhaps to help, or maybe just to gawk at the broken bodies. You never knew with the horror show.

He was hoarse from screaming. "The old one-two," he croaked, trying to explain, feeling the danger like an onrushing freight train in a bad dream. "First they set off a blast to create casualties, then they attack those who come to help. We've got to move now."

She gave him a look reserved for madmen and coldhearted bastards. A child was crying beside a headless corpse at their feet.

He jerked her along anyway, hauling her onto the curb and pushing her roughly ahead of him toward the shelter of the doorway, gauging the distance with the practiced eye of one long used to diving for cover. The portal was deep, an arched entrance that probably penetrated ten or twelve feet into the heavy walls, terminating in a sturdy side door reinforced with bands of iron.

Perfect cover.

They had almost reached the refuge of the door-way when a figure dressed in faded fatigues under a ripped sweater stepped from the deep shadows beneath its arch.

The man wore a mindless sneer beneath a drooping mustache, his hard black eyes glittering in the reflected light of the burning bus. He stared at them for a long moment, then did something with his hands, a mere flick of his hairy wrist, and disappeared again, swallowed up in the shadows as though he'd never been.

Rick Masterson heard the unmistakable metallic whang of the handle flying from the phosphorous grenade. He watched transfixed as the heavy, black-banded ovoid of olive-drab steel hit the curb with a dull thump, splashing to a stop in a pool of blood.

The world lit up in a tremendous burst of white light that silhouetted the girl's perfect body before him. He felt hot metal driving through his exposed knee and shoulder, cocked his head in slow surprise, realizing that he had heard nothing. The one that gets you, he thought dully. The one you never hear . . .

A soft wind began to blow at his back and he turned to look at the silent street, the bodies of the newly dead and the even more recently dead than that, all still illuminated in the bright, bright light. All moving now, getting up, brushing them-selves off, looking around.

The street still ran with their blood, the lifeless heaps of rags that had been their bodies still lay where they had fallen. But the figures rising from the pavement seemed untouched. Rick Masterson struggled to understand what was happening. The girl in the yellow slicker stepped away from him, adjusting her Delta Airlines bag on her shoulder and reaching for his hand. He let the broken lump of flesh that had been her body fall to his feet and reached out for the glowing image before him. Their hands touched and her smile faded. She jerked her hand away as though she had been burned.

"You are a real bastard, aren't you?" she asked in a curiously conversational tone.

He nodded dumbly, knowing that it was true.

She hesitated, then leaned over and quickly pecked him on the cheek. The light was beginning to fade and something dark and cold was descending. "Stay here," she said. "You've still got time."

"Wait!" he called as she turned and clicked away down the street on her high heels. "Don't go."

Her yellow slicker glistened in the waning light as she disappeared with the others into a rising column of white smoke. Rick turned around, confused. Something else was moving in the doorway. Something he dreaded, but had to see all the same. He squinted, trying to see into the black shadows of the tunnel. The dreadful thing stepped forward. Blood red eyes glowed in the inky darkness.

Rick Masterson shrieked in terror as the horrible presence reached for him.

CHAPTER 1

Spirit Lake

DEAD.

Sara stood in the deepening shadows that filled the study of her father's lodge, staring at the faded clippings on the desk. A chill autumn wind swept in through the broken pane of glass nearest the latch on the dirt-streaked French doors, swirling a cloud of brown leaves about her naked ankles. The heads of a dozen animals slain long ago in Harold Raynor's never-ending quest for trophies gazed down from their places above the massive rough-hewn mantelpiece, their glittering taxidermist's eyes reflecting the gray light of the waning afternoon.

The cold breeze riffled the yellowing pages of the open scrapbook, presenting a fast-forward vignette of the life and times of Harold Raynor; hunter of big game, destroyer of honest men, father of Sara. The collage of flapping pages reminded her of a sequence in a film she'd once seen, the sheets of a calendar blowing away to denote the passage of months and years, and she laughed at the absurdity of it.

Dead.

It was incomprehensible.

The sharp breeze fell away as suddenly as it had sprung up, leaving the meticulously pasted scrapbook open to a folded page from *The San Francisco Examiner*. The hard, cold eyes of her father stared out at her from beneath a thick line of type. FINANCIAL LEADERS MOURN LOSS OF EXCHANGE FOUNDER. Sara closed her eyes, trying to imagine the half-dozen cruel men who had once filled this room with whiskey and cigar smoke mourning the loss of Harold Raynor. Failed. No one had mourned Harold Raynor's passing, least of all his colleagues. She laughed again, a small, tight sound that echoed hollowly across the empty room. Correction: least of all his beloved daughter.

She turned away from the desk, averting her eyes from the faded photo of herself taken on the lake some long-ago summer, and looked at the teenagers.

They were stretched before the hearth now, sleeping in each other's arms beneath the patterned Navajo blanket she had bought from the dealer in Tucson the year she left the university. Beside them lay a small pile of pilfered objects; a few pieces of the everyday silver and two small ornamental bronzes in the style of Frederic Remington, which, she supposed, they considered valuable. She stepped closer to them, smiling at their innocence and wondering if they knew that the blanket, on which they had been loudly and enthusiastically fucking when she had entered the room, was worth ten times the total of all the other "valuables" they had so industriously collected.

The boy stirred in his sleep, one outstretched arm knocking over the row of empty beer cans he had carefully lined up on the stones. His eyes opened and he squinted into the deepening shadows where Sara now stood, as though he were suddenly aware that he was being watched. The girl snuggled closer to him, whimpering softly from somewhere within the thick tangle of golden hair spread on the blanket, and his darkly lashed eyelids fell closed again as he moved closer to her. She grunted pleasurably and pushed her buttocks back against him and Sara felt a sharp pang of remorse. She drifted closer, gazing upon the suggestive outline of their touching hips beneath the blanket.

Dead.

Never to be enfolded in the hot, urgent press of a sleeping lover's embrace again . . . Fucking dead.

The sun was almost down, the last feeble glimmerings of daylight tinging the tops of the approaching cloud bank a delicate shade of pink.

Sara stood on the dock in her thin nightdress, noticing how the planks beneath her feet had taken on the silvery patina of age, and wondering if they would still support the full weight of a grown man.

The dock held many pleasant memories for her. Summer picnics with the girls from St. Claire's, music from her portable radio thumping out across the smooth blue surface of the lake. The powerful Chris-Craft runabout bobbing at its mooring, beads of moisture from the brightly colored water skis and damp coils of manila hemp glittering like crystals on its waxed mahogany decks.

In the summer, the boys from the Marina, gangly teenage bodies tanned all golden beneath shocks of sun-bleached hair, would cruise by in their sleek outboards to joke with the girls, inviting them to ski, or to come to forbidden beach parties on the island at the far end of the lake. Sara had stayed out all night on the island only once—the time her father had been unexpectedly called away.

She closed her eyes, summoning up the memory of that August night in her seventeenth year: the boy's name had been Ted, the son of wealthy parents; wealthy enough anyway to be summering at the Marina, the exclusive collection of rustic bungalows dotting the shore at the southern end of the lake.

Originally built by her father for his own convenience in meeting with executives of his various boards during the hot months, the "bungalows" were actually spacious, fully equipped residences, each featuring, among other amenities, its own private dock and servants' quarters. Although modestly appointed in comparison to the Lodge, as her father's sprawling lakefront house was known, the bungalows were nonetheless luxurious digs by any standard.

Sara could not remember when the bungalows had first been made available for lease to select families anxious to report back to influential friends in the banks and exchanges that they'd vacationed "up at Harold Raynor's place in the Sierras," as if the fact that her father's agents permitted them temporarily to occupy space on his private lake in exchange for outrageous rental fees somehow bespoke his personal approval of them. She knew from friends at school that the half-dozen yearly leases were jealously contested among the rich and powerful from that time forward, and she had even heard rumors of bitter lawsuits over the rights of families to pass their seniority on the long waiting list to their heirs.

Ted, the boy she had gone to the island with, had been sweet and handsome. A junior at Princeton, and nearly two years older than she, he had arrived at the dock helming his father's lovingly restored Lightning, a sleek classic racing sailboat fitted out with green canvas flotation cushions of the softest foam.

Of course, he hadn't had the slightest idea who she was—the result of a game she frequently played on holidays with Tammy and Sue, her best friends and constant companions, both of whom resembled her somewhat in terms of general size and complexion. All through school, the two of them would draw lots at the end of each term to see who would spend the summer playing Sara, a privilege that included license to be as rude and snotty as they wished to anyone on the lake or in the small mining town at the foot of the mountain, as well as the use of her credit cards.

Sara had learned the hard way that the sons of prominent families wanted no part of Harold Raynor's daughter, except perhaps in the capacity of escorts to some well-chaperoned, boring cotillion or deb ball. At any rate, Ted hadn't known who she was. His playful invitation to the pretty blond girl he'd seen splashing her feet in the water at the end of old Raynor's dock had begun as a moonlight sail and picnic and, to her everlasting surprise, had ended with the two of them deliciously undressing each other by the light of a bonfire on the secluded island.

That night Sara had played Sue Harris, the daughter of a Detroit mill foreman, who was attending St. Claire's on a scholarship and who had had the good fortune to become friends with Sara Raynor, daughter of the third richest man in North America.

Unlike many of the boys Sara had dated under similar guises, Ted Steele had not tried to impress her with his own family's wealth and had exhibited none of the rich-kid pretensions to which she had grown accustomed when impersonating Sue or Tammy. His complete lack of an "attitude" combined with the earnest way he had gazed out over the dark waters as he told her of his secret ambition to find a way of avoiding a dull apprenticeship in the family business and becoming a serious artist had won her over before they were halfway to the island. By the time they had roasted their hot dogs over the driftwood fire he'd built on the rocky shore, Sara had known that Ted Steele, with his sparkling blue eyes and wild black hair, would be her first lover. That is, if he would have her.

She had been wearing an old Cornell sweatshirt and a pair of cutoffs and she couldn't stand her hair. She had been convinced at the time that the natural blond curls the other girls pretended to envy made her look juvenile and had wondered miserably if Ted Steele would even want to kiss her.

But he did want to. And he had whispered sweetly in her ear and pulled her softly to him, and she had heard his breathing, hoarse and rapid as they kissed and kissed again. She had not minded one bit when his hand had glided up under the Cornell sweatshirt to discover that she was braless— a brazen last-minute decision that had practically been forced upon her by Sue and Tammy as they had giggled beforehand over the gory details of how she was supposed to seduce him.

There on the beach by the light of the bonfire, Sara had forgotten everything she was supposed to do and say, simply nestling close to him and nodding shyly when he had stopped and looked seriously at her to inquire if she wanted to go any further.

He had spread the boat cushions on the rocks then, and knelt facing her, and she had been horrified and fascinated to see her hands reaching out unbidden to unbuckle his belt and peel the close-fitting canvas shorts down over his slim hips. She had gazed down at him for a long while before finally reaching to touch him, the sudden, heavy feel of him sending shocks of electricity coursing through her veins and making her knees go weak.

They had stayed like that for long minutes, touching and exploring each other and giggling like naughty little children until, finally, they had collapsed onto the soft green cushions together.

He had looked at her once more, stammering out a clumsy half question about birth control, and she had lied that she was on the pill, the stupid answer making her feel somehow worldly and in control.

Daylight was touching the eastern sky by the time they had started back up the lake. The sailboat ghosting silently along through the heavy morning mist had made Sara feel as if she were in a dream. She was sitting in the bottom of the boat leaning against Ted's knees, her hand clutched tightly in his, half listening as he whispered about the letters he would write to her and trying miserably to decide how to tell him who she really was.

They had just rounded a point of land a mile below the Lodge when she heard the clatter of helicopter blades overhead and saw the lights of emergency vehicles flashing eerily in the fog. Assuming there had been an accident at the Lodge, she had urged Ted to make the boat go faster.

Laying on full sail, they glided in to the dock behind the Lodge a few minutes later and she had leaped from the boat to find her father standing there with the gold-chased Belgian deer rifle cradled in his arms. He was glaring past her at the boy in the boat and she had run at him, screaming as the heavy rifle swung slowly up to his shoulder. . . .

The wind was rising on the lake now and there was a hint of early snow in the air. Sara still stood on the dock, following the flight of a solitary hawk across the water. It skimmed effortlessly a few feet above the choppy surface, en route to its nest hidden among the brooding pines of Solaris Peak. Bitter tears of remorse stung Sara's eyes and she fought against the ache in her throat as she watched the flight of the magnificent raptor, so strong and free and alive. The hawk beat its outstretched wings, the powerful downstrokes dipping to the frosted wave tops until it suddenly rose, touching an invisible column of rising air and gaining altitude for the passage above the distant bungalows of the Marina: they would be shuttered now against the coming of the winter storms and all the bright sailboats and striped lawn chairs and wrought-iron tea tables stored away until next June. Sara felt a deep void of loneliness sweep through her soul, the utter loneliness that yet another solitary winter on the lake would bring.

The sun had gone, overtaken by the approaching storm clouds. The lake's normally dark blue waters turned an even deeper shade, until its surface was distinguishable only by the blowing whitecaps. Sara considered returning to the Lodge to share the ephemeral companionship of the teenagers on the hearth, wishing, as crude and unkempt as they were, that they would stay the winter. Knowing even as she wished it that they dared not linger— the grounds were clearly posted and a deputy from the local sheriff's department regularly visited the sealed house, which had long since become the property of the Raynor Corporation, and which with increasing rarity still served as a base for occasional summer sales conferences by its executives.

Her eyes stayed fixed on the hawk, now no more than a dark speck rising above the white fences of the distant bungalows.

That was when she saw the light.

It flared briefly from a ground-floor window of the nearest bungalow, a radiant flash of yellow standing out against the unrelieved blackness of the steep, thickly wooded mountainside behind the Marina. The flare gradually abated, settling to a warm golden glow that beamed out across the troubled surface of the lake like an inviting path of moonlight. Sara imagined she felt her heart pounding in her chest. Someone had lit a fire in the house. Someone who had come to the lake, perhaps to spend a week or two before the deep snow fell, perhaps the whole winter.

She caught herself midway into one of her constant fantasies, the same fantasies that had caused Father to tease her so when she was still just a very little girl, before . . . before her mother had gone away and not come back. Sara smiled at her own foolishness then. No one was going to spend the winter at Spirit Lake.

No one except her.

And she was dead.

Something moved in the trees behind the Lodge and she turned away from the water to look. A dark shadow glided across a patch of pale lawn, blending into the deeper pools of darkness beneath the eaves. She felt a sudden chill and shuddered despite herself.

There were demons about.

CHAPTER 2

Refuge

T H E fire flared satisfyingly in the gray stone hearth, quickly taking hold of the fatty pine kindling and seeking purchase on the three heavy splits of tamarack pine stacked on the iron grate. Rick Masterson stood, brushing flakes of bark from his corduroy jeans and feeling the residual stiffness in his battered left knee. Ignoring the pain, he crossed to the big pine dining table where he had left the flashlight and turned the beam onto the sheet of scribbled instructions that Jimmy had pressed into his hand over breakfast at their favorite hangout in L.A. that morning.

Jimmy, a renegade rich kid, who at five-two looked like nothing so much as a miniature version of John Candy, was Rick's best friend as well as his full-time assistant and sometime sound man, tech, and shotgun. It was Jimmy who had found him screaming and delirious amid the bloody carnage of the street in Dubrovnik; found him and kept him from bleeding to death.

During those first touchy days in the intensive-care ward of the Paris hospital where he'd been airlifted following the bombing, Jimmy had hovered over him like a mother hen, talking incessantly because some well-meaning doctor had told him that the sound of a familiar voice might help pull Rick out of the coma. Jimmy had talked mostly about the idyllic summers he'd spent at Spirit Lake as a kid and how, when Rick was well enough, the two of them would come up here to spend a lazy summer sailing and fishing in the clean mountain air.

That had been in March.

The French doctors had kept him in Paris until June, when, still encased in plaster from neck to calf, the network had sprung for the private jet that had taken him to L.A. for the excruciating series of operations that had gradually pieced back together the shattered remains of his right arm and shoulder and replaced the joint in his left knee with a titanium implant. By the time he had walked out of the orthopedic clinic at UCLA, it was October. The summer was gone and Jimmy had been "temporarily" reassigned to another news team. The doctors had told Rick he might be able to return to work in the spring and the network had put him on indefinite disability leave at full salary, heavily influenced no doubt by the talk of a Pulitzer that had begun circulating even before he had been Medevaced out of Dubrovnik by the UN rescue team.

After the hospital he had spent a week knocking

around his Burbank condo, watching game shows and being kept awake by the omnipresent clatter of low-flying police helicopters. And, on the few occasions when he had been able to sleep, there had been the nightmares. Terrible dreams that he could never remember, they had started while he was still in the hospital in Paris, seeming to worsen as his physical condition had improved. Whatever they were about, the dreams always filled him with unreasoning dread, causing him to sit up screaming in the night, his sheets drenched in sweat. At three o'clock in the morning on the first day of the second week, following the most recent—and most frightening—dream, he had called Jimmy to ask about using his father's place at Spirit Lake.

Rick smiled, remembering Jimmy's face as he had turned the keys to the bungalow over to him in the coffee shop on Ventura Boulevard that morning. "I still think you're nuts, buddy," he had said, mopping up a pool of strawberry syrup with the remains of a folded pancake and holding up his pudgy fingers to enumerate. "I mean, here you are the lone fucking hero of the Yugo war and a lead-pipe cinch for the Pulitzer. *People* magazine wants to do a lead article on you and the network is talking Movie of the Week. You got two book offers, an open invitation to the Playboy Mansion, and four or five months to lay around in the sun and show your scars to broads in bikinis by the pool, and you wanta take off to a place where the sun don't shine. Why, man?"

Rick hadn't told him about the nightmares. Not directly at least. "I'd just like to get away from all of that crap for a while," was what he had said. "Go someplace real quiet where I can maybe fish a little or fool around with my cameras and try out a couple of new ideas . . . someplace where I can sleep without taking a pill."

"You still not sleeping?" Jimmy's round baby face had filled with concern.

"Just a case of nerves," he had lied, absently massaging the injured shoulder. "Like that time you freaked out on me in Angola. Remember?"

"Angola?" Jimmy had suddenly pushed his plate away. "Shit, man, don't ever talk to me about Angola. I didn't sleep for months after Angola. Hell, I couldn't *eat* for a week." He'd closed his eyes, trying to exorcise the horrible image the name conjured up in his mind, and Rick regretted having drawn the analogy.

Angola had been three years earlier. Rick and his small crew had been hanging out for weeks in the remote Namibian capital of Windhoek, trying to get a lead on the bloody border war that had been raging for more than a dozen years between then South African–controlled Namibia and the Marxist regime to the north, when they had unexpectedly been invited to accompany a squad of South African regulars on a dangerous reconnaissance mission into Angola.

Force-marching by night across the no-man's-land separating the two countries and fording a shallow river just before dawn, they had stopped at the edge of a broad, grassy plain where a herd of perhaps two hundred magnificent African elephants were clustered in family groups, browsing among the foliage of trees made lush and green by the newly fallen rains. It had been an incredible sight, the elephants, the red ball of the rising African sun ... and then the Cubans had arrived— the line of their heavy Soviet-made T-54 battle tanks suddenly flanking the field from the surrounding forest—and all hell had broken loose.

As the first volley of machine-gun fire broke out from the lines of approaching tanks, Rick had assumed the South Africans had been spotted and were the object of the withering fusillade. He had watched with growing amazement as elephants began to fall and a line of black soldiers had run out into the field to swarm over the dying beasts, hacking out their tusks with bloody axes and leaving the carcasses to rot in the sun. In the midst of the slaughter he had turned to look at Jimmy and seen the little man's mouth working soundlessly as the South African officer in charge of the mission tapped their camera with his baton and pointed with barely contained rage to the killing field. "There's your bloody native war of independence and freedom, Yank," he had screamed. "Go ahead, get it on video. Get it for all the world to see."

They *had* gotten it all, including the Angolan army helicopter swinging in low over the field to pick up the ivory and the South Africans rising up from the bush to fire their shoulder-aimed rockets at the idling tanks. The whole bloody mess. The horror of the corrupt military forces turning their weapons of destruction on the helpless animals

had been magnified in Jimmy's mind by the after-
math. The network had refused to air the footage.
Too gruesome for TV had been their claim.

Rick had been pissed.

Jimmy, however, had been shattered, had not
slept for months afterward, and often woke in the
night screaming. He had looked at Rick in the coffee shop that morning, trying to see the pain that
lay beyond his friend's eyes. There was something
else, too; surprise that something had finally hit
Rick, the king of the hard-asses. "You really that
fucked up, man?" he had worriedly asked.

Rick had shrugged. It was true. He was fucked
up. And although he hadn't said it then, he knew
with growing certainty that Angola was part of it.
Unlike Jimmy, Angola had not shattered him. Sure,
he had been disturbed for a few days, mostly
angry over the fact that the hard won footage
hadn't aired. But shattered? No. Now he realized
that he should have been. That something had to
be very wrong with anyone who had seen what he
had seen and had been able to walk away as if
nothing had happened.

He didn't know how he knew that, or why it was
bothering him now. He thought it must have something to do with the beautiful girl who had died in
his arms in Dubrovnik. If he closed his eyes, he
could still see her face. Hear her final words ...

But he hadn't told Jimmy any of that. "I'll get
over it," was all he had said. He had smiled thinly,
hoping to allay his friend's concern. "I just need a
little downtime, that's all. Thought I'd fool around
with the old Nikon. I used to be a halfway decent
still photographer, you know."

* * *

Now, in the rustic bungalow with the fireplace beginning to warm up the room, he scanned Jimmy's note until he found the item he was looking for. "There's a Honda generator in the boat house," he read aloud. "They say a chimpanzee of average intelligence can operate it, but I've never been able to figure the damn thing out myself. Doubt you'll do any better. Rotsa ruck, butthole."

"Same to you, pal." Rick smiled at the juvenile sentiment, fleetingly wishing Jimmy were with him. Still grinning, he shoved the note into the pocket of his green Pendleton and swung the flashlight around the room. Big and clean, with hooked rugs on the broad pine floorboards and a selection of comfortable-looking furniture, including a sturdy wooden coffee table you could spread a meal on and an oversized sofa draped with colorful blankets. Double-glazed sliding-glass doors opened from the paneled wall opposite the fireplace onto a balcony overlooking the lake. The beamed ceiling was spotted with big skylights that would flood the room with illumination during the day. Rick nodded his approval of the layout, thinking that the morning light ought to be great for photography. He really did intend to take some pictures, and this place was going to be just fine . . . assuming, of course, that he could manage the generator.

Hefting the flashlight in his good hand, he stepped out through the heavy front door and shone the powerful beam onto the white Jeep Cherokee drawn up to the steps, the black Anvil cases filled with his camera equipment, and his luggage, all inside waiting to be unloaded. He groaned inwardly at the thought of lugging everything into the house right now and bypassed the Jeep, intent on locating the generator.

Rick stepped onto a thick brown carpet of pine needles at the edge of the drive and stopped to look out at the lake and the dark outlines of the surrounding mountains, noting with satisfaction the total absence of artificial lights and man-made sounds. Well, he told himself, you said you wanted to get away from it all. This is away from it all.

The wind was blowing harder than it had been when he had arrived just a few minutes earlier and he could feel the first thin pellets of snow from the oncoming storm stinging his cheek. Better get the power on before the blizzard, he told himself. He could hear the slap of water against pilings as he walked down a rock-bordered path to a white clapboard building at the edge of the lake.

He stopped before the building's only door, a solid slab of wood with a bright new Yale lock clipped to a heavy duty hasp, and fumbled with the batch of keys, finding the right one on the second try.

The inside of the windowless boat house was pitch-dark and he played the flashlight around, searching for something that looked like a generator. A red fiberglass ski boat covered with a blue tarp hung suspended over black water in the center of the double slip, surrounded on three sides by a narrow walkway. An overhead garage-type metal door on the lake side completed the building. The walls were hung with life vests, water skis, ropes, and other boating paraphernalia, but he could see nothing resembling a generator. He hesitated for a moment, remembering Doc Olson's warning about the prosthetic knee's propensity to give way without warning until the surrounding muscles were completely healed, and pictured himself pitching headfirst into the black, freezing water.

Sidling carefully along the narrow walk to the opposite side of the boat house and playing the flashlight along the cluttered walls, he discovered the generator, a powerful new Honda, tucked away in an alcove beneath a well-stocked worktable. The four-stroke engine came instantly to life with a single turn of the control-panel key, flooding the boat house with light from a naked bulb above the workbench. Rick checked the fuel gauge, which showed the tank was full, and shook his head at Jimmy's little joke. The boat house, like everything else he had so far encountered at the bungalow, was built for maximum comfort.

The worktable was equipped with a very expensive set of well-oiled Snap-On tools—presumably for tinkering with the boat—and he examined a cork board filled with half a dozen snapshots of summers on the lake. Rick quickly picked out Jimmy's round moon face in three of the photos. There was his friend at age ten or so, proudly displaying a wriggling fish for the camera. In another shot a teenage Jimmy sat on the back of the red ski boat, kissing an equally pudgy girl. The third photo was a candid shot that had obviously been taken without the knowledge of its subjects. In it,

Jimmy sat at the helm of a small sailboat, gazing up with naked adoration at the face of an intense, dark-haired young man who was showing him a complex knot tied in a length of line running to one of the sails.

Rick had spent a good portion of his life trying to capture elusive emotions on film and he was moved by the power of the simple photograph. Jimmy, who was obviously supposed to be looking at the knot, stared instead at the handsome older boy, who, with his eyes cast down to the line in his hands, was completely unaware of his student's worshipful gaze. The picture was a prizewinner. Rick wondered who had taken it, who the young man in the sailboat was. He couldn't recall Jimmy ever having mentioned an older brother.

The wind was howling around the boat house as Rick locked the door behind him and hobbled across the pine needles to the bungalow. Lights shone from the windows now, casting a warm, inviting glow on the surrounding trees. He ducked into the Cherokee long enough to grab the canvas duffel bag containing his clothes and toilet articles, deciding to let the rest wait until morning. Right now he wanted only to stretch out on the big sofa before the fireplace and wind down from the long drive from L.A. He wondered how long it would take for the generator to crank out enough juice to fill the bungalow's water heater. Suddenly the idea of a long, hot bath was extremely appealing.

*　　*　　*

The dark thing beneath the eaves was unde-cided. It had been peering in through the windows of the shuttered lodge for a long time now, watch-ing the teenagers sleeping by the hearth, calculat-ing its chances of taking one of them. It was a difficult decision, for though its hunger for the flame of life that glowed tantalizingly through their soft living skins was great, the fearful pain of being summarily cast out of an unwilling host was even greater.

The pair before the dying fire was young and strong, and the thing knew from experience they would be extremely difficult to enter, their bright, ravenous spirits flooding every atom of their living flesh with the power of their own youth. Though it was not of flesh, the thing was a predator all the same. And like most predators it preyed most suc-cessfully on the sick and the injured and avoided the strong, especially when there was more than one with which to contend.

The thing was very old and very wise. As an elemental—the creatures the original natives of North America referred to as the Old Ones—it had wandered the dark forests surrounding the sacred lake even before the rivers of molten rock had vomited forth from the great fissures on the mountain-side in the dim ages of prehistory. Once, it had exercised dominion over every living creature within its range and been worshiped by the native tribes, which had delivered up living human hosts upon demand for its comfort and pleasure. But that had been long ago. It had long since been reduced to scavenging for warmth among the ani-mals of the forest, a dull, unsatisfying experience that left it aching for the sensory fulfillment of corruptible intelligence. The thing most desired a human host with eyes to see, legs to travel, contacts with other humans that might be exploited as future hosts. Unfortunately its hosts did not long survive, the passion and madness inspired by its possession gobbling up the bright flames of their souls like a malignant cancer.

It had returned hopefully to this large human habitation, which had for a brief span of time been its favorite hunting ground, in search of another wounded soul. Disappointment had raged within its consciousness as it realized that the supply of evil men upon whom it once had thrived was now exhausted.

The dark thing had ridden the last of them, an octogenarian who had been a colleague of the man who built the habitation, to the far ends of the earth, nibbling sparingly at his soul until it was entirely consumed. Leaving the old banker's vile corpse in a regal suite atop a famous Parisian hotel, it had started the long journey back to its favored hunting ground within the unwilling vessel of the Texas prostitute who had spent the dying man's final hours rifling through his belongings for cash and other valuables. She had, at first, seemed ideal to the thing's purposes. The unprincipled woman had proven to be a poor host, however, the consuming inferno of her raging cocaine habit making control of her all but impossible, snatching away morsels of her soul faster than the thing could fasten its jaws upon them. She had hanged herself in a Los Angeles hotel room nearly three years before, and the thing had returned to its sacred lake only after many trials, humiliated and hungry, and vowing never to leave again.

The thing by the window came suddenly alert, sensing the nearby presence of another human spirit. It scanned the dark shadows surrounding the lodge, snorting in frustration as it picked out the pale form of the disembodied female figure from the curtains of blowing snow that swept across the wooden construction at the edge of the lake. Vague memories of the female as she had been in life stirred uncomfortably in its mind. Memories of the time when the habitation had been filled with the rich scent of prey. Now it wondered briefly why she stood at the water's edge, gazing out into the storm. It dismissed the nonproductive thought, turning back to the window for another tantalizing look at the sleeping teenagers inside the abandoned habitation. Without a body, the woman on the dock was neither a threat nor a source of food, and thus of no interest. It tightened itself around the burning knot of hunger at the core of its being and slipped along the rough log wall, seeking a way into the house, where it could probe the sleeping humans more carefully. Perhaps one of them was flawed or injured in some way that was not readily evident from this distance.

CHAPTER 3

Nightmares

T H E horror show.

Rocketing along in the left seat of a Bell Jetranger. Ground speed one hundred and fifty miles per hour. Altitude ten feet.

Rick Masterson's toes clenched the insides of his imported Italian climbing boots, the nonslip composition soles pressing hard against the dubious solidity of the carpeted floorboard that ended abruptly three inches ahead of his boot tips. Beyond, nothing separated him from empty space but the sweeping arch of the helicopter's bubble-like Plexiglas windshield. Somebody had once compared the sensation of flying in the front seat of a high-speed helicopter to being perched on a kitchen chair atop a flagpole with a goldfish bowl on your head—the whole flimsy contraption hurtling forward through space at more than two hundred feet per second.

Masterson had no time to reflect on the mathematics. The chopper was screaming down a street of bombed-out apartment blocks in Beirut and people were shooting at it, grim figures in faded fatigues popping up from balconies like ducks in a shooting gallery. Jimmy sat in the back, his camera trained on Rick's head and shoulders as the landscape ripped past behind the reporter's shoulders. "This is Beirut at its worst," Rick began, "a city of constantly warring factions which—"

CRRRAAACK!

A burst of automatic-weapons fire starred the Plexiglas windshield, the razored fragments whizzing through the interior of the cabin in a sparkling shower. A bright spot of blood blossomed below Jimmy's left eye, spurting through his upraised fingers as the helicopter suddenly lay over on its side and made an impossible maneuver between two multistoried office buildings. The stunt had been Rick's own idea.

Bad idea.

The Jetranger stuttered in the turn, blades whirring scant inches above the rubbled street, engine screaming in protest against mechanical tortures it was never designed to withstand. Rick's heart paused in midbeat as something exploded behind him. The aircraft shuddered again, then abruptly righted itself and shot down an empty boulevard, clawing for altitude. Rick grinned, turning to congratulate the former CIA pilot on his skill in having neatly saved all their asses from certain destruction.

A golden haze filled the cramped cockpit and the girl in the yellow slicker sat in the pilot's seat, manipulating the controls. She turned her astounding blue eyes on him and smiled her beautiful smile. "That was close, Rick. Very close. You nearly killed poor Jimmy in order to make your broadcast more interesting that day. Was it worth it, Rick?" Something cold touched the back of his neck and he whirled to stare into the black void filling the rear compartment. Burning red eyes glared at him from the darkness and he felt his bladder let go, the hot liquid flooding embarrassingly over his lower body.

Rick screamed, sitting upright in the steaming tub, sloshing water out onto the tiled bathroom floor. His eyes blinked rapidly as he clawed his way out of the bath and stood naked before the misted mirror. The nightmare . . . he remembered Beirut, the helicopter . . . then nothing.

Grabbing a towel from a rack by the basin, he swabbed it across the mirror, staring at his bloodless face. Held a trembling hand before his eyes.

Jesus!

Beirut had been real. Following the abortive sortie into the midst of the warring Christian and Muslim factions, Rick had ordered the pilot to fly directly to the hospital at the American University, preoccupied with staunching the flow of blood from Jimmy's cheek and not noticing, until someone on the ground had pointed it out, the six-inch sliver of steel protruding from between his own shoulder blades, less than an inch below the collar of his flak jacket; a stray fragment from the Jetranger's ruined engine, which had torn itself apart after inhaling a couple of nine-millimeter bullets.

Close. Very fucking close.

He looked into the mirror again, straining to remember the rest of the nightmare. He knew the part he couldn't remember was worse than the replay of nearly having gotten himself and his entire crew killed because Rick Masterson wanted to be top dog.

Much worse.

He ran his fingers tenderly over the shiny ridge of inflamed scar tissue arching across his shoulder and disappearing beneath his left armpit. The nightmares had started in the hospital . . . after Dubrovnik. He closed his eyes and the girl's fresh young face smiled at him. He had wanted only to lure her into bed with him.

Shit!

Rick sat in front of the fireplace dressed in an old pair of marine corps sweat pants and a faded terry robe bearing the embroidered logo of the London Hilton. He was making a list on a yellow legal pad, as he ate a stale 7-Eleven sandwich and sipped a beer; the latter items all that remained of the meager supplies he had picked up on the road the last time he had stopped for gas.

The wind was batting fat flakes of snow against the bungalow's double-glazed windows and he hoped he'd be able to make the twenty-mile trek down the mountain to the little town of Silver Peak in the morning.

Several hours had passed since the incident in the bathroom and he had finally managed to put away his fears, concentrating instead on building up the fire in the main room and selecting a bed-room from the five available. The selection of a room hadn't been difficult. The bungalow's master bedroom, situated directly above and to the right of the high-ceilinged main room, had its own balcony, promising an even better view of the lake and mountains than the downstairs. He had spent a good bit of time arranging his sparse collection of jeans and sweaters in the drawers of a big double bureau in the bedroom, then had forced himself to unload the Jeep. Pleasantly exhausted from the activity, he had settled down to eat his cardboard sandwich and construct a shopping list for his trip to town.

Rick had passed through Silver Peak on his way to the cabin late that afternoon, finding the weath-ered collection of gas stations, saloons and houses exactly as Jimmy had described them: Dodge City West. According to Jimmy, the tiny settlement had been a mining boomtown for about fifteen minutes sometime back in the late 1800s. Like most such places—and the West was spotted with them—most of the people of Silver Peak had run out along with the silver mine that had given the town its name. Silver Peak was only saved from becom-ing a ghost town by the efforts of a few crusty diehards who liked the clean air and open spaces of the Sierra Nevada. The hardy survivors had held out against the financial ruination of the closed mines by taking advantage of Nevada's local option law to vote in legalized gambling and prostitution. Several of the old saloons with fanciful names like the Boomtown Palace and the Silverado had been restored to their former glory and a rather famous brothel had opened on the outskirts of town, with the result that Silver Peak, Nevada, had become both an attraction for Japanese and European tourists anxious for a glimpse of the "real" Old West, as well as a drawing card for local cowboys, roughnecks, and horny servicemen from the sprawling air base near Reno.

In dispensing advice on the trip to Spirit Lake, Jimmy had suggested that Rick might want to detour en route to do his serious shopping in Reno, sixty miles to the north, or in Carson City, the state capital, which was marginally closer via a more treacherous mountain road to the west. Both cities featured all the amenities of civilization, including supermarkets and shopping malls. The idea of doing business in the old mining town was more appealing to Rick, however, and that was where he planned on going in the morning. Heeding his friend's warning about the frequent winter storms that could drop enough snow in a single night to isolate the lake for weeks at a time, he planned on laying in enough groceries to last him at least a month.

Mike Gomez sat up in the cold darkness of the Lodge's huge main room. The fire had died some time ago, and the teenager had to fumble for his cigarette lighter in order to see.

Shivering against the chill, he slipped out from under the rough fiber of the dusty old blanket and found his jeans and sweater on the floor where he'd dropped them. Missy was still sleeping by the hearth, her chest moving rhythmically beneath the covers, and he moved with exaggerated caution in order to avoid disturbing her. He pulled on his clothes and tiptoed to one of the tall bookcases flanking the fireplace, selecting a thick volume from the tightly packed shelves and carrying it back to the hearth.

Sitting on the still-warm stones, he extinguished the lighter, which was getting too hot to hold, and fumbled in the dark bulk of his backpack for their remaining can of Vienna sausage. He popped the top off the can in the dark, fished out exactly half of the tightly packed sausages by feel, and wrapped them in a hotdog bun. After setting the can carefully to one side for Missy, he bit ravenously into the cold sandwich, washing down the greasy mouthful with a swallow of warm beer from a half-empty can. He listened to the wind howling around the lodge and wondered if the old Camaro he had parked in the pines beside the building would be okay in the cold. He was specifically worried about the secondhand battery he had scrounged from the filling station in Salinas the night before he and Missy had run away together.

He smiled in the dark, wishing he had been there to see the look on her old man's pasty face when he had discovered that his precious little girl was gone, run off with a "beaner" whose parents once did stoop labor in the lettuce fields. Well, he had it coming, him and his fucking three-piece suits and his Mercedes Benz.

Big fucking deal!

Mike Gomez was determined to make it to Chicago, where his brother, Georgie, had already made a start toward busting the family's generations-old cycle of poverty by landing a good-paying job with an aerospace subcontractor. Georgie had talked to his supervisor about Mike, and the man had practically guaranteed that he'd get him on as a junior draftsman when he came to Chicago. Sixteen bucks an hour! With that kind of money, Mike and Missy could get a really nice apartment and live right.

They'd discussed it for weeks, meeting secretly during odd hours when Missy was supposed to be at cheerleader practice or the library to plan every detail of their escape from her father and their future together. He'd work and go to night school for his associate degree in drafting or computer repair while she finished high school. Then they'd be set and her old man would have to admit he'd been wrong, the bastard.

Mike's face flushed as he remembered the humiliation of going to Missy's big house on the night of her junior prom. He'd been wearing a rented powder-blue tux and carrying a seventeen-buck corsage in a gold box and all, just like his cousin Elena had told him he was supposed to do. It was going to be a perfect night, Missy's dream date. . . . Except that Missy hadn't been there. Instead her asshole father had come out onto his phony plantation-house porch carrying his fucking pipe and told him that Missy wouldn't be seeing him anymore. That was when he'd launched into his bullshit about how she was going off to some exclusive Eastern college the following year and they wouldn't have anything in common, what with Mike being a greaser and all. Oh, he hadn't said it exactly like that, but Mike Gomez knew the drill. Nice girls, respectable girls whose families owned property and horses and big houses in the ritzy hills above Monterey, didn't go out with beaners from the wrong side of Salinas.

Cramming the rest of the sandwich into his mouth, the boy felt for the lighter. It had cooled down enough to handle and he flicked it and pulled the heavy book into his lap. Opening the tooled leather cover, he read the flyleaf of the book, noting its title and squinting at the wavy inscription above the author's name. Having never heard of either *The Sun Also Rises* or Ernest Hemingway, and having no idea what the words *First Edition* signified, Mike ripped the page from its binding, crumpled it into a ball and set it on the hearth. When he had similarly removed half a dozen more pages, he piled them in the fireplace, stacked kindling on them, and touched the lighter to the pile.

The fire worked its way quickly through the heavy paper, lighting the kindling and filling the room with dancing shadows. Mike rubbed his hands briskly before the fire, staring at the flames and smiling to himself. The sudden burst of heat felt good in the chilly, high-ceilinged room. He would build up the fire until the room was thoroughly warmed and then awaken Missy. They could pick up Interstate 80 in Reno and, if they drove through the night, might even reach Chicago late tomorrow. . . . If the battery held out and they could sell some of the stuff they'd found in the abandoned lodge.

Lost in his own thoughts, the boy didn't notice the shadow—blacker than the others—that detached itself from the bookcase near the broken window and slid silently across the floor to touch his bare foot. He flinched as something cold slid up his leg beneath his jeans, felt a slight tingling sensation around his rectum as it entered his body.

Mike sat staring at the flames for several long minutes. A muscle in his cheek twitched involuntarily and he cocked his head to one side. Maybe twenty hours to Chicago in a busted Camaro. What in the hell had he been thinking? Her old man probably had the cops out looking for them. He lapsed into another long period of gazing at the fire and a slow smile curled across his handsome face. He and Missy could just stay here for a while, maybe until spring.

All they'd have to do would be to get some food.

He wrapped his arms around his knees, rocking back and forth before the fire. His head jerked up and down at the perfect logic of the new plan and a thin strand of saliva dribbled onto his chin. Sure, they could take the Camaro over to Reno tonight, load up on food at one of those all-night supermarkets, and be back before dawn. He giggled approvingly at his own sudden brilliance and another thought entered his head. Maybe he'd call Missy's dad from Reno. He could pretend he'd made a mistake, get the old fart to drive up here to this lonely mountain lake . . . and kill him. After all, he reasoned, it was the only way to be sure he wouldn't bother them anymore.

Storm

I T was snowing harder.

Rick stood at the open front door, shining the flashlight out onto the Jeep. An inch of the white stuff had already accumulated on the windshield and he wondered whether it would be a mistake to wait until morning to go down the mountain for supplies. He'd clicked on the bungalow's radio earlier—part of a well-equipped stereo rig hidden behind paneled doors with a big-screen TV and VCR—and caught the tail end of a weather report forecasting heavier-than-expected snowfall for the local mountains.

He glanced at the Rolex: 9:30. Still early. He tried to picture himself snowed in, scrounging through the bungalow for scraps of food to last him till the spring thaw, got a comic picture of Jimmy arriving to discover his skeletal remains propped against the pine dining table. Jimmy chomping on a baloney sandwich and shaking his baby moon face. "Poor dumb bastard must've starved to death. Too bad he didn't know about that closet full of canned goods and Fritos. . . ."

Rick smiled ruefully at the image. In fact, he'd already checked the kitchen and adjoining pantry for any supplies that might have been left by the previous occupants of the bungalow. He had found the cabinets stocked with enough spices to warm the heart of any gourmet chef. Just spices. Aside from that, the pantry shelves had yielded exactly half a jar of instant coffee, a box of Uncle Ben's rice, and two cans of stewed tomatoes. Not much to get through the winter on.

Besides, he hated stewed tomatoes.

He shone the light on the Jeep again. If the snow kept up for the rest of the night, the mountain road might well become impassable by morning. Weary as he was, he wasn't at all anxious to go hungry, much less starve, and the present snow accumulation created no problems whatsoever for the four-wheel-drive-equipped Cherokee. Deep snow would be another problem altogether. Having made his decision, he shut the door and went upstairs to search for a pair of gloves.

Sara stood watching the Lodge from the edge of the patio. Much earlier, from the dock, she had seen the sinister shadow slip from beneath the eaves, knowing it was aware of her presence and was deliberately ignoring her. She had watched for a long time—the one thing about being dead, she had observed, was that time was never a problem—losing sight of it in the blowing snow, and had moved up from the dock just in time to see it slither swiftly to the hole in the French doors and disappear inside.

Firelight was flickering behind the streaked panes now and she moved closer to the house, terrified of the thing she had come to think of as the demon, yet curious to learn what it was up to. She had observed it prowling the grounds several times in recent years, but to her knowledge at least, it had never entered the house before. Perhaps the broken window ...

One of the French doors was suddenly flung open and the teenagers stumbled out into the snow. The girl was weeping, trying to hold the boy back. He cursed her and, shaking her off his arm like a troublesome puppy, stomped off into the darkness alone.

The girl stood forlornly in the thin blanket of snow now covering the patio, her shoulders heaving. The racket of a grinding starter motor sounded from the trees at the far side of the house and a big engine roared to life. Headlights flared against the tops of the trees and a horn blared impatiently. The girl looked uncertainly into the trees, then ran toward the lights as the horn sounded again.

Sara had watched the entire spectacle with growing concern for the teenagers. The demon thing entering the Lodge, the boy's sudden belligerence, and his decision to leave the warmth and safety of the Lodge could only mean one thing. The dark spirit had claimed him for itself. Without thinking of the possible consequences to her own safety, she willed herself forward into the woods.

*   *   *

Rick guided the Jeep down the tree-lined drive leading from the bungalows to the blacktop road that circled the lake. He stopped at the end of the drive and rolled down his window to look out at the road surface, which was covered with two inches of fresh, untracked snow. Reaching down to the console beside the transmission, he pulled up on a small black lever. An orange light on the dash flicked on to indicate that the four-wheel drive was engaged. He was in the act of rolling up the window when the distant sound of a revving engine caught his attention. He listened, trying to decide whether he had imagined the sound in the howl of the wind. Hearing nothing further, he shrugged, closed the window, and drove out onto the road. If there was another car up here, he hoped for the sake of its occupants that it was also four-wheel-drive-equipped.

The boy's car, an ancient red Camaro coupe spotted with rust-colored primer, sat idling in the circular drive before the Lodge, its worn wipers batting ineffectively at the heavy clumps of wet snow accumulating on the cracked windshield. The boy, his face appearing maniacal in the glow of the dashboard lights, waited impatiently for the girl to cross the open space from the woods surrounding the house. Sara's throat constricted as she watched the pretty blond teenager hesitate at the passenger door, then open it and get into the car.

"No!" Sara's scream was lost in the roar of the Camaro's blown-out V-8 engine.

The door slammed shut and the old car spun away in a dizzying half circle around the snowy drive. Throwing aside her own terror, Sara willed herself into the car as it hurtled down the long driveway toward the lake road. A deep ache settled into her throat as she watched the snowy landscape rushing past the Camaro's windows. She had long ago vowed never to venture outside the confines of Spirit Lake again.

The lake road intersected with another strip of blacktop half a mile beyond the bungalows. From this point, one could continue on to the northern end of the lake or turn onto the second road, which led down the mountain to Silver Peak. Rick stopped at the junction's stop sign from force of habit rather than any expectation that he might encounter another vehicle, then turned onto the mountain road. As he did so he felt the Cherokee's knobby tires slipping ever so slightly in the turn, a sure sign that the blacktop wore a thin coat of ice beneath its surface covering of snow. Vowing to be extra cautious on the steep hairpin curves and sheer overhangs he remembered from the drive up, he gradually accelerated the surefooted vehicle until the speedometer indicated a steady twenty-five miles an hour. At that rate it might take him a long time to reach Silver Peak, but reach it he would.

The headlights bounced back into his eyes as the road gradually curved to the right around a jagged cut in the mountainside, and he kept the Jeep as close to the inside of the turn as he could without scraping off a mirror against the black rocks. Glancing out through his side window, he could clearly make out the line of demarcation where the white-coated road fell away into a black void. There were no guardrails on the road and he approached the steep downgrade beyond the first curve in second gear, letting the Jeep set its own pace and allowing the transmission to handle most of the work of braking.

The tension of driving nearly blind was already beginning to tell on his aching shoulder and he forced himself to relax as he tried to remember whether the sharp hairpin curve that he knew lay somewhere ahead in the blowing snow veered right or left. The fleeting thought crossed his mind that he would have been better off back in the bungalow with the stewed tomatoes. "Too late now," he chided himself. To the best of his recollection there was no place on the winding road wide enough to allow the Jeep to turn around.

Control.

The thing Sara thought of as a demon huddled miserably in a dark corner of Mike Gomez's mind, surrounded by blinding flashes of the rage that had initially allowed it to access the boy's body. Rage it had played upon to creep into his soul.

It found the contents of the boy's mind at once delightful and fearsome. At the conscious level—the level it had stirred to a murderous frenzy—delicious visions of impossible tortures to be visited upon a mild-looking human in a conservative suit whirled about like psychic tornadoes, the sheer exuberant energy of them confounding the thing's attempts to gain control of the maddened teenager.

Below the raging eye of the hatred that was now growing like a virulent cancer within his mind, the boy's normal subconscious thought stream further confused the thing's attempts to manage him. Other thoughts flowed around the malignant core of hatred where it had taken refuge, a serene blue river of innocence and goodness whose very depth terrified and repulsed the thing. The boy's emotions were driven by his love for the girl, and his subconscious mind envisioned nothing more sinister than himself driving a sleek new sports car down a sunny street with her beside him. Mike Gomez felt guilty and ashamed at having broken into the mountain lodge, his mind justifying those actions only by his desperation to be with Missy, free from the dictates of her overprotective father. At an even deeper level, myriad half-formed images were still forming: their arrival in Chicago, where he would begin an idyllic life working in a bright, airy factory, mailing money to his parents to make them proud, living in a modern apartment with the decor of television advertisements, pampering Missy beyond her wildest expectations. . . .

The thing had already tried twice to bridge these strong emotions in concentrated assaults aimed at seizing overall control of the boy by overwhelming his fragile psyche with its own black energy. Twice it had fallen back exhausted as the host's subconscious mind had fought off the alien presence that threatened to suffocate it.

Following the second such assault, something had snapped inside the boy and he had rampaged out of the lodge and into the bitter cold night, temporarily blind to all rational behavior by his naked hatred for the girl's father. The boy's unexpectedly violent reaction to the thing's harsh probe of his festering rage was not at all what it had intended.

It realized now that it had miscalculated—something that would never have happened when it had been at the peak of its powers—and settled upon a different approach altogether. Temporarily relinquishing the idea of gaining total control over the boy's mind with one all-out assault, it had temporarily withdrawn. Now it cautiously extended a single dark tendril into the core of the boy's brain, feeling for the bright sheath of his optic nerve. First it would see. The rest would follow.

The tendril penetrated the delicate membrane of tissues surrounding the thick nerve, plunging deep into the tightly bundled fibers beneath. It felt the host body shudder, and thrilled to the tingle of the sparking neurons flowing directly to the brain from the neural receptors. Then it was staring out through Mike Gomez's eyes at the onrushing image of the snowy mountain road ahead of the speeding car. The creature extended another tendril into the brain, delicately probing for access to the central nervous system. Slowly and carefully feeling for the precise spot . . .

The boy was out of his mind.

Sara studied him as he hunched over the wheel of the speeding Camaro, his bloodless hands clenched clawlike on the chipped plastic, shudders racking his muscled young body at random intervals. She knew the demon was struggling for possession of him, its relentless probings of his mind driving him to the wildest extremes of dementia. Her mind screamed at the thing to stop, but she knew she was powerless to intercede.

Another long spasm racked his body and Mike Gomez alternately laughed and began screaming obscenities, simultaneously letting go of the steering wheel and pounding his fists on the cracked plastic dashboard. He turned his head toward the girl and Sara could see that he was chewing an increasingly large hole through the tissues of his right cheek.

Beside him, the terrified girl sat staring at the bloody and contorted face, calling his name over and over and pleading with him to slow the speeding car as they approached the junction to the mountain road. The boy suddenly stiffened as the demon made another all-out assault on some critical neurological center, and Sara felt the car attempting to brake. She shut out the sound of the girl's high-pitched scream as the bald tires lost purchase on the snowy road and the Camaro drifted onto the shoulder, sliding through the stop sign, knocking it flat.

For one precarious moment the car spun sideways, its headlights swinging through the snow to illuminate a massive boulder that promised imminent destruction to both the vehicle and its living occupants. Then it suddenly straightened and rocketed into the first curve of the treacherous mountain road. Sara's startled gaze lifted to the rearview mirror between the teenagers. The glowing yellow eyes of the demon glared back at her in triumph from Mike Gomez's face, and she swallowed hard, realizing that she had seen those hard, evil eyes once before.

When she had been alive.

CHAPTER 5

Silver Peak

RICK Masterson's grip loosened on the
padded steering wheel and he allowed himself a
deep sigh of relief as the Cherokee rolled smoothly
around a final curve and the lights of Silver Peak
twinkled up from the small plateau at the foot of
the mountain. With the exception of his nerves,
stretched taut by forty-five minutes on the treacherous road, the trip had been completely uneventful.
The snow was tapering off to occasional flurries
mixed with rain here at the lower elevation, and he
levered the shift out of four-wheel drive.

The clock on the dash showed nearly eleven as
he rolled onto the town's main thoroughfare, com-
prised at this end of small, darkened houses that
had the look of former mining shacks. He scanned
the poorly lighted street, wondering whether he
would actually find anything open at this hour.
His shoulder and knee were both throbbing, and
the thought of pushing on for another hour or

more to reach either Carson or Reno was decidedly unappealing.

The street jogged left, then right again, at a spot where the town's original founders had obligingly diverted it to make room for a towering structure of clapboard and tin, a rock crusher, which, in its present dilapidated state, now leaned precariously over the roadway, threatening passersby with imminent collapse.

Rounding the building, he spotted a faded Texaco sign lit by a single bulb. He slowed to examine the low, single-story building beneath the light. Its facade sported a long, crudely hand-painted signboard reading G. HAPWELL, GENERAL MERCHANDISE. The flicker of a television screen lit a window behind the Laurel and Hardy gas pumps, and Rick pulled into the drive, the Jeep's tires crunching loudly on the frozen gravel.

A smile lit his face as he peered out at the store through the streaked passenger window. A bright orange "open" sign glared at him from an upper corner of a display window filled with dusty fishing tackle. Levering himself out of the Jeep, he hobbled stiffly to the battered screen door and pushed on the glass door behind that. It was locked.

"Shit!" Rick's temper flared at a level equal to the shooting pain in his injured leg, and he banged loudly on the door with his fist. He heard the sound of a chair scraping across wooden floor-boards and a moment later a grizzled face that reminded him of the bearded old-timer who played comic relief to the hero in some long-for-gotten Western TV series appeared behind the glass door.

"We're closed, mister," grumbled the old man.

"Your sign says you're open," yelled Rick, pointing to the window.

The old-timer squinted up at the "open" sign as though it were an artifact from a lost civilization. "What are you, some kind of young smart-ass hippie?" he hollered back through the glass.

"Look, I just need some supplies. I'll make it worth your while to open up for a couple of minutes."

"Come back tomorrow. Be open for ten hours and it won't cost you a dime." The old coot pulled down a torn green shade and Rick could hear the tired floorboards creaking as he walked away.

"Aw, fuck it!" Rick yelled. He turned and stomped away toward the Jeep.

That was when his knee collapsed.

One second he was walking, the next he found himself lying on the rough ground, the frozen gravel scraping uncomfortably against his cheek. Cursing fluently in three different languages, he pulled himself to a sitting position and looked up to see the old-timer hovering over him with a double-barrel shotgun.

"You ain't drunk, are ya?"

"Fuck you," said Rick, struggling to get up, the process made difficult by his knee, which had suddenly stiffened like a frozen mackerel.

"Gimpy knee, eh?" The old man grunted, lowering the shotgun and extending a nicotine-stained hand toward the man on the ground.

Rick stared at the proffered hand for a long moment, then grudgingly took it and pulled himself to his feet.

"Had a cousin with a gimpy knee like that once. Took a piece of shrapnel fightin' the fuckin' asshole Nazis in France in forty-four." He glared at Rick, his faded blue eyes twinkling in the light of the Texaco sign. "Where'd you get yours?" he asked without waiting for a reply. "Fell down the steps of some whorehouse, I expect."

Rick just stared at him.

The old-timer spat an amber wad of steaming tobacco juice into a dirty pile of snow and stomped back into the store without another word. "Well, come on in if you're comin'," he hollered through the open door. "I ain't got no mind to heat the whole goddamn town."

Janet McMurty—Janet from Another Planet to the regular denizens of Silver Peak's dozen-odd saloons—stood in the shadows of a dilapidated clapboard mine building, watching the stranger entering Hapwell's store across the street. Glancing up at the steep mountain peak towering above the town, she felt a sudden claustrophobic foreboding growing within her, like an icy hand clutching at her innards.

Janet was no stranger to such feelings and the sight of the ominous black clouds piling up behind the mountain did nothing to set her mind at ease about the unforeseen arrival of the stranger and the dark aura she could clearly see hovering about him. Although she was well acquainted with the myriad shades of depression, despair, and hopelessness that steeped the environs of places like Silver Peak—places where thousands had suffered and died and dead-ended in their relentless quest for unattainable riches—she had never witnessed anything quite like the black presence cloaking the handsome, young man across the street, and she was frightened.

She watched the store carefully, waiting until the door banged firmly shut behind the stranger before stepping out into the dim circle of light cast by one of Silver Peak's few street lamps. A sudden gust of freezing wind shook the naked yellow bulb atop its spindly wooden pole, filling the empty block with leaping shadows. She shuddered, uncertain whether the chill she felt was due to the cold or to the lingering effects of the presence hovering about the man who had entered Hapwell's store. Unwilling to explore further, she gathered her woolen shawl about her thin shoulders and hurried away toward the line of shuttered saloons farther down the street. A blinding migraine headache—the kind her grandmother, who had also had the "gift," had referred to as "purple bastards"—tore at the top of her skull, and she knew that she must find a drink.

His name was George "Hap" Hapwell. He was seventy-three years old and lived in the cluttered store—which stocked everything from mining supplies to disposable diapers—with six cats and a twenty-five-inch Muntz television set that he had bought new in Los Angeles in 1956. He would have liked to get a new one, but as a survivor of the infamous Bataan Death March in the Philippines in '41, he refused as a matter of principle to buy anything made in Japan or, for that matter, on behalf of his wounded cousin, Germany. The locals all thought he was crazy, which didn't stop them from patronizing his store—which was, he gleefully noted, the only one this side of Reno offering more than what he colorfully described as "cheap Jap tourist shit."

Hapwell imparted all of that information—plus a detailed history of how he had joined the marines as a runaway kid, survived five years in a Japanese POW camp, returned home with his pockets bulging with back pay, married a conniving bitch, divorced her, killed a man in a knife fight over a two-dollar poker hand, became a merchant seaman, sold bum real estate in Florida, won a fortune in Vegas, lost another fortune treasure-hunting in Brazil, ran his Cadillac off a cliff en route to a rodeo in Winnemucca, and decided to stay in Nevada to prospect for gold—in the twenty minutes it took Rick to select and stack his purchases on the old-fashioned wood counter at the front of the store.

"If you don't mind my asking," Rick said when he had finished and Hapwell was toting up the bill on the back of a paper bag with a stub of spit-moistened pencil, "how did you end up owning a store? Strike it rich in the goldfields?"

The old man looked up at him and winked. "Never made a dime prospectin'," he said, cackling. "Rich widder left this place to me in her will. That'll be eighty-seven fifty."

Rick reached for his billfold, his eyes scanning the counter for a nonexistent American Express or VISA logo. He was used to traveling the world on the network's plastic and it had not occurred to him until this moment that cash might be in order in a place like Silver Peak, Nevada.

"I don't suppose you take credit cards?" he asked hopefully.

Hapwell's eyes turned flinty and he shook his head as though he were regarding a particularly dull-witted child. "Don't look like that much of a crazy man, do I?"

"No, I suppose not. The thing is—"

"What kind of plastic you got?" asked the old man, reaching for something hidden beneath the counter.

Rick sheepishly exposed a case filled with credit cards. "You name it, I've got it."

Hapwell leaned forward to squint at the case, then produced a faded plaid jacket and a crushed Stetson from some hidden recess behind the counter, and stomped toward the door on turned-over cowboy boots. "Well, come on," he snapped. "I ain't got all damned night."

The demon was in control.

Sara gazed at the burning eyes regarding her in the rearview mirror, trying to remember where she had seen that look before. The boy's erratic behavior had abruptly ceased some minutes earlier and now he was hunched over the Camaro's steering wheel, expertly guiding the old car down the steep slopes, applying precisely the right amount of braking pressure to carry them smoothly through the descending series of hairpin turns.

The girl in the front seat had stopped pleading. Now she sat silently gazing out at the curtains of driving snow that swept through the bright cone of the headlights.

Sara's stomach tightened. This was the first time she had left the lake in years, but she knew this treacherous road all too well. A sick feeling gripped her as the familiar outlines of a curve appeared out of the blowing snow and she suddenly knew that something horrible was about to happen. The car entered the turn smoothly enough, its speed modulated to the exact maximum that would allow the slick tires to retain traction on the icy surface.

BLAM!

The right front tire, an old, mismatched radial pilfered from a wreck stored at the rear of the Salinas ARCO station where Mike Gomez worked part-time, exploded like a rotten banana.

Sara's thoughts, as the car spun lazily around in the center of the curve, and then plunged tail-first over the railless embankment, were drowned by the shrill scream of the teenage girl.

She was suddenly certain that something like this had happened before.

Something that had involved her.

Outside, the snow had stopped and a dazzle of stars were drilling bright holes in a black velvet sky. Rick, his breath jetting out of him in frosty puffs, hobbled painfully after the old-timer, who had crossed the street and started briskly down a covered wooden sidewalk fronting a series of shuttered two- and three-story buildings.

"Where are we going now?"

Ignoring him, Hapwell stopped before the facade of a darkened brick building and punched a buzzer located discreetly in the painted molding beside the door. After a moment the door swung open to the sound of country music and laughter, and an attractive, dark-haired woman in tight Levi's and a clinging pink sweater smiled out at the two men. "Hap, you old coot, where have you been? I was just about to send Denny after you."

"Bidness," grunted Hapwell, pointing a thumb over his shoulder at Rick. He slipped through the door, deftly ducking the kiss the brunette tried to plant on his forehead. "That damn-fool tourist machine of yours still workin'?"

The woman wrinkled her brow and turned to Rick. "Hi," she said, "my name's Phylis. Do you know what he's talking about?"

Rick took her slender hand and shook it. "Rick. And no, I haven't the foggiest idea."

"Well, you'd better come in out of the cold," she said, stepping aside. "I'm sure we'll figure it out sooner or later."

Rick, whose ears were beginning to go numb in the frigid mountain air, smiled his gratitude and stepped into a short hallway. A burst of laughter sounded from a half-open door behind the woman and Willie Nelson began singing "Mama, Don't Let Your Babies Grow Up to Be Cowboys." Phylis looked Rick over appraisingly, then latched the outer door behind them and led him through the open door.

He found himself standing at a side entrance to a huge, high-ceilinged room. Red velvet wallpaper decorated the walls behind an elaborately carved and mirrored wooden bar whose centerpiece was a massive full-length painting of a reclining nude. In the center of the room, rows of brightly lit slot machines flanked a small dance floor surrounded by tables covered with checkered cloths. Fifteen or twenty locals in the no-nonsense work clothes of ranchers and miners huddled at one end of the bar or clustered around the jukebox, bottles of Bud or Corona clutched in their callused fists.

"So, what do you think?"

Rick tore his gaze from the extraordinary details of the room to find the woman watching him.

"Well," he said diplomatically. "It's . . . pretty amazing."

Her laugh was warm and throaty, conjuring up images of a young Bacall in one of his favorite films. "Hap says it reminds him of a New Orleans cathouse." She smiled. "Actually it's a semiauthentic restoration of the Silver Peak Hotel bar, circa 1870. I spent more than a year doing the research. Of course"—she laughed—"the origi‗ Silver Peak didn't have electronic slots and ve eo poker, bu you have to have those to survive up here. Short tourist season and long winters," she added.

"This is your place, then?"

"Such as it is. I've got thirty rooms upstairs I'm hoping to renovate, too. But you wouldn't believe the expense."

He looked back at the hallway with the latched door. "How come the speakeasy routine?"

"Keeps out the riffraff." She smiled again. "Actually we don't cater to the tourist trade in the winter. In the first place, there isn't any, and in the second place, I'm shorthanded." Her brown eyes narrowed and she looked at him with mock severity. "You're not a tourist, are you?"

Rick laughed. "Not if it means I have to go back outside."

"Good answer. Evasive as hell, but good."

Across the room, the white-aproned bartender took a steaming plate from a window at the far end of the bar and set it before a man in grimy coveralls. The delicious odor of french fries and charred meat filled the air and Rick felt his stomach grumbling. "You serve food, too?"

Phylis smiled and led him to the bar, where the miner was decorating a gargantuan T-bone with ketchup. "Just steaks and burgers in the winter." She glanced frankly at his expensive clothes. "Nothing fancy, I'm afraid. When I opened up here three years ago, I was only going to operate the grill during tourist season, but it turns out there's no place to get a decent meal in this town until May." She clapped the miner on the back and he grinned at her through a mouthful of fries.

"Great grub, Phylis."

"You hungry?" she asked Rick.

"Man, am I ever," he confessed.

"Well, grab a stool and name your poison." She slipped through an opening in the bar and picked up an order pad, pulling a pencil from a heavy coil of dark hair tied at the back of her head. "As I said, steaks and burgers. Monday nights the menu expands to include fried chicken."

"Steak." He grinned. "Rare." He looked at the beer drinkers farther down the bar and added, "And a Corona."

"Good choice. I'll be back with your beer in just

a minute." She jotted down the order and hurried to the kitchen window at the far end of the bar.

Unbuttoning his parka, Rick turned around on the stool and surveyed the room. The steak-eating miner nodded to him, as if to confirm the fact that anyone who was okay with Phylis was okay with him, and Rick nodded back. A high-pitched whistle split the air and he looked over to the row of slot machines to see Hapwell motioning impatiently for him to join him there.

Rick crossed the room and found the old-timer standing before an automated bank-teller machine emblazoned with the logo CASINO CASH.

"Okay, junior, break out that plastic and we'll see if it's any good," he snapped.

"I'll be damned," said Rick, gazing at the machine and pulling out his billfold. He slipped his gold VISA card into the slot, punched in the appropriate numbers, and was rewarded with three crisp one-hundred-dollar bills. He slipped two of the bills into the wallet with his card and receipt and held the third up to Hapwell. "Hope you can break a hundred." He laughed.

"Gimme that," the old man hissed. He shoved the bill into the pocket of his jacket, glancing suspiciously around the saloon to see if anyone else had observed the transaction. "Lots of rough types in here," he growled, leading Rick back to the bar and taking a stool beside him.

Rick saw Phylis approaching with his Corona. "Buy you a beer?" he asked Hapwell.

The old man grunted, laying his Stetson on the bar, and Rick held up two fingers. The attractive saloon owner retraced her steps to the cooler at the other end of the bar and returned to place frosty bottles before both men.

"So," said Hapwell when he had taken a deep swallow of the Corona. "What's your story, pilgrim?"

Rick shrugged, noting that Phylis was unabashedly leaning on the bar awaiting his reply. The grimy miner's fork halted midway to his mouth and he turned his head to listen in as well.

"Well, I was in an . . . accident several months ago and I've been—"

"An accident?" Hapwell interrupted. "I thought it was a terrorist bomb took you out."

Rick stared at the old man, who calmly took another swig of his Corona, wiped his scraggly chin whiskers with the back of his hand, and beamed up at Phylis like a proud father.

"They say he'll probably get the Poo-litzer Prize," Hapwell proudly informed her. "Ya oughta get him to put his autograph up over the bar."

"Wait a minute!" said Rick. "You know who I am?"

"Knowed it the minute I got a good look at you in the light down at the store." Hapwell chuckled. "Look just like your picture on the television." He turned to Phylis for confirmation. "Don't he?"

She nodded and patted Rick's hand. "Don't take it too hard, Mr. Masterson. Hap doesn't miss much."

"Yeah," Rick said, "but if he already knew who I was, why did he let me think I wasn't going to get any groceries?" He turned to the old-timer. "And why did you ask what 'my story' was?"

Hapwell drained his bottle and held the empty up for another. "Just 'cause I seen you on the TV don't mean you was good for no groceries," he said. "Besides," he added, "you looked like you needed a hot meal, and they wouldn'ta let you in here on your own in that Beverly Hills outfit you got on."

Rick looked down at his turtleneck sweater and jeans. "What's wrong with my outfit?"

"Too new. Too expensive . . . too clean."

Phylis laughed. "Speak for yourself, Hap. He looks just fine to me." Her eyes caught Rick's and she suddenly blushed becomingly. "I just meant I would have let you in anyway," she hastily explained.

Hapwell snorted disgustedly and she excused herself to fetch more beer as the bartender appeared with two steaming plates.

"I didn't hear you order anything," said Rick as Hapwell borrowed the miner's ketchup bottle and began smothering his steak.

"Didn't have to," said Hapwell. "I'm in here every night right after Ted Koppel." He knifed a chunk out of his steak and popped it into his mouth. "So what *is* your story?"

"I think what he wants to know," said Phylis, who had appeared carrying two more frosty Coronas, "is what you're doing in Silver Peak. There's no place to stay up here and it's hardly the tourist season." She set the beers on the bar and lowered her voice to a confidential tone. "In case you haven't noticed, no one in a town this size is allowed to have any degree of privacy whatsoever. And, so far at least, you qualify as a major mystery. Do you have a relative here, a secret lover? Or did you just make a wrong turn outside Carson City?"

Rick laughed and pulled his plate toward him. "Well, Phylis, I'm sorry to disappoint you," he said.

"But the answer is none of the above. Los Angeles just got a little hectic after all my hospital time, and a friend offered me the use of his family's place up at Spirit Lake for a while. End of mystery."

He sprinkled salt on his fries and began to eat, looking up after a moment to see both Phylis and Hapwell staring at him. The miner had moved to the other end of the bar and was whispering something to a group of cowboys. They stopped talking to stare at Rick, too.

"What?" He was beginning to be annoyed.

"Nobody winters up at Spirit Lake," said Hapwell. He reached into his pocket and tossed the hundred-dollar bill onto the bar. "Leastways, not on my groceries."

"Are you crazy?" said Rick. "Why not?"

"Man ain't safe up there alone in the snow," Hapwell muttered. "Not since seventy-eight . . ." His eyes took on a faraway look. "Used to pack in up there on horses to hunt bighorn," he began. "Me'n Tall Hudson and Tommy Whitehorse . . ."

Phylis shot Hapwell a look and his voice trailed off. He picked up his beer and took a sullen swig.

"It isn't safe to winter up at the lake," she said to Rick, "because the weather is much too unpredictable. If the road gets sealed off—and that can happen anytime from October on—there's no way out. The Forest Service can't even get a helicopter in to you because of the danger of setting off avalanches. I'm surprised your friend didn't tell you all of this before you came up."

"Well, he did try to discourage me," Rick admitted, "but he didn't say anything about it being particularly dangerous."

"Goddamned flatland tourist summer renters," muttered Hapwell. "Don't know shit from Shinola."

"Shut up, Hap," Phylis snapped. The old-timer fell silent and she glared at the cowboys, who had drifted closer to their end of the bar and were listening intently to the exchange. "Denny," she yelled at the bartender, "put some music on. This place is like a morgue. You," she ordered the cowboys, "go mind your own business or I'm closing up early."

The plaintive strains of "Angel Flying Too Close to the Ground" filled the barroom as the chastised drinkers scattered like sheep before Phylis's stern gaze. When they had moved out of earshot, she leaned across the bar and placed a soft hand tipped with lacquered crimson nails on Rick's arm.

"Look, Mr. Masterson . . . Rick," she said. "Everyone around here is very touchy about the lake. There was a terrible tragedy up there several winters ago and none of us wants to see it happen again."

"What kind of tragedy?"

Phylis's eyes darted to Hapwell, who glared defiantly back at her.

"Go ahead and tell the man," he said.

"Some . . . people . . . were trapped at the lake following an early winter storm," she said carefully. "A young woman went up there on a lark after the place was shut down for the winter. The story is that she went to the lake with enough supplies for a weekend. By the time the weekend was over, more than six feet of snow had fallen and the road was blocked by avalanches.

"Anyway, the girl's father was a very wealthy man. As it turns out, she was supposed to be spending the week with him in Switzerland. When she didn't arrive there, he started looking for her. He finally figured out that she had gone to the lake. He came up here then and learned that the road had been out for a couple of days. He set up a headquarters in Silver Peak to organize a rescue effort."

Phylis paused and poured herself a cup of coffee from a pot behind the bar. "That year," she continued, "the storms kept coming in one after another. Nobody could do anything, not the Forest Service or the mountain rescue team. They even brought in a group of marines from the training center at Sonora who were especially trained for cold-weather and mountain work."

She hesitated, now very obviously choosing her words carefully. "After everything else had failed, the father offered some of the local men a lot of money—"

"Ten thousand apiece," Hapwell interjected.

Phylis shot him a deadly look and turned back to Rick. "—a lot of money, to pack him in over the mountains on horseback. Some of the men from Silver Peak were killed in an avalanche. The rest turned back. They barely made it back here with their lives."

"And the father?" Rick was listening intently now, the half-eaten steak forgotten and growing cold on his plate. Far from being discouraged by the chilling story, his journalist's ear was completely attuned to it.

"The father went on into the mountains alone," Phylis said, raising her eyes and looking again at Hapwell. The old man was contemplatively sipping his beer. "He was never seen alive again."

"And the young woman?"

"The local mountain rescue team finally managed to make their way into the area a couple of weeks later, after the weather finally broke. They discovered the girl alive. . . . Unfortunately she . . . died . . . before she could be brought out."

Hapwell began to laugh uproariously. "Well, that's the prettiest damn version of that story I ever heard tell of," he said. "Denny," he yelled. "Bring my old buddy Jack Daniel's over here."

The bartender arrived carrying the bottle and a shot glass and looked meaningfully at Phylis. She nodded and he poured Hapwell a drink. The old man downed it in a single swallow and shoved the glass across the bar for a refill.

"Hap, you take it easy now," Phylis warned. "Remember what Doc Hollister said about your blood pressure."

Hapwell nodded meekly, sipped the second shot and looked at Rick with glittering eyes.

"Wait a minute," said Rick. "What happened to the girl? Why did she die?"

Phylis shrugged. "No one is quite certain. She was . . . irrational . . . by the time the rescuers got to her."

"Bullhockey," yelled Hapwell, unable to contain himself. He downed the rest of his shot and glared at Phylis. "Since the idee here is to talk this young agent out of wintering over at Spirit Lake," he said, "maybe he oughta hear more. Like the whole rest of the story."

"The idea," Phylis said evenly, "is to inform Mr. Masterson of the hazards he might encounter as the result of a severe winter storm."

"Look," said Rick, holding up a weary hand. "I really appreciate your concern, both of you, but I'm a big boy and a pretty smart one, too. Now, even though I was really beat tonight, the first thing I did when I saw it starting to snow was haul myself down here for supplies. I've got a whole mess of groceries on the counter over at Hap's place, my car is equipped with four-wheel drive and off-road tires, and the house I'm staying in has it's own generator and what looks to be about a six-year supply of firewood out back, so it's highly unlikely that I'm going to either freeze or starve to death up there."

He grinned and cut into his steak. A dribble of cold blood pooled beneath the nearly raw meat. "Now, if it'll make either of you feel better, I'll pack up some extra canned goods, just to be on the safe side, and I'll listen very closely to the weather reports. Chances are I'll be going back to L.A. in a few weeks anyway, but regardless, at the first sign of a really big storm, I'll come down. Fair enough?" He raised his fork, preparing to bite into the steak.

Hapwell and Phylis looked at each other. The old man seemed about to say more, but Phylis shook her head in warning. "Here," she said, taking Rick's plate. "Let me warm this up for you."

CHAPTER 6

The Mountain

DEAD.

Sara stood at the edge of the curve, peering down at the wrecked Camaro far below. It was upended in a bank of snow among the pines like a macabre Christmas miniature, the bald tires pointing skyward, the roof crushed down nearly to dashboard level.

She felt disoriented and slightly sick at the memory of the crash. After the car left the roadway, it had plunged straight down for nearly a hundred feet before hitting the first outcropping of unyielding black rock in its path. The girl's scream had died abruptly as her neck and back had been mercifully snapped with the first shock of the crash. What was left of the car had continued on down the slope after that, tumbling end over end for another five hundred feet before coming to rest in the snowbank.

The teenagers had to be dead, she told herself,

their souls must have slipped out unseen from the crumpled wreckage before the car had even stopped tumbling. She remembered seeing the boy's body cruelly impaled on the steering column at the same instant the girl had died. Then he had been flung from the car and she had not seen him again. It had all been so confusing, the sounds of the crash, the expectation that the car would burst into flames at any second. . . . Then she had inexplicably found herself back here, standing on the road at the apex of the treacherous curve.

She had willed herself to the edge of the cliff then, following the trail of fading skid marks until they disappeared, searching the canyon for the car. She had watched it for a long time afterward, waiting for the fire. Although she clearly smelled the strong odor of raw gasoline, there had been no fire.

Somehow she had expected a fire.

She looked around her now, remembering clearly that she had stood here, on this particular spot, before . . . waiting. But waiting for what? Her mind went blank and she wondered vaguely what had become of the demon thing that had been in the boy.

A sudden wave of freezing cold passed through her body and she looked down to realize that her feet were sinking into the soft snow. She knew that wasn't right somehow, but she could not remember why.

She wished someone would come and take her away from this awful place.

Someone in a car with a warm heater.

Someone who would take her home.

* * *

The white Jeep Cherokee sat idling at the entrance to Hapwell's store. The supplies had been loaded in the back, along with a pair of ridiculous wood-and-leather snowshoes that the old-timer had drunkenly insisted Rick take along with him before he had passed out. Rick had thrown them in with the groceries just to humor the old man.

Rick was anxious to be on his way now. Sharp pains were shooting through his shoulder and he was reluctant to take any of the medications that had been prescribed for his pain until he was safely back in the bungalow.

He stood by the open driver's door as Phylis stepped out onto the narrow porch that fronted the store.

"Is he going to be okay?" he asked as she gently closed the screen door behind her. He had loaded the supplies while she had put Hapwell to bed.

Phylis smiled and walked over to the Jeep. "Oh he'll sleep it off. Probably wake up with a king-sized headache and be meaner than hell tomorrow . . . Look, if you don't feel like driving back up tonight, the offer of that spare room still stands."

Rick climbed into the Jeep and looked at her standing there in the dim light of the Texaco sign. She had brought up the subject of the spare room, one of two she'd already restored in the old hotel above the bar—the other was hers—while they were still back at the saloon. Phylis was a damned attractive woman, he thought. Nice, too. Maybe too nice for the likes of a Rick Masterson right now.

He had realized that while they were sipping coffee at one of the tables with the checkered cloths in the nearly empty saloon, he listening to the story of how Phylis Rand, aged twenty-eight, had come to Silver Peak while old Hapwell was still belly up to the bar, loudly and cantankerously renewing his acquaintance with Jack Daniel's.

Phylis had been a Las Vegas dancer who had visited the old mining town five years earlier as a weekend tourist. She had fallen in love at once with the easygoing, good-natured locals and the faded boomtown architecture of the place, fully expecting to come back someday for another round of sight-seeing. A year later, after a bank of defective stage lights dropped on her during a performance at Caesar's, she had returned to the quirky little town to recuperate and come to grips with the fact that her dancing career was at an end. She had stayed on, using the casino's generous insurance settlement to buy the Silver Peak Hotel, which she now dreamed of restoring to all its former grandeur.

Curiously, it was Phylis's dream, rather than her obvious concern for his safety and her mothering of the grizzled old storekeeper, that had made Rick decide against taking her up on the tantalizing offer of a cozy room just down the hall from hers. Rick knew himself well enough to understand that when it came to women, he was a shatterer of dreams, a footloose adventure junkie who disappeared from nice women's lives without notice or explanation in his endless quest for the next story. That aspect of himself had never bothered him until now—in fact, he had considered it an asset—

but then a lot of things had never bothered him until now. He closed his eyes, picturing the girl in the yellow slicker.

He had only wanted to fuck her. . . .

"Sure I can't change your mind?" Phylis was leaning on the sill of the Jeep's window, one shapely breast lightly touching his injured arm.

Startled by his own uncharacteristic feelings, he shook his head like a tongue-tied schoolboy. "I'd, uh, better get back up there," he finally mumbled.

"Okay." She stepped away from the Jeep and tapped the hood lightly. "Drive carefully and don't forget Monday."

"Fried chicken." He grinned, feeling like a high-school nerd. "It's a date."

He slipped the vehicle into gear, then stepped on the brake. "One more question," he said, leaning out the window. "Just out of curiosity, what else was it that old Hap wanted to tell me about that girl who died up at the lake that you didn't want him to?"

She shrugged prettily. "It really wasn't anything much," she said. "I just didn't want the whole town to come off like a bunch of superstitious yokels when the important thing was to warn you about the weather conditions."

"Come on, what was it?" he teased. "Inquiring minds want to know. Is there a Bigfoot up there or something?"

Phylis's expression turned serious and she shook her head. "The girl they found, the survivor—"

"Who didn't survive," Rick corrected.

"Yes, well, she didn't just die before the rescue party got her out. She committed suicide."

"Oh," Rick said. He hesitated, running back over the story in his mind. "Why?"

Phylis shook her head. More of a shudder actually. "Well, when they found her, she was in pretty good shape physically. Since there had been no food available for weeks and the father was still missing, there was some speculation that he had actually made it to the lake and that she had kept herself alive by . . . well, by eating him. They found evidence of what might have been human remains in the kitchen. That's why they think she killed herself."

"Oh."

"It's only a theory," Phylis said. "Anyway, it's not a pretty story to tell a man who's about to cut into a rare steak. Not, for that matter, a good story to tell in a restaurant. Bad for business. Besides, nobody knows for sure what really took place up there. The girl was the only one and she's dead, poor thing. After what happened, though, none of the locals will go near the lake in the winter."

"And this all happened back in seventy-eight? I can't believe I didn't hear about it at the time."

Phylis shook her head again. "No, it happened a year or two before that—1976, I think. Hap and his buddies last packed in up there to hunt bighorn in the winter of seventy-eight." She paused, shivering in the cold. "I suspect they got to drinking their Jack Daniel's around the campfire and scared themselves silly. Anyway, that's another story, an old man's story. I'm sure he'll be happy to bend your ear sometime when he's not too drunk." She smiled again. "As for why you didn't hear about it at the time, the father's corporation assumed ownership of the place. They moved in a corps of security and PR types right after the tragedy and pretty much smothered the story. I guess they figured that cannibalism was bad for business, too."

"Look, can I drive you back to the hotel?" he asked, noticing that she was shivering in the cold.

She shook her head. "No thanks," she said. "It's not that far and I kind of enjoy walking under the stars."

Rick nodded, slipped the Jeep into gear, and drove out onto the frozen street. She watched until she saw the twin glow of the taillights flare as he touched the brakes at the junction of the mountain turnoff, then she turned toward the saloon. A dark figure snatched at her from the shadows and she found herself staring into the bloodshot eyes of Janet McMurty.

"Janet, you nearly scared the life out of me! What in the name of God are you doing wandering around out here in the cold?"

Janet, the hem of her flowered granny gown flapping about her skinny legs, pulled her into the center of the street and pointed a trembling finger in the direction of the departing Jeep. "Evil," she croaked. "Dark and evil."

Phylis leaned closer, smelling the reek of raw whiskey on the older woman's breath. Janet, with her homemade granny gowns, her wispy, flyaway hair and her strange ways, was one of Silver Peak's more colorful town characters, albeit the only female one, and Phylis felt sorry for her. "Come on, dear," she said, placing a protective arm about the pathetic creature's shoulders. "Let's go over to my place. I'll fix you a nice cup of tea and then have Denny drive you home."

Janet looked up at her lovely friend with adoring eyes, allowing herself to be propelled along the wooden sidewalk like a naughty three-year-old. "Can I have just a little drink?" she asked in a small voice.

The lower reaches of the road leading back up the mountain were free of snow, and Rick made good time along the first few grades. He slipped a CD into the dashboard player, finding the Broadway cast album from *Cats* a welcome change from the Silver Peak Saloon's strict diet of Willie Nelson, and remembering with a grin Phylis's story of how the cowboys had revolted en masse at her inclusion of a Manilow album among the jukebox selections.

The Jeep's heater blasted warm air on his feet as the soothing strains of Betty Buckley's voice filled the car with good feelings, and he found that the grin was still on his face. His arm tingled where Phylis's breast had touched it, and the throbbing in the bum shoulder seemed to have abated just a little.

He peered ahead through the windshield as the road curved sharply into another steep upgrade and saw the ominous crystalline reflection of snowflakes on the upcoming stretch of blacktop. Shifting the transmission into four-wheel drive, he completed the curve and allowed the Jeep to slow to a steady thirty-five as the radiator pointed up the next grade. The knobby off-road tires gripped the slick surface with no signs of slippage and he allowed himself to relax, enjoying the starlit view of the rugged snowy mountains.

Halfway up the mountain the grade flattened out

into a short straightaway that led directly into another sharp hairpin, and his eyes followed the bright sweep of illumination provided by the Jeep's quartz-halogen headlight beams. Snowcapped rocks along the inside of the curve, patches of buckled roadway peeking through a layer of fresh powder . . .

A pale figure standing in the center of the road.

"Oh Christ!" Rick downshifted to second, tapping gently on the brakes and feeling the knobby tires beginning to slide on the icy surface, the Jeep's back end breaking away in slow motion. The figure loomed directly ahead of him now, a young girl with flowing blond hair, the glare of the onrushing headlights silhouetting her body through the flimsy material of her thin garment.

Spinning the wheel into the skid, Rick touched the accelerator, peering past the girl to the edge of the canyon beyond. The Jeep flashed past her, gaining traction at the last possible moment and veering back toward the sheer rock wall bordering the opposite side of the road. Metal crunched up front and he heard the tinkle of glass as the vehicle nosed into the rocks and the engine stalled.

"Shit!"

He sat there slumped over the wheel in the warm Jeep with Buckley's mellow sounds still cooing in his ears. Bolts of pain shot through the injured knee, which had banged the bottom of the dash, and his shoulder unaccountably throbbed again. He swiveled his head around to look out the back window and saw her standing there like an evil angel in the red glare of the brake lights.

Just standing there.

*　*　*

"You damned idiot!" he growled, yanking up on the handbrake and flinging his door open. Cold air flooded the interior as he stuck his head out and yelled at her. "Hey, you, what are you trying to do, get yourself killed!"

The girl stood in the center of the road, unmoving.

Rick got out of the car and stepped onto the slippery white surface. The red light picked out every detail of the gown pressed to her body in the freezing wind. She seemed to be staring at him.

"Hey, are you okay?"

When she still did not answer, he walked to her, limping heavily on the banged knee. He reached out to touch her bare shoulder, found it freezing.

"Miss?"

The girl looked up at him through frightened eyes. He knew the signs of shock, was suddenly worried that she might be lapsing into hypothermia as well.

She was barefoot in the snow, for godsake!

Rick looked around the desolate area, scanning the dark road for some sign of how she had gotten there. Aside from a pair of shallow depressions in the blowing snow, there was nothing. Stripping off his parka, he draped it over her, touched her lightly on the shoulder again. Even like this, he thought she was the most beautiful female he had ever seen. What in the hell was she doing out here? A car wreck, a fight with her boyfriend?

"Look," he said gently, "my car is right over here. Let's get you inside and warmed up and I'll drive you to a doctor."

The girl looked at him and a hint of a smile played at the corners of her bloodless lips. She offered no resistance as he led her to the Jeep and got her into the passenger seat. Rounding the vehicle, Rick quickly inspected the front fender, noting with relief that the damage done by the rocks was confined to a broken parking light and some scraped paint. He climbed back into the driver's seat, turned the key. The engine sprang immediately to life. He set the heater at its highest setting and slammed the door. "Look, is there anyone else up here with you?"

She looked at him strangely, then shook her head.

"Okay," he said, shifting the Jeep into reverse and gently easing out on the clutch. "There's no room to turn around up here," he explained, backing out onto the narrow road and starting slowly up the mountain, "so I'm going to have to drive up to Spirit Lake then turn around. Okay?"

He glanced over at the girl and found her warming her hands before the heater vent. She smiled at him—a real smile this time—and cocked her ear to the *Cats* album, which had never stopped playing.

"That song is just beautiful," she said.

"Ah, you do talk." He smiled encouragingly. "I was afraid you were in shock or something.

"What's it called?" she asked, running her hands across the dashboard, picking up a CD and gazing in wonder at her reflection in the liquid colors running across its surface.

"The song? It's called 'Memories.' It's from *Cats*."

"I just love it," she said.

"Yeah, you don't have to be a Betty Buckley fan to like that one," he agreed.

She looked at him strangely. "What?"

"Betty Buckley, the singer."

"Oh," she said, turning to gaze out the window.

Rick watched her carefully for a long moment before he caught on. Hell, she was just a kid, twenty, maybe twenty-one. *Cats* was probably way before her time. He suddenly felt very old. "How are you feeling now?" he asked.

"Much better, thank you," She turned to look at him and he was struck again by her beauty. She shivered inside his parka and cupped her hands over the vent. "I just can't seem to get warm."

"I can believe that," he said. "How did you get all the way up here in the first place?"

She turned away again and gazed at the starlit night. "I was with some people . . . in a car," she said.

"And they just left you out there on that road all by yourself?" he asked suspiciously.

She nodded as if the fact of her abandonment were of no particular consequence, holding up the CD. "What's this?" she asked brightly.

"*Elvis in Concert,*" he answered, glancing over at the title imprinted on the album.

Her eyes lit up. "Elvis?"

"Really," he said, taking the disc from her hand. "Don't tell me you're an Elvis fan?"

"Oh yes." She said it with such genuine emotion that he turned to see if she was making fun of him. If she was, there was nothing in her expression to indicate it.

"Elvis it is." He popped the CD into the player and watched fascinated as she closed her eyes and began to twist her shoulders in time to "Blue Suede Shoes." Her high breasts moved seductively beneath the open parka and he had to force his eyes away. Just as well, he thought, the road was still plenty slippery.

It took him another fifteen minutes of intense concentration to negotiate the last few miles of snowy road to the junction at the intersection of the lake and mountain roads. Rick pulled to a stop on the shoulder and looked over at the girl. She hadn't budged or uttered another word in response to his several pointed attempts to discover who had left her on the lonely mountain road, or why, sitting huddled up in the passenger seat with his parka wrapped around her, listening to the Elvis album. Smiling, he reached for the stereo controls and turned down the volume. She looked at him in surprise.

"This is the turnaround," he said. "I'll get you back down to Silver Peak and we'll find a doctor. You can call your folks if you'd like."

She looked out the window and her face brightened. "Can't you just take me home?" she asked.

"Home?" Rick was confused.

"Yes, please." She pointed up the lake road in the opposite direction from the bungalows.

"You're staying up here?"

"Well, of course. I . . . live here."

He looked up the road, noticing the recent tire tracks leading into the junction from the direction she had indicated. He *had* heard a car earlier. He began to laugh, realizing that the local yokels of Silver Peak had had a little giggle at his expense.

Nobody winters at Spirit Lake. Oh well, he thought, at least the steak had been good. But, Jesus, cannibals!

The girl was looking at him strangely now. "I'm sorry," he apologized, still chuckling to himself. "Someone told me that no one ever came up here in the winter and I believed them."

She smiled.

"How far is it to your place?"

"Not far," she said, running her fingers through her thick blond hair. "Do I look awful?"

Rick shook his head and put the Jeep into gear. "For someone who was freezing to death twenty minutes ago, you look absolutely gorgeous." A frown creased his brow and he peered at her in the dim light. "I'm not so sure we shouldn't at least have a doctor look you over."

Something that might have been fear showed in her eyes and she shook her head. "I'm fine," she said. "Really. I just want to go home."

Rick scrutinized her. She did sound all right. And if she lived here at the lake, her family was probably worried about her. "Okay," he said, putting the Jeep into gear again. "But I don't want to hear about it if you come down with pneumonia."

She smiled and moved her shoulders in time to the Elvis CD. "I know everybody else thinks disco is so cool, but I just love Elvis," she said. "I practically grew up listening to him."

"Can't help but love the King," Rick agreed. He turned up the volume on "Don't Be Cruel" for her and pulled out onto the lake road. "You believe he's still alive?"

She looked at him with a knowing smile. "What a silly question," she said. "Of course Elvis is alive."

Home

T H E white Jeep Cherokee rolled to a stop before a set of massive stone pillars flanking a drive darkened by the shadows of brooding ponderosa pines.

Rick peered up the long drive, unable to see the house that lay at its end. "You live *here?*" he asked, a slight note of incredulity in his voice.

The girl nodded and touched his arm. "Yes. Thank you very much for helping me."

"Rick," he said, taking her hand, which was still icy despite the fact that she had been huddling before the heater vent for close to half an hour. He put his hand on the Jeep's stick shift, preparing to start up the long drive.

"I'll get out here, Rick," she said, fumbling for the unfamiliar door handle.

"Without shoes? No chance." He turned into the unplowed driveway before she could protest further.

The girl sat silently watching the shadows pass

as the Jeep crunched up a long tunnel of trees,
emerging before a massive house overlooking the
lake.

"Doesn't look like there's anybody home," he
said, peering at the darkened windows. "Are you
sure you can . . . ?"

Cold air flooded the car as the passenger door
swung open and he looked across to see the girl
standing outside.

"Thank you again." She smiled, then turned and
started toward the house.

"Wait a minute," he called. "I don't even know
your name."

"Sara," she said. "Just Sara."

"Well, I hope I see you again, Sara. It's nice to
know I'm not all alone up here."

She smiled again and gave him a little wave,
then disappeared into the deep shadows of the
unlit front porch.

Rick was halfway back to the bungalow before
he realized that she still had his parka. He was
tempted to turn back, but the throbbing in his
shoulder had become a deep, abiding ache. He
could drive over and pick up the parka in the
morning. It would give him a chance to check on
the girl . . . Sara. Thank God he hadn't hit her, or
run the Jeep off the cliff in his effort to avoid her.

He still wondered about the unexplained set of
circumstances that had led her to be on the
deserted mountain road clad only in a thin nightgown. Probably boyfriend trouble, he concluded.
He shuddered at the thought of what might have
happened if he hadn't come along and picked her
up. God, but she was beautiful, though. He grinned

foolishly, remembering how she had looked silhouetted in the headlights on the road. Her thin gown had left very little to the imagination. Chiding himself for the lustful thoughts he was having about a kid who had to be at least ten years his junior, he tried to refocus on the earlier events of the evening. Phylis Rand was a pretty spectacular lady, too.

A woman, not a girl.

The dark thing had stayed.

Clinging to the inside of Mike Gomez's mind, it fought the boy's panicked spirit, which was struggling to free itself from its ruined body. The body lay splayed where it had fallen, on a patch of frozen ground a hundred feet up the slope from the upended Camaro, having been thrown free of the car several seconds before the final impact in the snowbank. Aside from the gaping chest wound, occasioned when the steering column had been driven backward into the driver's seat, the body was in remarkably good condition. As long as the boy's spirit was forced to remain imprisoned within its shell, the elemental could continue to feed on it.

It needed the energy that Mike Gomez could give it. Gaining control of the teenager had sapped its strength to the point of danger, strength it now needed to aid in its quest for a new and more serviceable host.

The thing felt about in the darkness for another fragment of the host's tortured spirit, clamped its jaws, and noisily sucked the warming fire. The body twitched as dead muscles spasmed in the cold.

In fact, Mike Gomez's self was still intimately connected to his broken human shell. He could still feel everything. His mind screamed out for Missy, but somehow he knew she had already gone on without him.

Sara stood in the chill shadows of her father's study, softly humming the strange new melody she had heard upon entering the man's car. Something had happened to her tonight. Something that had allowed her to become almost human again, if just for a short while. She remembered having waited at the curve on the mountain road before, years earlier. Waiting. Once she had even gotten into another car. This time it was different, though. Rick had not tried to touch her, but neither had he been afraid of her.

Not like all the others.

She looked down at the faded photo on the desk. The smiling girl on the sunny dock looked back from beneath the dusty glass, mocking her. She turned to face the streaked mirror hanging on the back of the open door to Harold Raynor's private bathroom. Her own face stared at her, a hollow-eyed version of the girl in the photo. The familiar tangle of thick blond hair cascaded over her shoulder, and she automatically raised a pale hand to brush it away from her forehead. She gasped sharply as the hand began to fade, gradually becoming transparent in the mirror, along with the rest of her body.

Within moments her image had disappeared entirely from the mirror. The warm parka that she had been wearing slipped to the floor with a whisper and she felt the chill of the room on her bare shoulders.

Crossing slowly to the window, Sara peered across the black waters of the lake, looking for the light she had seen before. She was certain the stranger at the other end of the lake had somehow been responsible for her transformation, short-lived though it had been. Perhaps if he stayed the whole winter . . . The thought died half-formed. Sara knew she could never hope to become the smiling girl on the dock again. That was over. It would be enough to know that she would not have to spend yet another gray winter alone. Yellow light flooded the windows of the distant bungalow and she willed herself to the end of the dock. "Rick," she whispered. "Please don't go away and leave me here alone."

Rick's head came up abruptly and he looked around the bungalow's pine-paneled kitchen, puzzled. He had just hauled the last of the groceries in from the Jeep and was dutifully stowing the few perishable items he'd been able to find in Hapwell's store in the refrigerator when he clearly heard his name called. He cocked his head toward the nearest window. Heard nothing but the wind in the towering pines surrounding the bungalow.

He glanced at the Rolex. Nearly 3:00 A.M. No wonder he was hearing things. He dug a couple of pain pills out of his pocket, washed them down with a swallow of milk straight from the carton, and tried to remember how long it had been since he had last slept. Not counting the few minutes in the bathtub the previous evening, he figured he was going on twenty hours now. Shoving the last of the stuff that couldn't wait into the fridge and leaving the rest scattered across the countertop for the morning, he hobbled to the big sofa in front of the fireplace.

Everything hurt.

He hadn't yet made the bed upstairs and he wasn't about to start scrounging around for sheets at this hour. Just toss a couple of logs on the fire and crash on the sofa with the blankets. He hefted a couple of pieces of tamarack onto the grate, grimacing at his own exhaustion, and aware for the first time in months of what it was like to be honestly bone-tired.

The pills were already beginning to take effect as he dropped onto the sofa and pulled off his shoes. He experimentally closed his eyes, glad to see that the girl in the yellow slicker was nowhere about.

Nothing was going to keep him from sleeping tonight.

The thing in Mike Gomez's head stirred. Something was happening outside the freezing cadaver. Raising its dripping jaws from what remained of the boy's soul, it extended a dark probe into the slack fibers of the optic nerve and peered up into the night sky through a half-frozen eye. At the cloudy limits of its peripheral vision, a strong beam of light shot down from the road above, bathing the upended Camaro in an eerie glow. "Son of a bitch!" said a distant voice. "I told ya them was skid marks. Look, there's a car down there."

The beam of light slid across the snowbank and came to a stop on the boy's contorted face, nearly blinding the creature in a sudden dazzle of refraction from the ice crystals already forming within the freezing eye.

A shadow moved at the edge of the cliff high above and the faraway voice rose a full octave. "Oh Mother of God, there's a body. Looks like a kid."

A second shadow appeared behind the dazzling light and a deeper voice resonated down the canyon. "Fuck it, I ain't climbin' down there tonight," it growled. A match flared at the edge of the cliff and a cruel laugh echoed off the stone canyon walls. "Ain't as if the little bastard is goin' noplace before first light."

Something in the timbre of the second voice shot a thrill of anticipation through the predator in Mike Gomez. Suddenly alert, it pushed a sensitive probe through the boy's nostril and was rewarded with the faint pungent aroma of cigar smoke. Glorious memories of the rich prey it had enjoyed at the human habitation by the lake flooded its senses and it withdrew into the body, coiling into a tight knot and shivering with the anticipation of inhabiting a new host so soon. It knew it must do something to entice the prey to it. Do it quickly. Gathering together all its carefully hoarded reserves of strength, it channeled them into a single tremendous effort, then fell back exhausted.

"He moved," the first voice screamed.

"Eli, you're as full of shit as a Christmas turkey," the man with the cigar growled. "Gimme that thing!"

The elemental waited, pushing vainly against the stiffening muscles of Mike Gomez's body as the light played fitfully over the frozen corpse.

"I swear to God, Sheriff," whined the higher voice. "I seen him move."

Footsteps shuffled away on the road above and a radio crackled unintelligibly. After a few minutes the footsteps returned and a thick coil of rope dropped down the side of the cliff. Its descent was followed by the sounds of falling rocks and labored breathing as heavy boots scrabbled for purchase on the steep ground.

"That son of a bitch better be alive," the deep voice grunted, "else I'm gonna kick your crazy ass all the way back to Silver Peak."

The thing inside Mike Gomez smiled and coiled, prepared to spring.

CHAPTER 8

Dreamscape

T H E horror show.

Riding along in the back of Pop's '65 Chevy wagon, the tailgate window r_ed down. Your Heinz fifty-seven-variety mutt, Bucky, is drooling on your arm, and Freddie, your best friend in the whole world, has got you giggling so hard you can't stop 'cause he just cut a world-championship fart. A fart so loud and abrupt, it's sure to go into the Fart Hall of Fame. Your mom's in the front seat, turning around to grin questioningly at you. There's a pink scarf fluttering around her hair in the breeze from the open window and she looks so pretty you'd cry if you weren't already giggling so hard.

Rick Masterson was ten years old again, starting out on what was going to be the best weekend of his life. Relaxing against the cool rim of the

Chevy's chrome-stripped tailgate, a huge black inner tube cushioning his feet, he was speeding down the potholed Mississippi highway on his way to Panama City, Florida, a glorious noisy place filled with outrageous amusement rides and junk-food stands.

Pop was at the wheel, pedal to the metal, looking like something from outer space in his weird Hawaiian shirt with the pink flamingos, his Ray•Ban polarized clip-ons snapped rakishly over his wire-rim accountant's glasses. Frankie Vallee was wailing something about big girls on the radio, and Pop was doing a funny falsetto sing-along and flipping up the clip-ons to give Mom a Groucho Marx leer. It just didn't get any better than this.

Not ever.

Rick's giggling subsided and he wriggled a bare foot over the top of Mom's pink American Tourister night case, slipping his toes up under Freddie's fat butt and catching him totally by surprise.

"You fag!" Freddie squealing, his mouth a round hole smeared with mustard from the three hot dogs he'd just crammed down, and leaping away from him. Bucky barking joyously, jumping over legs and arms and sleeping bags and comically losing his balance as the Chevy's cream-puff suspension bottomed out on a pothole.

And then everything in the Chevy bouncing up to the roof like the law of gravity had just been repealed.

Rick turned his head toward the front of the Chevy. Caught a glimpse of Mom saying something. Pop's clip-ons sliding down his nose. Turned to look at Freddie. Screamed at the sight of the open tailgate, pieces of luggage and beach floats bounding across the highway.

But no Freddie.

Screaming as Pop brought the Chevy to a long skidding halt, running barefoot down the tar-hot highway. Stopping on the red-dust shoulder to look down. Cars stopping. People staring at the bloody thing in the dirt.

Then Freddie screaming. Screaming so loud and so high it hurt your ears. Screaming for an hour and never stopping until the funeral home ambulance from some nearby little dogshit town pulled up and a skinny redneck in a dirty white shirt got out puffing a cigarette and spit into the dust, reckoning to his cross-eyed partner whether it was worth the drive to Gulfport to get the kid to a hospital, or just wait a few minutes and take him on to the funeral home.

Then Pop, coming out of nowhere, his arms and shirt drenched in Freddie's blood, grabbing the skinny driver by his scraggly cracker neck and threatening to murder the no-count son of a bitch on the spot . . .

Rick was huddled in the back of the Chevy wagon, trembling uncontrollably in the arms of the fat black lady who'd run down from the nearby field road. Black lady cradling him in her huge, butter-soft arms and singing softly to him over Freddie's screams as Pop and a couple of truck drivers gently loaded him into the ambulance. "Hush little baby, don't you cry. . . ."

Rick rubbed his eyes, feeling the comforting press of arms around him, smelling the cornmeal on her hands. He touched the slick fabric of the black lady's raincoat, wondering why she wore such a garment on a blazing hot summer day. . . . Looked up to see the girl from Dubrovnik smiling at him, her yellow slicker glaring fluorescent in the bright Mississippi sunlight.

"The old one-two, Rick," she crooned sadly, pointing out through the back of the wagon.

Bucky.

Forgotten in the heat of the emergency. Good old Bucky, dolefully whimpering and wagging his tail, standing in the middle of the traffic-stalled road . . . in the path of the onrushing ambulance.

Rick screamed in his high, ten-year-old voice, his pitch precisely matched and drowned by the wail of the ambulance siren. The red demon eyes of the nameless thing behind the wheel peering out from a void of perfect blackness, swerving ever so slightly to center the dumb, helpless dog exactly in the track of the heavy vehicle. . . .

"Oh God!"

Rick sat bolt upright on the sofa, blinking at the shadows from the flickering fireplace, which was casting an insane light show about the walls of the darkened room.

"Rick!"

He spun around, looking for the voice that had called him, fell back onto the sofa, closing his eyes.

"Christ, don't," he pleaded.

"Rick." He felt a cool hand on his forehead. Not daring to open his eyes again.

"It's all right, baby," cooed the voice, soft and gentle as a whisper. "Sleep now."

He fell into a black, merciful sleep and dreamed a strange, erotic dream about Phylis Rand. She was standing in the middle of a curve on the snowy mountain road, gusts of freezing wind blowing her thin nightgown against the hollows of her perfectly sculpted body. . . .

Sara stood among the dancing shadows of the bungalow's fireplace, watching the sleeping man. She had drifted across the lake earlier—her flight as swift and effortless as that of the lonely hawk—wanting only to see him again, to gaze upon his face and wonder what miraculous force had made it possible for him to see her. Except for one maddening period years earlier when she had found herself returning nightly to the mountain road to wait—for what or whom, she never discovered—she knew that she existed only in her own mind. But Rick had seen her tonight.

It had to mean something.

She had arrived at the bungalow, intending merely to hover outside the windows in hopes of catching a glimpse of the man inside. Instead she had heard him writhing in his sleep, crying out in small tortured breaths like a child. Moved by his obvious distress, she had projected herself into the room where he lay, placed her cold, bloodless hand on his brow, wanting only to soothe his pain. Then, with no thought that such a thing was even possible, she had been abruptly drawn into the last horrible moments of his dream—had stood in the hot red dirt along the strange highway of some long-past time and watched his ten-year-old view of his perfect world unalterably changed forever. Seen the tiny dark spot of cynicism take root on his soul. Been dazzled by the beautiful golden creature who had suddenly appeared to cradle and soothe his child's body in her arms.

Terrified by the vision, yet fascinated, too, she had tried to withdraw. It was then that the girl in the glowing yellow slicker had turned to smile at her and, with a wave of her hand, allowed her to glimpse the tortured scenes that plagued Rick whenever he allowed himself to slip into sleep— scenes that Sara intuitively understood made him somehow like her, that *could* quite easily turn him into what she had become.

Or worse.

Looking into the frightening shadows of his tortured soul, Sara also sensed the cold, dark thing that lingered in the black hole that had grown and festered in him over the years, waiting to make him its own. She had felt its rage and was frightened of it, knowing it could take her as well, if it chose. It was stronger than the lake thing she thought of as the demon, much stronger. And cunning, too, a seething intellect fueled by pure malevolence. She had pulled away when she could stand no more, cautiously returning to the hard reality of the bungalow's main room to gaze down upon the sleeping man before the fire, feeling she could help but not certain how.

There was something else.

Sara also knew that within the sleeping man on the sofa, his thick black hair gleaming in the firelight, there was a chance for her.

If only he would stay.

"Little fucker's stiff as a board." Sheriff Jim "Bull" Ryan spat disgustedly into the snow and leaned over Mike Gomez, flashing his light into the boy's dead eyes. "Fucking runaway, I'll lay you ten to one."

Eli, his deputy, was poking around the overturned Camaro, shining his own powerful flashlight through the shattered windshield. Missy Ferguson's horribly smashed face stared back at him. "Oh Christ, Sheriff, there's another one in here. A girl."

Eli turned away from the wreck and leaned over a clump of bushes to retch into the snow. "Just kids," he gasped with genuine emotion.

Ryan wasn't paying attention. He'd seen so many stiffs in his twenty years as Silver County's chief law-enforcement officer that the sight of a couple of snot-nose runaways splattered on the rocks as the result of their own stupidity raised no emotion in him beyond a worsening of his usually vile mood. There was something about this kid on the ground that interested him, though. Something . . . different.

He leaned over the corpse, playing his light on the dead eyes. Something moved behind the cloudy lenses, something dark. He was certain he had seen it. As certain as Eli had sounded when he'd thought he'd seen the body move from up on the road. He felt in his hip pocket for the plastic disposable gloves he had carried ever since the beginning of the AIDS epidemic. No telling what kind of bugs this little bastard had inside him. He slipped on a glove, grabbed the boy's chin, and stared into his eyes.

He saw it again, a flash of movement. And something else, too. He squatted rock still over the body for several moments, staring.

"Hey, Eli, get your sorry ass over here," he finally bellowed.

The little deputy came stumbling across the rough ground and knelt beside him.

"Tell me what you see," said Ryan, flashing his light into the boy's eyes.

Eli squinted and shrugged his shoulders. "Nothing, Sheriff."

"What do you mean, nothing?" Ryan shoved the deputy roughly away from him. "Get back on up to the road and wait for the meat wagon."

"Sure, Sheriff, whatever you say." The little deputy scrambled away, delighted at the opportunity to escape to the warmth of the Ford Bronco patrol unit idling on the mountain road above.

Ryan rocked back on his heels, withdrawing a fresh cigar from his fur-lined uniform jacket. He bit the end off the smoke, touched a match to it, and spent several long minutes sucking in thick, acrid smoke, watching with his piglike eyes as the deputy clambered up the steep incline. As soon as Eli's slender form disappeared over the cliff edge, Ryan flashed his light into Mike Gomez's face. Grabbing the boy by the chin, he peered again into the lifeless eyes.

* * *

Phylis lay awake in the gleaming brass four-poster that was the pièce de résistance of the restored high-ceilinged bedroom apartment she maintained above the old saloon. Somewhere far in the distance a siren wailed—the sound itself an odd occurrence in Silver Peak—and she wondered if Rick Masterson had made it safely up the mountain to Spirit Lake. She had been lying awake for hours thinking about him.

From the first moment she had seen him standing in the open doorway, she had known. Everything about him, his voice, his mannerisms, even the way he smelled—a suggestion of new leather behind a hint of mint-flavored toothpaste—had turned her on. She smiled to herself now as she remembered how she had stood behind the bar trying to be nonchalant while her knees were wobbling like a nervous teenager's. The first time she'd touched him, deliberately laying her hand on his to emphasize some minor point of conversation, the sensation had been positively electric.

"Christ, Phil," she murmured aloud in her negative voice, a firmly ingrained habit she had developed in Vegas to psych herself up before going out to perform for a packed showroom, "you must have scared the poor guy to death, inviting him to spend the night after you'd known him for all of sixty minutes. He probably thinks you're the county tramp."

"You know that's not true," she told herself in the other more sensible voice, the one she used to overcome the fears raised by the negative voice—

fears about the size of the house, the condition of her ankles, the tape anchors that were supposed to keep her breasts inside the scanty costumes the casino managers had insisted she dance in, whatever. "I only invited him because that road is dangerous," she insisted. "He said so himself. Besides," she added, "the poor thing looked exhausted."

The first voice was frankly amused. "Never kid a kidder, Phil, old buddy," it said. "You wanted to get him up here so you could flounce around in that Frederick's of Hollywood getup you've had tucked away in the wardrobe for the past two years. Heck, you would have had the 'poor exhausted thing' panting like a Great Dane in heat before you'd finished showing him where the towels were, and you damn well know it."

"Bitch," said the second voice.

Phylis yawned, getting sleepy at last.

"The thing is," she said in her first voice, "how *are* we going to get him up here?"

She pulled the down comforter over her head. "I don't know," she said. "We'll think of something."

CLANK, CLANK, CLANK, CLANK!

Phylis sat up, startled by the strange sound. Red lights flashed against the walls and someone yelled outside her window, followed by the sound of a revving engine. Swinging her feet over the side of the bed, she hurried to the double casement fronting Silver Peak's main street and looked out. A black-and-white sheriff's vehicle, its roof lights flashing, sat in the middle of the street as the town's battered tow truck lowered the wreck of a badly smashed red Camaro into the vacant lot beside Hapwell's store. Bull Ryan stood with a stub of cigar clenched in his teeth, watching the operation. He suddenly turned and leered up at Phylis, reflections of the red emergency flashers glittering in his fat-encased eyes.

She dropped her gaze to the plunging neckline of the lacy nightgown she was wearing, painfully aware that the way she was leaning over the sill was providing the crude sheriff with a nearly unobstructed view of her breasts. Her face burning, she stepped quickly back into the shadows and drew the shade.

Ryan's harsh, guttural laughter rang in her ears as she made her way back to bed.

The Lake

M O R N I N G.

Rick turned over onto his back and looked up into a dazzling beam of light aimed directly into his eyes. "Jesus," he groaned.

He rolled stiffly away from the shaft of sunlight beaming in through the skylight and tried to sit up. The shoulder throbbed and the knee creaked as he got his feet onto the floor. "Father forgive me," he muttered, "for I have sinned."

The fire had gone out during the night and he shivered in the chill as he tossed new kindling and logs into the grate. Limping to the kitchen in his socks, he started a pot of coffee on the propane gas range and went to the window, squinting against the brightness outside.

A sky so richly blue it hurt his eyes glared back at him from the even bluer waters of the lake, the whole surrounded by a sparkling blanket of virgin snow. On the surrounding mountainsides endless ranks of ponderosa pines, their dark green branches delicately tipped with the glittering white stuff, trooped down to the sapphire water, fringing its edge in palisades of thick brown trunks. Small birds chirped and flitted among the trees, adding a continuous joyous chorus to the scene. A hundred feet from the bungalow a family of whitetail deer stood drinking at the lake. All in all, it was the most breathtaking scene Rick Masterson had ever witnessed.

Forgetting his aching joints, he slid open the glass balcony doors and was rewarded with a blast of cold, pine-scented air. He took a deep breath of the fragrant stuff and, shielding his eyes against the glare with his hands, scanned the lake. Light flashed against a pane of glass to the north and he was just able to make out the faint outlines of the sprawling house where he had dropped the girl the night before. He smiled, thinking about her, and wondered if she had awakened with a cold. He still didn't see how she could have gone barefoot in the snow without getting frostbitten.

The bungalow's upstairs bathroom was gloriously hot and steamy.

Rick stood beneath the pulsating shower head and let the scalding needles of spray pound him until his skin was red and tingling. He closed his eyes and was pleasantly rewarded with an image of Phylis Rand leaning over the bar of the Silver Peak Saloon, a tantalizing bit of cleavage peeking through the vee of her soft pink sweater. He grinned foolishly, suddenly aware that he was becoming aroused, and wondered why he hadn't dreamed of her the night before. His forehead wrinkled into a frown and he realized that he hadn't dreamed of anything, not that he remembered, at any rate. It occurred to him that that was good. That was very good. This place must be agreeing with him. Thank God something was after all these months.

The hot water ran out all at once, dousing him with an icy blast from the shower head. He yelped and jumped out of the shower, toweled down with a rough bath sheet, and stood in front of the steamy mirror for a cold shave. Grinning at his misty reflection in the glass, he decided that he must look substantially better than he had the night before. Anyway he felt great.

Stepping out into the adjoining bedroom, he sniffed the aroma of fresh coffee and hurried into fresh jeans and a sweatshirt. He wondered what Phylis looked like fresh from the shower. "A damn sight better than you do, pal," he replied to his own unspoken question.

After a breakfast of ham and scrambled eggs washed down with several cups of coffee and mopped up with three thickly buttered slabs of wheat toast, Rick pulled on a sweater and stepped out onto the snow-sheltered porch. He groaned under the weight of the massive breakfast, figuring he'd consumed enough cholesterol to give the entire network-news staff double coronaries and vowing to make a run into Reno or Carson, where, hopefully, he'd find a market that offered something a bit less bypass-oriented than the old-time staples available in Hap Hapwell's general store.

He entered the boat house to find the little Honda generator purring softly, although the fuel gauge was reading near empty. Topping off the tank from one of the red jerry cans he located beneath the workbench, he made a mental note to add gas to his shopping list. He was replacing the half-full can beneath the bench when he noticed the small square of paper that had slipped down from the bulletin board above. Curious, he stretched his good arm to reach into the tight spot, retrieving the square with two fingers.

It was another snapshot.

Rick looked at the faded picture in the dim light of the boat house. This one was old, the glossy finish cracked, the colors faded. In it, he recognized the same dark-haired young man whose photo with Jimmy in the sailboat was tacked to the bulletin board. But Jimmy wasn't in this photo. In this one the youth stood before an old Jeep, looking directly at the camera. Jimmy's older brother? A brother he'd never mentioned. An image of Jimmy flashed into his mind. Jimmy, the pudgy, moon-faced kid who had been a gofer at the network's Los Angeles headquarters five years ago—before Rick had come in from assignment in Nicaragua and the kid had started following him around like a homeless puppy. . . .

"Well, I'll be damned!" Rick nodded, suddenly understanding why the kid had started tagging after him in the first place, persisting until—more out of frustration than anything else—Rick had gotten him on his team as a tech. "I must be about the same age as the kid's brother."

Tacking the photo to the bulletin board, Rick bent and peered under the bench again. The frayed corner of another photo—one he never would have noticed if he hadn't been looking—peeked from behind the two-by-four that served as a floor-level brace for the legs of the sturdy bench. He got down on his hands and knees to retrieve it.

The new photo was of the same vintage as the previous one, evidently taken on the same day. In it, a girl in a brief bikini sat perched on the hood of the same Jeep. She was laughing at something out of the range of the camera's lens, her thick tangle of blond hair swirled carelessly across one tanned shoulder.

The heavy breakfast grumbled uncomfortably in Rick's stomach as he stared at the picture of the girl he had picked up on the mountain road the night before. He caught his breath and looked again. A little mental math told him it couldn't be the same girl. Jimmy looked to be about ten years old in the picture with the young man in the boat. The kid had just turned twenty-five last August. That meant the picture had to have been taken about fifteen years ago. Yet the girl in the picture was twenty or twenty-one—the same age as the girl on the road. "Not possible," he said, pinning the new picture up beside the other.

He had locked up the boat house and was halfway up the walk to the bungalow before the explanation hit him. Jimmy had told him Spirit Lake was a family place, a place where the same people brought their kids and their kids' children

year after year. The girl on the road was somebody's kid sister, just like the guy in the boat was
probably Jimmy's big brother. Wait until he got
back to L.A. and told Jimmy. The kid would probably
get a charge out of it.

A sudden breeze ruffled the loose sweater, blowing a draft of icy air up his back, and he determined that he'd better retrieve his parka, the only
real cold-weather garment he'd brought with him.

Although the straight-line distance between the
bungalows and the lodge near the north end of the
lake was just a little over a mile, the distance by
road was closer to three. North of the junction, the
narrow blacktop road entered a thick pine forest
that at times reduced the view of the lake to mere
glimpses of blue water behind the thick stands of
conifers.

Rick drove along slowly, enjoying the sound of
the Jeep's tires crunching through the fresh snow
and admiring the view he'd missed the previous
night. The way he felt this morning confirmed in
his mind the wisdom of having come up here to
get away from the troubles that had plagued him
in Los Angeles, and he wondered if he would be
able to hack it out in the field again when the time
came for a new assignment. Somewhere on the
long road from Dubrovnik he had come to the realization that there was something intrinsically
wrong with spending one's life immersed in bloodshed
and disaster, and though he frequently reassured
himself that his singular ability to function calmly
in situations that would drive most men to distrac-

tion was merely a defense mechanism, he couldn't help thinking at times that there was something in his makeup that craved the carnage, making him purposely seek out situations that other people—sensible ones—ran from.

He thought about it, trying to determine what it might be, but came up with nothing. His life until the time he had gone to work for the network had been unremarkable. The only child of middle-class parents, he'd grown up in a quiet Memphis suburb, had played second-string football in high school, mostly because it pleased Pop, and gone on to Emory University near Atlanta, where he had intended to major in English literature.

At the end of his sophomore year he'd attended a weekend lecture by a respected broadcast journalist because the girl he'd been going with at the time had dragged him along. As often happens in such cases, the eloquence of the speaker had fired his imagination with visions of life on the cutting edge of world events. The following Monday he'd presented himself to the head of Emory's journalism department to announce his wish to change majors.

The bemused dean, who had also attended the inspirational lecture, showed him a stack of applications from students who had preceded him in expressing their desire to become broadcast journalists that day and asked why he thought he could make it in a business that was always tough, often dirty, and sometimes downright dangerous. Rick had looked the man in the eye and said it was what he was born to do. Out of sixty applications inspired by Walter Cronkite's lecture, his was the only one accepted.

He'd thrown himself into the program with great zeal, taking courses in photography on the side and, ultimately, becoming editor of the school's weekly paper and doing midnight stints as a deejay for the campus radio station.

Upon graduation from college, he'd landed a job covering the police beat for a small Omaha radio station and had moved into television two years later as a reporter for a local network affiliate in Kansas City. He'd come to the notice of the network when, having received the dubious honor of being the station's only reporter asked to work one cold and snowy Christmas Eve, he'd packed his crew and camera onto snowmobiles to follow up a lead from the state-police radio band about a group of motorists stranded on a lonely stretch of interstate highway in what turned out to be the Midwest's worst blizzard of the century—arriving just in time to witness a young woman giving birth in the back of a farmer's livestock trailer, surrounded by bales of hay and farm animals.

The "Miracle of Christmas" story, as it had come to be known throughout the industry, had been picked up and broadcast around the world, and Rick Masterson was suddenly somebody. The following summer he had been hired by the network and sent to Nicaragua to document the story of the refugees caught in the cross fire between warring factions struggling for control of the country.

Now, driving through the peaceful woods around Spirit Lake, Rick concluded that there was nothing in his background to account for the reputation he'd acquired as a coldhearted bastard. It was just the goddamned job. He was good at what he did and he knew it, and that meant putting the story first, regardless. He wasn't sure where he'd come up with that particular philosophy, but it worked. He felt a surge of uneasiness over the fact that—except for Jimmy—most of the network production and tech people groaned when they were assigned to his crews. But that was their problem. He could hardly be held responsible for the cameraman who had died in South Africa the year before or, for that matter, the kid who'd lost his leg in that Coast Guard drug shoot-out off the Bahamas the year before that. That kind of shit happened all the time and was hardly proof—as some of the techies had been overheard to grumble— that he'd gladly waste one of them in order to get ten seconds of great footage. He'd never heard any of them complain about the money. Besides, if he was the insensitive hard-ass they had him cracked up to be, why was he now having nightmares about all of it?

The Jeep rounded a gentle curve and emerged from the deep woods along the lake's western shore to parallel a snow-covered beach. Shoving aside all the mind clutter he'd come up here to forget about, Rick rolled down his window to admit a blast of chilly air and scanned the scenic vista of mountains and sky surrounding him.

Sunlight blazed against the windows of the big lodge just across a narrow bay from the road, and he squinted against the sudden glare, looking for some sign that the inhabitants were up and about. The place seemed absolutely still in the cold morning light, and he worried that Sara might be sleeping in after her ordeal. Oh well, he decided, surely there would be someone about who could at least return his parka.

The long drive leading up the avenue of pines was still unplowed. Slowing at the entrance, Rick noticed that the expanse of snow covering the surface was marked only by the distinctive knobby tread of the Jeep's off-road tires—from his arrival and departure the night before—and the partially snow-filled tracks of one other vehicle, whose narrow gauge suggested a smaller car without chains or snow treads. He guided the Jeep onto the drive and followed his own tracks up to the circular turnaround fronting the house.

Arriving in darkness the night before, he hadn't gotten a true picture of how big the place really was, the low profile of the main building extending more than a hundred feet across the front, and the snow-covered roofs of several outbuildings showing through the nearby trees. He whistled softly at the sheer size of the estate, realizing that the half-frozen girl he had picked up on the mountain road must be wealthy. Correction, filthy rich. He figured that the taxes alone on this place would probably eat up his own not insubstantial salary. "Poor little rich girl," he said aloud, thinking of the shivering and pathetic creature he'd rescued from the lonely mountain road the night before, "obviously even all of Daddy's money can't make her happy." He allowed himself a vicious grin. "Maybe I ought to ask for a reward."

Pulling to a stop before the lodge's sheltered main door, he peered into the dark shadows hiding the front door and started to get out of the Jeep. It suddenly occurred to him that the place might be guarded and he blew the horn instead—remembering how he'd once gone uninvited onto the grounds of a palatial estate owned by a wealthy Chicago labor boss and been caught flat-footed by a pair of vicious Dobermans.

He waited for several minutes, and when no snarling dogs appeared, he opened the Jeep's door and got out, crunching through the encrusted snow of a flagstone walk to the lodge's dark entrance porch.

CHAPTER 10

The Lodge

DARK.

Dark and unkempt. That was Rick's first impression of the entrance porch to the lodge. Stepping in out of the bright morning sunshine, he was assailed by a wave of subfreezing air and the stale, unpleasant odor of slowly decaying vegetation. The grated concrete floor of the porch was inches deep in damp pine needles, the brown windblown mat of them drifted up against the heavy front door and its supporting rock walls in a way that suggested it had been weeks or perhaps months since anyone had gone into the house through this entrance.

Puzzled, Rick looked around him. No other doors were visible, yet he was certain the girl had come this way the night before. To his left, the porch continued around to the side of the house via a narrow, unswept walkway beneath the eaves, and he assumed she must have gone that way after he had seen her disappear into the shadows. Reluctant to start prowling around a strange property uninvited, he turned back to the door and searched for a bell or buzzer. Finding nothing, he raised his good arm and knocked on the door.

It swung open at his first touch, revealing a long, unlit corridor richly paneled in expensive hardwood above a gray fieldstone floor. To his right, the paneling supported a dozen coat hooks formed from the antlers of deer. At the far end and to the left, another door was visible.

"Hello?" His own voice echoed back to him from the corridor, which, it suddenly occurred to him, might be just an extension of the porch, and not a part of the house proper. He called again, "Anybody home?" and, when no one answered, stepped into the corridor, making as much noise as possible.

The door at the far end of the corridor stood partially open and he looked through to see a vast, high-ceilinged room, one wall of which was taken up by a massive stone fireplace that soared forty feet to the beamed ceiling above. Light filtered into the room through dirty windows, affording a dim view of the sparkling lake beyond.

"Hello, Sara?" Rick stepped into the room, taking in the dusty hardwood floor, the bizarre collection of animal heads on the wall, and the tomblike chill in the air. He crossed slowly to the fireplace, where someone had been drinking beer and, from the look of it, camping out, nudging a half-empty can of Vienna sausages with the tip of his shoe.

What in the hell was going on here?

Something popped behind him and he whirled to see a wisp of smoke rising from a glowing ember in the fireplace. Kneeling as well as the damaged knee would allow, he placed his hand upon the hearth stones. Still warm. Not too long ago there had been a fire burning here.

Hoisting himself back to his feet, he looked down at the small pile of silverware and statuary by the sofa, picked up the brightly colored Navajo blanket by the floor, and examined it. An expensive piece. Very expensive. He carefully folded the blanket, laid it across the sofa, and walked around the perimeter of the room, noting the shelves filled with valuable books, the broken pane of glass at the French doors.

One corner of the room by the windows overlooking the lake contained an antique mahogany desk of tremendous proportions, and he crossed to it, quickly scanning the dusty collection of yellowing papers on its surface, the scrapbook opened to the full-page obituary of someone named Harold Raynor. He had just started to read the article when he sensed a presence behind him. He turned to see the dim outline of a hulking figure silhouetted in the doorway leading to the paneled corridor.

"Hello," he called, edging away from the desk. "I didn't think there was anybody here."

The sinister figure in the doorway did not move. It stood silently regarding him from the shadows, blocking his way out.

Rick smiled. "Look, I'm sure this looks a little strange, but my name is Rick Masterson. I'm staying at one of the bungalows down at the other end of the lake and I—"

"Masterson? You that TV-news guy?"

"Yes," said Rick, relieved. He stepped forward to

meet the figure in the doorway, halting as a huge man in a fleece-lined sheepskin jacket emerged from the shadows, pointing a long-barreled revolver at his chest. For a long moment the man's hate-filled eyes glared at him and Rick was certain he was going to shoot. The man's beady eyes flickered to a mass of dark shadows gathering on the wall behind Rick and his entire body twitched convulsively. The hatred suddenly faded from his eyes, replaced by the bored look of officialdom.

"I think you're full of shit, mister," said Sheriff Bull Ryan. He turned back the lapel of the sheepskin jacket and a badge glinted in the dim light. "My name's Ryan and I'm the law around here. So far all I see is a fucking trespasser." His bright little eyes scanned the room from behind folds of unhealthy fat, taking in the broken window, the empty cans, and the pile of valuables by the sofa. "Looks like simple breaking and entering and first-degree burglary to me."

"Burglary? Look, I've got ID," Rick said. He slid a hand around to his hip pocket, reaching for his billfold.

"Hands over your head," growled Ryan, spinning him roughly around and snatching the billfold.

"If you'd just give me a goddamn second," said Rick, "I can explain—"

"Shut the fuck up. If I want you to explain anything, I'll ask you."

Rick closed his mouth and stood with his hands raised as Ryan rifled his billfold. After a moment the sheriff spun the reporter back around and scrutinized him. The big revolver stayed leveled at Rick's chest.

"Okay," he said. "Explain."

Rick winced at the pain shooting through his injured shoulder, but he wasn't about to give the asshole with the gun the satisfaction of asking if he could lower his hands. One look at the man's eyes, greedy and cruel, told him what he was up against. He'd dealt with official bullies like this one in half a dozen two-bit countries scattered around the globe and he knew that his type thrived upon anything they interpreted as a sign of weakness.

"Well," he said, "I was driving up from Silver Peak last night and I found this girl on the road."

Ryan's eyes narrowed. "What girl?"

Rick shrugged. "She said her name was Sara and that she lived here. I dropped her off out front and she came inside. I'd given her my jacket and I came by to pick it up this morning. The front door was open, so I came in." He paused, gauging the big man's reaction to his words. "I'm staying up here in one of the bungalows as a guest of Charles Randall," he added, casually dropping the name of Jimmy's father, an internationally known investment banker. He knew from long experience that if anything was bound to impress a creep like Ryan, it was a connection with someone rich and powerful.

The ploy seemed to work because the sheriff slowly lowered the gun and handed Rick's billfold back to him. "You can put your hands down," he said, turning his back on Rick and surveying the room more closely. He crossed to the fireplace and kicked at the row of beer cans on the hearth with a size-thirteen boot. "Little fuckers," he muttered. "Got what they deserved if you ask me."

"Look," said Rick. "If I could just find the girl and get my jacket, I'd like to be going."

"Mister, there ain't no girl," said Ryan, turning to glare at him as if he were some kind of an idiot. "Least not anymore."

"I don't think I understand."

"Fucking kids," said Ryan, pointing the revolver at the mess in front of the fireplace. "Come up here from Carson and Reno and break into these empty houses to fuck and do their drugs. Carload of 'em run an old piece-of-shit Camaro off the mountain road last night. Two of 'em was killed, a boy and a girl."

Rick felt his breath catch. "The girl, a blonde, early twenties?"

Ryan wagged his floppy jowls. "Nah, little bitch couldn'ta been more than sixteen." He stared at the fireplace for a long moment. "I expect the one you picked up on the road must've been with 'em. Got herself out of the car some way before it went over. She look to you like she might've been in a wreck?"

Rick nodded. "Yeah, she was barefoot in the snow and looked scared as hell. . . . I tried to take her to a hospital, but she insisted on coming here."

"Probably had another car stashed up here," said Ryan. He bit the end off a fat green cigar and spit it into the fireplace. "Got her little tail out of here as fast as she could, I expect."

Rick's mind was racing to catch up with the sheriff's imaginative reconstruction of the previous night's events on the mountain. It didn't work for him. "Wait a minute," he protested. "In the first place, the girl I picked up didn't seem like the kind to just walk away and leave her friends for dead in a wrecked car."

Ryan touched a match to his cigar and glared at him through piggish eyes.

"Secondly, there was only one set of tracks in the driveway besides mine when I got here a little while ago, so there couldn't have been any second car."

The sheriff said nothing.

"Finally," Rick concluded, "the girl said she lived here." He looked meaningfully toward the unexplored portion of the house. "Maybe she had a concussion or something and she's passed out in one of the other rooms."

Ryan exhaled a cloud of stinking smoke and pointed the glowing cigar at him.

"Look here, Mister . . . Masterson, now I know you're this big, hot-shit TV reporter and you must have some real rich friends if they're letting you stay up here in one of them fancy-ass bungalows down to the Marina, so I'm tryin' to be real nice to you. Part of the service." He jammed the cigar into the corner of his mouth, exposing a row of yellow teeth, and holstered the revolver. "But this is police business and you don't have a goddamn clue as to what's goin' on up here, so I suggest you go on back down to your own end of the lake and do whatever it was you come up here to do."

"But the girl said she lived here, in this house," Rick insisted.

"Mister, ain't nobody lived here in this house since 1976. They're all dead."

"What?"

"This house belongs to the Raynor Corporation out of San Francisco. Since old man Raynor croaked, they pay the county to keep it up for corporate meetings and shit during the summer—at least they used to come. Corporation ain't held no meetings here for a couple of years now. Anyway, your little girlfriend, whoever she was, done come up here to get fucked and do a little dope, and now she's gone. Case closed, except I gotta bring a woman up here to clean the place up or the company'll shit their pants." Ryan kicked disgustedly at the mess on the floor. "It'll take me a week to find somebody to do it. Probably have to go to Reno or Carson."

"Why?" asked Rick.

Ryan laughed, a nasty wheezing sound, and hawked a gob of green phlegm into the fireplace. "'Cause the damn fools down in Silver Peak all think this place is haunted." He chuckled. Not one of 'em'll set foot up here in the winter. Hell, I gotta send a fuckin' deputy up here with 'em every spring just to get 'em to clean the johns and run a vacuum." He tore a square of cardboard from a beer carton and jammed it into the broken window-pane on the French door. "You better go on and get out of here now so I can close up."

"Mind if I take a quick look around for my parka?" Rick asked. "She might have left it here. It's the only cold-weather gear I brought with me," he added.

Ryan scowled dubiously, considering the request. "Make it damn quick," he finally said.

Rick quickly scanned the big room, returning to the area of the massive desk. He spotted a half-open door in a dark corner behind the desk and stepped across to find that it hid the entrance to a small bathroom. His parka lay in a heap before the mirrored door. He picked it up and returned to the desk to find Ryan waiting for him.

"Got it."

Ryan aimed a fat thumb toward the corridor door Rick had entered by. "Okay, out."

Rick nodded, pausing to slip into the parka. That was when he saw the photograph on the desk. The girl, Sara, or at least the girl who looked like her. The same girl whose faded picture he had found in the boat house. He started to say something to Ryan, then thought better of it. There was something about the man he didn't like. There had been something in the sheriff's first look, a moment when Rick had been sure Ryan was about to kill him. The moment had passed, but whatever had prompted it went far beyond the ordinary cruelty and stupidity that shone dully from his glittering little eyes.

Something . . . evil.

Ryan followed the nosy reporter out through the long corridor leading to the lodge's front door and stood watching from the dark shadows as he circled the sheriff's vehicle and climbed into the white Jeep Cherokee.

He waited until the Jeep turned around and started down the drive before turning back to the empty house. Pausing before the open front door, he peered into the dark corridor leading into the main room they called the study. Just looking in from the outside, straining to see into the darkness, was giving him a splitting headache.

Ryan had never liked going into the house, which was one reason he hadn't been up since the summer. It wasn't that he believed the saloon stories that goddamn old fart Hapwell and his friends told; Sheriff Bull Ryan believed in eating, drinking, and fucking over anyone or anything that got in his way, and that was all. Still, the old Lodge gave him the creeps. Ever since what had happened up here in '76 . . .

A sly grin twisted his fleshy lips and he took the fat cigar from between his teeth and stared at the glowing tip. A dark thought popped into his head. Maybe he should just torch the goddamn place. Then he'd never have to come back again to walk through those dead rooms. The memory of what he'd discovered in the kitchen when he'd finally been packed up to the lake by snowmobile that day back in '76 still turned his stomach. Christ! He'd never seen such a stinking mess in his whole life—and that included two tours in 'Nam, where he'd seen so much shit he'd thought nothing would ever shock him again.

Pulling his heavy jacket tight around his bulging gut, he spat on the littered stones of the porch and reentered the house. Something inside his head was telling him to torch the place, just like he'd torched those gook hooches up in Quang Tri Province. The world would be better off without it and he'd never have to come back here again, Raynor Corporation or no Raynor Corporation. He couldn't understand what they wanted to keep the goddamn eyesore for anyway . . . they never even used it anymore.

CHAPTER 11

A Meeting of Minds

S A R A stood in the empty study regarding the cold fireplace. She had drifted into the room during her solitary wanderings among the familiar passages at the rear of the house just as Rick and the vile sheriff were leaving. Her heart had leaped at the sight of the young man pulling on his parka before her father's massive desk, and she had been on the verge of reaching out for him. The sheriff's brusque order for Rick to leave the Lodge had weakened her resolve, however, and she had hung back in the shadows until they both left.

A tiny wisp of smoke rose from the last of the dying embers on the hearth, a veil as insubstantial as herself swirling up the chimney. The big sofa before the fireplace had always been Sara's favorite spot, a place to curl up with a good book or to make meticulous entries in the little diary she had faithfully kept in life. She smiled at the cooling embers, wishing there was a roaring blaze in the fireplace now. A crackling fire had always made the room, with its collection of rare volumes— which she had been forbidden to touch—and its piteous menagerie of stuffed animals, seem less forbidding.

A footstep sounded on the floorboards behind Sara and she whirled to see the hulking figure of the sheriff lurking in the shadowed doorway of the entrance hall. She had seen this man many times before, usually when he arrived at the house to check the doors and windows or to supervise the annual cleaning and repairs each spring, and she was not frightened of him. Neither did she like him, however. Waves of negative energy positively oozed from Bull Ryan's gross being and she had witnessed him removing small items from the property on more than one occasion.

Sara usually withdrew from the room when the man was about, somehow sensing that his predatory nature made him dimly aware of her presence. This time, however, something in his demeanor prompted her to stay. He stood in the doorway now, staring straight at her, his small eyes glittering as though he could actually see her here by the fireplace. He shook his big head after a moment and blinked like a man waking from a deep sleep.

Stepping deliberately into the room, he crossed directly in front of her without a glance in her direction and halted before the shelves of rare books. One hand was thrust deep into the pocket of his sheepskin coat and she wondered if he was going to steal another of the valuable volumes.

*   *   *

Bull Ryan stood before the ceiling-high shelves of dusty old books, staring dully. His right hand reached out to caress the tinder-dry binding of a collection of Shaw's plays and a twisted smile played at the corners of his mouth. The paper was dry, so dry. The plastic cigarette lighter in his jacket pocket tingled against the fingers of his left hand and he envisioned striking a flame, then touching it to the Shaw and watching with satisfaction as hungry sparks danced and spread among the dense ranks of books, the blue-and-orange sheets of fire reaching to the ceiling beams, jumping from there to the Lodge's roof of dry redwood shakes. The beautiful flames spreading out to engulf the entire building in a monstrous red blossom of destruction.

Ryan's smile broadened. It seemed so . . . right. After the fire there would be no more need for him to drive the treacherous mountain road with whimpering cleaning ladies, no more lonely patrols to see if the property was safe, no more snot-nose kids breaking in. . . . Hell, even the Raynor Corporation would be happy. He knew for a fact that they'd insured the place to the hilt. That wasn't the important thing, though. The important thing was the fire itself. The look and smell of it would be . . . awesome.

Sara watched with growing curiosity as the big man stood swaying and muttering to himself before the wall of bookshelves. A strand of clear saliva dribbled from the corner of his ugly mouth and dangled from his chin as he slowly withdrew a brightly colored cigarette lighter from his coat and spun the striking wheel with his thick thumb. A jet of blue flame hovered above the lighter and he moved it closer to the books.

"No!" she screamed, realizing at once what he was about to do and hurling herself at him. Without the familiar shell of the house to protect her, she would be consigned to wander the empty grounds of the Lodge alone for eternity, denied even the scant comfort that the familiar surroundings provided . . . denied the occasional human contact that might someday help free her from her present state.

An icy blast of pure rage sliced through the core of Ryan's being and he staggered back away from the bookshelf with Sara's soundless scream still echoing in his head. The gas-fired cigarette lighter flew from his hand, its flame extinguished before it hit the floor, and skittered under the sofa.

Terrified at what had just happened, Ryan pulled his revolver from its holster and whirled about to face the seemingly empty room. His eyes darted from shadow to shadow, searching for a target. Something had hit him from behind. Something he couldn't see but that he knew was there all the same. The locals' stories about the place flooded his mind, stories he had laughed at, despite the fact that coming here had always made him uneasy.

His breath was coming in short gasps and he rubbed a beefy hand across his flushed face, trying to remember why he had come back into the house at all. Something about a fire. He glanced quickly at the fireplace, confirming that it had now gone completely cold. That must have been it, he reasoned. He must have come back to check on the fireplace. After all, the Raynor Corporation paid him a fat yearly retainer for keeping tabs on the place. Wouldn't do to have it burn down, taking his little nest egg with it.

Something cold and soft touched his cheek and he turned again, muffling the tiny hiccuping sob that rose in his wattled throat and pointing the gun at empty space. "I'm warnin' you, fucker," he said in a tremulous, high-pitched voice. "Keep away from me!"

A tinkling laugh that might have been a stray gust of wind down the chimney echoed at his back as he took to his heels and ran for the entrance hall.

Sara watched from a dormer window above the drive as Ryan sprinted comically to his vehicle. She suppressed a mischievous giggle at the sight of the fat sheriff jumping into his idling patrol unit and roaring away down the long avenue of trees, all four wheels of the speeding vehicle churning up rooster tails of sparkling snow. She had never actually tried to haunt anyone before and the ease with which she had just reduced the swaggering bully to near hysteria was exhilarating.

Turning away from the streaked window, she glided through the dusty attic space above the lodge, threading her way past moth-eaten trophies, boxes of fishing tackle, and draped piles of discarded furniture until she found herself face-to-face with a gilt-framed portrait of Harold Raynor.

"Did you see that, Daddy?" She smirked. "I frightened him away all by myself. Aren't you proud of your little girl?"

Her father's cold eyes stared back from the cobwebbed canvas and she wished with all her might that she had the strength to rip the cruel, unchanging smile from his face.

She turned away after a brief moment, not letting herself think about what he had done to her lest it drive her into another state of depression like the one that had caused her to take her life.

Bull Ryan drove the black-and-white patrol unit hard, roaring down through the curves of the icy mountain road at speeds bordering on the suicidal, even for a road-hugging vehicle like the Bronco with an experienced driver at the wheel. "Goddamn!" he yelled into the empty interior of the car for the tenth time since he had left the Lodge.

Ryan was a man who was used to being in complete control at all times and he didn't like what was happening to him now. Things that he didn't understand.

He bit the end off a fresh cigar, patted his pockets for his lighter, and cursed again. Something had spooked him back there at the Lodge. Something he dared not even consider, for if it was true that there were such things as ghosts that could reach out and lay an icy hand upon a man's soul the way he had just felt himself touched, then there might be a God after all. He tried to push the nagging thought out of his mind as he fumbled with the dashboard lighter.

A God who sent people to heaven, or hell.

Ryan clutched the steering wheel harder, braking and veering the Bronco to avoid a gleaming patch of snowmelt at the center of a tight curve. The four-wheeler skidded, its front wheels shuddering across the rough surface, then straightened and roared out onto the next steep downgrade.

If there really was a hell, Bull Ryan reasoned, then he was going straight there for sure. All the shit he'd done in 'Nam alone—fragging that little butthole lieutenant, burning hooches just 'cause he liked the sound of the slopes wailing in the afternoon sun, and the feel of cutting a man in half with a heavy machine gun . . .

"Shit!"

They said you could be forgiven if you wanted to, but Ryan couldn't see anybody forgiving the things he'd done, even the minor stuff since he'd come back from 'Nam, the shakedowns and scams that went all the way back to the days when he'd been a bitter young deputy . . . the busload of hippies he'd put into the canyon 'cause one of them, a long-haired freak in beads, had given him the finger and called him a pig popped into his mind.

"Shit!"

He slowed for another long hairpin, thinking about what had happened at the Lodge. First he'd found that prick of a news guy poking around up there, then, after he'd gotten rid of him, he had been overwhelmed by a sudden uncontrollable urge to burn the place down. Although he hadn't admitted it to himself immediately, he felt sure that was what had been in his mind, at least for the moment that he'd been standing there looking at all those old books. He clearly remembered holding his lighter—the lighter that was now missing from his pocket—to the old books. What the fuck was that all about? he wondered. And that voice in his head, the icy touch. He'd come close to pissing his pants.

Ryan looked down at his hands on the steering wheel. He could see them trembling, even though he was clenching the padded vinyl ring as hard as he could.

"Shit." He had to do something. He felt as if he was losing his mind.

The elemental feeding on Ryan's soul peered out through its host's eyes. It was not alarmed at the view of rushing rocks and icy road it saw through the Bronco's mud-spattered windshield. The speeding vehicle was new and the host was in control, if only marginally.

It withdrew the probing tendril and returned to its feast, plunging its hideous jaws into the sweet decaying meat of the man's spirit. While dimly aware of Ryan's surging thought stream, it had no interest in controlling him for the moment, contenting itself instead with regaining the strength that had been sapped by the lean times it had endured. Later, after it had nibbled away the diseased parts down to the bright fresh core of the man's spirit, it would contaminate more of him, causing him to commit acts so heinous that his previous exploits would pale in comparison. For the present, however, there was enough of the delicious rot for several more meals. So much, in fact, that it had ignored the host's refusal to set fire to the human habitation, a thought it had implanted in his brain merely to see if he would obey.

The elemental twisted its dripping jaws into something that might have passed for a grin had it been human, reflecting on the absolute perfection of its kind. It possessed the ability to reside undetected in a truly evil soul indefinitely, feasting painlessly on the dead and diseased parts until they were completely gone. Then, when the soul had been cleansed to its purest essence—and assuming there was enough of it remaining to make the effort worthwhile—the thing could take control of the host, forcing it to commit acts so unspeakable that what remained of the living soul would quickly die and putrefy, providing a memorable last meal with which it might fuel its search for a new host.

The creature in Ryan's brain did not know what cosmic forces had decreed its existence, only that it served the purpose for which it had been designed in much the same way as did the vultures and other carrion eaters of the physical world. The thing served a purpose and that was reason enough for its being. Although it was aware that there existed orders of dark beings higher than itself, it did not care to dwell upon them or their purposes, avoiding the superior creatures at all costs.

The engorged thing at last fell back to digest its

meal, truly contented for the first time in ages. Although it could not sleep—its survival as a predator depending greatly upon its ability to become instantly alert—it allowed itself to drift into a semistupor, secure in the knowledge that it could feed again when it was hungry.

It still suffered a slight nagging sensation, recalling the close brush with extinction it had suffered when its host had encountered the other human in the habitation, and it vowed to be more cautious now that it was regaining its strength. Fortunately it had stopped feeding on its host long enough to look out and recognize the subtle signs that had instantly told it that another truly frightening creature—one of the dreaded higher orders of demons—was patiently stalking the other man.

Although it had not actually seen the other creature, an immense monstrosity of a type that it knew inhabited the deepest of the subterranean regions far below the earthly plane, the thing's extremely sensitive olfactory system had registered the dreaded scent and its night-seeing retinas had caught the dull traces of red light cast by the great demon's eyes in the deep shadows above the prey. That had been more than enough for it. Being a cunning survivor, the elemental had, of course, quickly dissuaded its own host from exercising its petty cruelties on the prey belonging to the more powerful creature with the glowing eyes.

It remembered without shame that it had been greatly relieved when the other human had left the habitation by the sacred lake.

*　*　*

Rick Masterson had spent the remainder of the morning unpacking his camera gear. Pausing only for a quick lunch of baloney sandwiches and beer on the sun-drenched balcony outside the bungalow's main room, he had assembled a lightweight hiking kit for the Nikon. Despite his haste in getting the equipment in order, it was nearly three in the afternoon when he got away from the bungalow and began his tramp along the southern edge of the lake.

Rick was not really too concerned about the time. Today's trip was for familiarization only and he didn't expect to get any photos worth keeping. Mostly he wanted to get the lay of the land and, perhaps, mentally compose some shots and sun angles for the series of winter landscapes he had been thinking about shooting. Also, he thought that a walk in the woods would give him some time to reflect on the morning's strange events. He was still concerned about the mysterious girl he had picked up on the road the night before, and was convinced from the strange coincidence of the old photographs that she must somehow be related to the owners of the huge lodge at the other end of the lake.

The shore curved away from his track half a mile below the bungalow as the lake swerved sharply to the west. Taking to the dark trees in order to circumvent a large granite outcropping that projected far into the water, Rick padded silently down a shaded path carpeted with a decades-deep accumulation of pine needles. Here and there he saw wild birds flitting among the treetops. Deer sign abounded where the path crossed a narrower game trail, and he thought he recognized the tracks of a big cat in a patch of clear ground at the base of a particularly large ponderosa. He let his thumb wander to the Nikon's shutter release, wondering whether he would have the nerve to stand and photograph an honest-to-God mountain lion should he encounter one out here. "Hell, you'd probably cut and run like a scared rabbit," he said aloud, surprised at the echoing quality of his own voice in the vast wilderness.

After a few minutes the trail opened out on the lakeshore again and he paused to look at a post-card-perfect scene of snowcapped mountains and sky reflected on the glassy blue surface. He knew the instant he saw it that this was a shot that would never be the same again if he waited a hundred years. Columns of white cloud towered above the mountains, scattering rays of misty white light across the treetops of a delightful little island situated precisely in the center of the lake.

Scanning the sky and figuring he had no more than half an hour in which to capture the scene before the dim globe of the weak winter sun slipped behind the mountain peak, he quickly slipped off the nylon pack slung across his shoulder, unsnapping a lightweight aluminum tripod and setting up the Nikon for a series of shots he was already mentally titling Shangri-la.

Beast

D A R K N E S S fell.

Rick packed the collapsed tripod into its nylon
case and looked at the Rolex. Although it wasn't
yet five, the shadows among the tall trees surrounding the lake were already taking on the inky
appearance of night.

It had taken him much longer than he had antici-
pated to shoot the idyllic lake scene and he had
finished just moments before, straightening from
the Nikon to watch the sun slip quickly behind the
granite mass of the highest mountain peak. As
always happens in the highest alpine regions, the
comfortable warmth of the day had departed
along with the light and he felt a sudden chill as
the deepening blue sky of the short Sierra twilight
rapidly descended on the lake.

Slinging the Nikon around his neck and chiding
himself for having failed to take into account the
abbreviated period of winter daylight, he stepped

onto the same path he had come down earlier and walked quickly back into the towering forest.

Full darkness descended upon him the moment he left the lakeshore and he cursed his own stupidity at not having brought along a flashlight. One false step on the lonely trail, he realized, and the weak knee could give way, leaving him stranded a long way from the bungalow with no prospect of human assistance.

"Dumb-ass!" He hurried along the faint path, keeping his eyes glued to the ground just ahead.

Sara watched the faint outline of the distant bungalow as the final traces of daylight slowly bled from the western sky. She had been out at the end of the dock for some time now, watching the bungalow for the comforting glow of firelight that would confirm that she was no longer alone on the lake.

She had been thinking about Rick Masterson all day, whiling away the hours in her secret place and fantasizing to herself.

In her fantasy she was still alive, wearing one of the pretty party dresses that now hung moldering in the closet of her bedroom, her thick golden hair freshly washed and gleaming about her shoulders. Her father, of course, was away on one of his extended business trips. Sara smiled to herself. Soon the bell would ring and Rick would arrive to take her dancing—she loved to dance, often whirling about in the silence of her room for hours while she hummed the old songs that had been her favorites in high school, songs by the Beatles and the Stones and Simon and Garfunkel . . . "Like a Bridge over Troubled Waters" . . .

She felt the familiar tight ache in her throat as the full impact of what she had lost so long ago struck her again.

"Damn!" The forbidden epithet escaped her lips before she could stop it and she wondered if she would be punished. Sara had vowed she would not let herself dwell upon her losses ever again, understanding that the negative energies of such thinking served only to keep her trapped in this halfway state of existence.

Her fantasy shattered, she raised her head and looked toward the bungalow again. It had grown so dark that now she was unable to see anything.

Her first instinct, one born of many such past disappointments, was that Rick had gone. Gone from her like all the others. She suddenly wished that it were possible for her to weep, remembering with great sadness how comforting it had been when, as an unhappy little girl, she had simply been able to curl up beneath the flowered Laura Ashley comforter on her pretty canopied bed—the one her mother had picked out for her—and cry her sadness away until the hurt was all gone.

Dropping her chin onto her chest, she turned back toward the Lodge, drifting effortlessly over the snow-spotted lawn. Perhaps she would feel better in her room. Perhaps, but not very likely.

She had reached the French doors on the patio—always preferring to come and go by way of the familiar entrances and corridors she had followed in life rather than simply walking through walls, a practice that had always struck her as icky and unnatural—and was about to enter the study when a thought occurred to her. Perhaps Rick hadn't gone away at all. Maybe something had happened to him and he needed her help. An image of the dark presence that hovered about him flooded her mind and she hesitated, aware that unlike the demon that had possessed the teenaged boy, the hideous thing that stalked Rick could destroy her as well.

Retracing her path to the edge of the dock, she stared out into the blackness where she knew the bungalow lay, and wondered if she should cross the lake to see about him.

Rick's knee hadn't gone out on him on the rough trail as he had feared.

Something far worse had happened.

"Dammit, I said get away," he shouted, hoping that the sound of his voice would frighten the snarling creature blocking the path ahead of him.

No dice.

The tawny mountain lion stood her ground, snarling menacingly and dropping to her belly to peer at him through golden eyes that picked up and amplified the sparks of emerging starlight now becoming visible above the tops of the trees. At eight feet from nose to tail, she was a formidable and potentially deadly enemy and he had no hope of either outfighting or outrunning her.

"Shit," he muttered under his breath, his mind racing frantically to recall what little he had learned about big cats from his two stints in Africa. Don't make any sudden moves, and if you can't scare the cat off with a loud noise, you'd better start praying. Not very damn much.

He had been walking briskly along the forest path, having made it nearly back to the edge of the trees, when he had first become aware that he was being stalked by something, the hairs on the back of his neck tingling exactly the same way they had the time he'd walked into a sniper's field of fire somewhere south of Managua more than five years earlier. In that instance he'd thrown himself to the dirt a heartbeat before the rifle shot had drilled through the empty space where he should have been, kicking up a geyser of dust just beyond his heels. He seriously doubted the same tactic would work here. He had begun walking faster instead, despite the danger of tripping and wrecking the bad knee.

He had walked himself right into the cat's trap, nearly stumbling over her at the point in the trail where she had run ahead to intercept him. Now she lay blocking the way a scant twenty-five feet from where he stood, her two-inch fangs gleaming in the starlight.

"Idiot!" Another barely audible whisper.

It hadn't occurred to him that the cat, whose tracks he'd seen earlier, might pose any actual physical danger to him. After all, North American mountain lions were not supposed to attack humans. At least he didn't think they were. He allowed himself a rueful grin. If that was actually the case, then this particular feline had evidently not been keeping up with her *National Geographic*s. Perhaps if he escaped he could write an article, "Dispelling the Myth That Hungry Mountain Lions Don't Really Eat People."

Okay, he told himself, get serious. This is very serious shit. He remained frozen in place, reviewing his options as the big cat twitched her tail, its soft swish stirring the pine needles into small eddies of motion behind her. He could try to back off, hoping she wouldn't follow, then hoping to find an alternate route to the bungalow without becoming hopelessly lost in the vast forest that surrounded the lake. Bad idea. Too much hoping involved.

Think of something else.

The Nikon was at hand, its powerful onboard flash able to be activated at the push of a button. He could possibly snap the cat's picture, hoping the flash would either blind or frighten her and giving him the chance to run like hell. Another bad idea. In the first place, he remembered a boozy hunter in the bar at his hotel in Nairobi relating a story about African lions charging the muzzle flashes of high-powered rifles, and coming away with bloody chunks of the shooter's anatomy in their jaws before going down. In the second place, he reasoned, the flash stood as much chance of blinding him as it did the lioness. Third. Well, running was pretty much a lost cause anyway. Even with a healthy knee, he'd hardly stand a chance against this magnificent creature.

"Shit!" he whispered again.

Sweat was trickling down his neck now, despite the rapidly dropping air temperature. The lioness growled impatiently, the muscles along her flanks tensing as she prepared to spring. Rick raised the flimsy nylon tripod case, preparing to fend off the attack with the ridiculous bundle of aluminum sticks inside.

* * *

The lioness hunched on the trail, every atom of her being focused on the man before her. She was in her sixth year, a healthy female in her prime, weighing in at close to a hundred and eighty pounds, and she was ravenously hungry.

She had come down from the higher elevations surrounding the lake the previous evening, driven to this usually reliable winter hunting ground by the scarcity of game in the rocky heights above. Upon entering the heavily forested valley, however, she had been disappointed to discover that something had already frightened off most of the larger animals she numbered among her prey. The air had been thick with the stink of wood smoke, the hated sign that men were about.

Lying up in a secluded outcropping above the lakeside bungalows of the Marina, she had watched the man's comings and goings for most of this day, descending on a parallel track into the thick forest to the south, when she had finally seen him strike out alone in that direction. Unbeknownst to him, she had lain silently among the trees, watching the whole time he had labored over the camera.

The lioness had never attacked a man before, always choosing to move to a distant part of her range at the slightest hint of wood smoke on the air or the distant echoes of gunfire. But she was ravenously hungry now, the growing cubs within her womb demanding extra fuel for her lean body. Fuel and a large kill she could drag to an area near the cave where she would be giving birth within a few days. She needed the man's flesh and her cautious daylong observations had convinced her that he would be an easy kill. His pronounced limp as he had moved down the forest trail earlier had not gone unnoticed, and now she could smell the stink of fear in him as well.

She opened her mouth, baring her fangs, and bunched the muscles in her haunches, ready to launch herself across the space separating her from her weak and frightened prey.

Rick Masterson watched in helpless fascination as the lioness opened her mouth, rising up in slow motion to become airborne, the long, muscled body twisting in flight to correct its trajectory almost before he had started his own clumsy sideways move to avoid her.

He hit the ground with a fair certainty that he was going to die, doubting that his remains would even be found. Mom and Pop back in Memphis wondering, long after he had been eaten and digested, what had happened to their blue-eyed baby boy. . . .

An unearthly shriek filled the air, followed by the sound of a heavy thud. A cloud of dusty pine needles exploded beside his head and he glimpsed a patch of tawny fur disappearing into the shadows.

Rick sat up and looked cautiously around the small clearing. He could hear the sound of branches breaking and brush crackling as the cat ran hell-bent for leather back toward the high country from which it had come. His heart was pounding in his ears as he levered himself to his feet with the aid of the tripod and hobbled from the trees as quickly as the injured knee would allow.

The terror-stricken lioness, her brain paralyzed by the single overpowering need to escape her unseen tormentor, leaped onto an overhang of dark stone, tearing the skin of her flank against the sharp projection of a dead tree limb. Without pausing to examine the painful wound, she jumped to the next higher shelf of stone and streaked up a narrow ledge to the flat expanse of open ground leading to the cave she had carefully selected as a birthing den.

What had happened to her in the forest moments before was totally beyond her experience. A black cloud had enveloped her mind and some icy thing with glowing red eyes had literally gripped her heart at the very instant that she had made her spring and was dropping, teeth and claws extended with the absolute certainty of a clean kill, toward the helpless man creature. In that instant her entire body had shuddered violently, throwing off her precisely targeted attack and dumping her, hurt and confused, onto the soft ground beside the prey.

Reaching the vicinity of the birthing cave, she paused briefly to lick at the dark blood oozing from her lacerated flank and peered back down the mountain to see if the frightful thing had pursued her. Satisfied that she was not being followed, and limping painfully, she abandoned the cave and slunk away toward the cold high country, determined never to enter this part of her range again.

Night Visitors

RICK reached the relative safety of the lakeshore, pausing only to look nervously over his shoulder. The brooding pines were silent behind him now and he felt fairly certain that the big cat was long gone. His shoulder throbbed painfully where he had hit the ground and the injured knee was growing progressively weaker due to the unaccustomed strain to which it had been subjected.

Unzipping the nylon case to remove the collapsible aluminum tripod, he extended the slender legs to their second stop, and tying them together with a neck cord savaged from his light meter, he fashioned a cane, which he figured might also double as a weapon in case the lioness returned.

Leaning heavily on the makeshift support, he rounded the curve in the shoreline and looked up the lake to see lights blazing in the bungalow.

Ten minutes of labored walking brought him to the boat house. He listened briefly to the sound of the generator purring behind the closed door and moved cautiously up the narrow walk to the drive. There was a dark vehicle parked in the shadows behind the white Cherokee.

He paused beside the Jeep and was blinded by a glare of light as the door to the bungalow suddenly swung open. A dark shape filled the doorway and a gruff voice called out to him.

"Where the damn hell you been, boy? We was just about to send out a search party."

Rick's heart rate subsided to near normal and he leaned wearily against the fender of the Jeep, grinning up at Hapwell, who stood glaring down at him from the porch.

"Hi, Hap," he said affably. "Come on in and make yourself right at home."

"Crap!" snorted the old-timer, spitting into the snow and turning to reenter the house. "Any man's fool enough to walk away leavin' his door unlocked is gotta expect anybody that feels like it to walk in. Besides, what'd ya expect us to do? Sit around freezin' our cans off until you showed up?"

Rick climbed onto the porch and stepped into the main room, noting that a huge stack of tamarack from the woodpile out back was laid beside the roaring fire in the hearth and the pine dining table was littered with grocery cartons. "Us?" he asked the old man, who had dropped onto the sofa and was already lifting a can of Coors to his bushy lips.

"Hi," said Phylis, appearing around the corner from the kitchen. "Hope you don't mind us barging in like this, but we thought we'd better check on you before the big storm hit."

Rick's nose twitched as he smelled the fabulous aroma wafting from the kitchen and he grinned at Phylis, who looked good enough to eat in her tight jeans and turquoise ski sweater.

"Storm?" He grinned foolishly. "What storm?"

"I knew it." Hapwell cackled. "Damn fool green-horn don't have a clue."

Phylis placed her hands on her hips and frowned reproachfully at Rick.

Rick smiled sheepishly. "Guilty as charged," he said as he removed a beer from a frosty six-pack on the pine table and sank onto the sofa with a groan. "What's he talking about?" he asked Phylis.

"There's a storm coming," she said. "A big one." She carried a steaming cup of tea in from the dining area and settled cross-legged into a soft leather chair at his end of the sofa. "We figured we'd better bring you a few more supplies, or better yet, see if we could talk you into coming back down to town with us."

"Damn fool never even turned on his radio for the weather report," Hapwell muttered in disgust.

"I'm afraid you've got me," said Rick, genuinely embarrassed at the stupidity of his oversight. "It's been kind of a crazy day," he started lamely.

"And just what in the damn hell was you doin' out wanderin' around in these woods after dark without so much as a flashlight?" the old man demanded.

"Well, to tell you the truth," said Rick, "I hiked down to the end of the lake to take a few pictures and I sort of lost track of the time." He hesitated, taking a slow sip of his beer, letting the cold liquid work on the dryness in his mouth. "You probably won't believe this, but I saw a mountain lion."

"Hell, boy," Hapwell snorted, "there's still good-sized pumas come down into these valleys this time of year lookin' for a good meal before they lay up for the winter. I've even faced down a couple or three in my time. You got any idea what a hungry cat can do to a man on the trail alone?"

Rick's ears burned fiercely. "I'd always heard they wouldn't attack humans," he mumbled.

Hapwell spit disdainfully into the fireplace, the shot hissing sharply against the hot grate. "Save that crap for the bleedin'-heart Sierra Club liberals down to the big city in their condominiums." He laughed. "Big she-lion'll gut you and eat your liver for lunch while you're still worryin' about whether she's on the endangered-species list." He laughed again and leaned forward to poke a dirty finger at Rick. "Up here all by your lonesome, *you're* the endangered species, boy. Don't you never forget that."

"Okay, that's enough of your mountain-man act, Hap. You know as well as I do that there hasn't been a really big mountain lion seen in these mountains for at least ten years, and even if there had been, it's an established fact that they *don't* attack people." Phylis turned to Rick and sipped her tea. "But that doesn't mean it isn't dangerous, Rick. Hap's right. You shouldn't go too far from the cabin, especially not at night. This country can be just as unforgiving as it is beautiful. One mistake and it will swallow you."

Rick nodded. "I'm just beginning to realize that," he said meekly. "I don't know what qualifies as a big cat hereabouts, but the one I saw didn't look like any lightweight, and if it wasn't hungry, it was doing a pretty fair impression of it. As for not checking the weather, that was pretty dumb of me, too. Is there really a big storm coming?"

"Big *mother* of a storm," Hapwell interjected.

Sara hovered in the warm glow of firelight from the bungalow's balcony window, basking in the companionable drone of human conversation from within. She longed to let herself into the cheery interior of the room, wanting nothing more than to curl up unseen in a corner to listen to the occupants chatting. She stayed outside, however, hovering among the branches of a leaning ponderosa pine and fearful that her intrusion might be detected by Rick in the presence of the others. So far he seemed not to know what she was and she dared not run the risk of frightening him away before she had an opportunity to explain.

Her mind drifted back to that long-ago August when she had pondered another such explanation, trying to decide how to tell Ted that she was not what he thought she was. She smiled, thinking how simple that had been compared with the task that now faced her. "Let's see," she whispered, rehearsing. "I've got something to tell you, Rick. You see, I'm not really the girl you think I am. Oh, it's not that I don't have all the thoughts and emotions and needs of any other healthy girl my age. It's just that I'm, well, kind of . . . not alive anymore."

She giggled at the complete and utter ridiculousness of her situation, deciding there must be a better way. She would have to think about it. For now, she was content in the knowledge that he was safe. She chided herself for her foolish concerns that something had happened to him, or that he had left the lake without her.

Inside the house, the pretty dark haired woman in the leather chair by the fire was saying something. Feeling a sudden flush of jealousy, Sara moved away from the window, knowing she could never compete for Rick's attentions with this vibrant living creature. She willed herself to drift slowly back across the lake. There must be a way to reach out to him . . . to let him know how much she needed him to stay here with her.

" . . . not only the danger of being snowed in, but also the fact that people sometimes experience . . . strange happenings up here in the winter," Phylis concluded, watching Rick's eyes for his reaction to what she had just said.

"Well, your point about the weather is well taken," he agreed. "I promise to give that some very serious thought and, at the very least, to keep my ear glued to the radio from now on. As for the 'strange happenings,' everybody keeps talking about them"—he laughed, leaning forward to place his paper plate on the coffee table and cleaning his hands on a napkin—"but nobody seems to have any specifics." The three of them had been eating the excellent spare ribs and corn on the cob brought up from the saloon's kitchen and reheated in the bungalow's oven while he'd been listening to Hap and Phylis's warnings about the major winter storm threatening to strike the area within the next forty-eight hours.

"Great meal," he said, reaching for the mug of scalding coffee and taking a tentative sip.

Phylis raised her eyebrows. "What do you mean everybody?" she asked. "I didn't think you'd spoken to anyone except Hap and myself last night."

"Well, there was a girl I picked up on the road after I left your place last night," said Rick. "Then this morning I ran into your local answer to Deputy Dawg."

"You met Bull Ryan up here?"

"Well, I'm not sure if *met* is exactly the right word." Rick smiled. "Let's just say I was unexpectedly frisked and rousted by him."

"That big bully," huffed Phylis. She turned to Hapwell. "I'm telling you, Hap, we've got to bring this before the town council. That . . . man is becoming impossible."

"Don't look at me, lady," Hapwell grunted. "I don't want no part of that mean sumbitch. I'm too damn old to go around askin' to have my ribs caved in for me on purpose. Besides, what's that got to do with why we're here?"

Phylis's face flushed as she launched into what was obviously a hotly debated local topic. "Dammit, Hap, the only reason Ryan keeps that cushy job of his is that no one around here has the guts to stand up to him!" She broke off, realizing that as Hap had correctly pointed out, she was onto a subject that had nothing to do with either Rick or the reason for their unexpected visit to the lake. "I'm sorry," she said, laying a warm hand on Rick's arm. "I'm afraid my opinion of our esteemed sheriff is the local joke around Silver Peak. How on earth did you manage to have a run-in with Ryan up here?"

"Well," said Rick, "evidently there was a wreck on the mountain road last night."

Phylis nodded. "It was awful. Two teenagers were killed when their car went over the edge. The county rescue squad brought them down early this morning—"

"Heard it took 'em three hours to cut the girl out of the car," Hap observed, stuffing a battered pipe with vile-smelling tobacco and leaning over to ignite it with a splinter from the fireplace. "You shoulda seen the blood. They was pieces of scalp still stuck to the windshield when they brung the wreck in."

Phylis shot the old man a look and he shut up, leaning back to suck noisily on his pipe.

"Apparently," Rick continued, "the girl I picked up on the road had been in the car that was wrecked, but she somehow managed to escape without being hurt. She was pretty cold when I found her, and a little confused, too, but otherwise okay. She pretty much insisted that I take her up to that big house at the other end of the lake. I dropped her off there and went back this morning to pick up my jacket. That's when I ran into Ryan. He tried to roust me for prowling, but seemed to back off real fast when I started dropping names."

He paused to take another sip of coffee, oblivious to the meaningful glances passing between Hapwell and Phylis. "At any rate," he continued, "Ryan mentioned something about a local superstition that the old house is haunted."

"This girl you picked up," said Phylis. "What did she look like?"

Rick shrugged. "Young, I'd say early twenties.

Pretty, with long blond hair. Ryan seemed to think she might have left a car up here. It was pretty obvious the other kids had broken in and were partying at the place." He wrinkled his brow, thinking about the pictures he'd found in the boat house and the one he'd seen in the old lodge. "I've got another theory about who she was, though."

He proceeded to tell them about the girl's claim that she lived in the house, also describing the coincidence of the photographs. When he was finished, the two of them were staring at him with their mouths open.

Phylis was the first to speak. "I'm sorry, Rick, but your theory is wrong."

"What?" He laughed. "Don't tell me you think she's a runaway, too. I mean, that line that Ryan was putting out just doesn't wash for me."

Phylis looked at him for a long time. "This girl," she finally said, "did she tell you what her name was?"

"Sure," said Rick. "Sara."

"Raynor," muttered the old man. "Sara Raynor."

"Raynor? As in the Raynor Corporation, the outfit that owns the house?"

Phylis nodded.

"See, I knew it!" Rick grinned in triumph. "I knew damn well that girl was telling me the truth. I told Ryan she wasn't the type who'd go off and leave her friends in a wrecked car, unless she'd suffered a concussion or something in the accident. Frankly I've been worried about her."

Phylis shook her head. "Rick, you don't understand," she said. She turned to Hapwell. "I think you'd better tell him the story."

Hapwell grunted. "Which one?" he asked.

"First things first," she said.

"Not without I get me a drink of whiskey first." He heaved himself up from the sofa and crossed the room to rummage among the several cardboard boxes of supplies stacked on the pine table in the dining area.

Rick looked suspiciously from the old-timer to Phylis. "Okay"—he grinned—"what's the joke?"

Phylis leaned forward, her hands clasped on her knees, to look into his eyes. She was not smiling. "There's no joke, Rick. But if what we're about to tell you is going to make any sense to you at all, then you have to hear it just the way Hap tells it. Otherwise . . ." She shook her head. "Well, just hear him out, please." A warm smile lit her lovely features and she placed her hand on his injured knee. "If it makes you feel better, you can think of it as the price of your dinner."

"Fair enough," he agreed, placing his hand on top of hers and pleased at the warmth he felt flowing into his knee. "It was a great dinner."

"Not many people know this story," Hapwell said when he had settled himself in front of the fire again. There was a tumbler of Jack Daniel's clenched in his gnarled hands and he was leaning forward, staring into the leaping flames. "Reason bein'," he continued, "that the feller what told it to me ended up gettin' hisself sent down to the state hospital. I hear tell they got him locked him up real nice and snug in one of them little rubber rooms." He turned his head and looked into Rick's eyes. "So this is a story told by a crazy man. And the only reason I'm tellin' it to you is 'cause it goes along with somethin' that me 'n two other fellers seen with our own eyes. And none of us was any crazier than is generally considered normal for folks livin' in these parts."

Rick sipped the whiskey in his own tumbler and carefully watched the old man's face for some sign that this was an elaborate put-on. Hapwell's grizzled beard glowed red in the firelight, the wrinkles etched deep into his brow indicating that he was struggling to find the proper words with which to begin his story.

"Now this was back in the fall of seventy-seven," he began. "It had already snowed some up here and this young feller—his name was Jeff, Jeff Fisher from down Sparks way—had just bought him a brand-new snowmobile.

"Well, this Jeff, he was itchin' to try that baby out. Candy-apple red it was, a Ski-Doo I think, the fanciest one they made.

"So, comes the first Saturday he could get off from work, he packs that little booger up in the back of his pickup and heads for the mountains to break her in. He pulled into my place 'round about two in the afternoon to fill her up with white gas, and we spent a few minutes lookin' at the new rig and jawin' about how much snow he was likely to find up here around the lake. After a little while he takes off with me warnin' him to watch hisself on the road, and I get on with my business. Done forgot all about him."

Hapwell took another deep swallow of his whiskey, topping off the glass from the open bottle on the coffee table. "Well, that night I closed up around the usual time, fed the cats, and went in back and cooked me up some eggs on the stove and settled down to watch a new two-hour *Columbo* I'd been waitin' for. The show had just got started good, with old Columbo diggin' into the case of the swimmin'-pool heiress when there's the damnedest racket you ever heard outside by the pumps.

"I grab up my old shotgun, figurin' it's a couple of drunk kids from down to the university come up here on Saturday night to hit the saloons and then run out of gas—crap like that happens all the time. But it ain't no college kids. It's young Jeff Fisher. He's outside with his pickup run into my light pole and there's blood runnin' down his face from a cut on his eye and he's poundin' on my door, blubberin' like a baby and beggin' me to let him in.

"Well, I open up and get him back there by the stove and pour some hot coffee down him, though I don't smell nothin' on his breath to show he's been drinkin', and after a while he comes around enough to tell me what happened to him up here on the mountain."

Hapwell paused to take another sip of his whiskey and fussed with relighting his pipe. Rick shot Phylis an amused glance, impatient for the old man to get on with it. To his surprise, she shook her head slightly, directing his attention back to Hapwell with a solemn nod.

"Well now, this Jeff Fisher was a big strapping young feller," said Hapwell, "a county lineman who worked mostly out in the back country keepin' the power lines clear of brushfires, rock slides, avalanches, and the like. I'm tellin' you all that so's you understand it wasn't like he was a man you'd normally expect to fall apart on you in a situation. But there he sat in my old chair by the stove that night with an old quilt wrapped around him, and he couldn't stop shakin'. Every time he'd start to talk his voice would go all high and funny and his eyes kept dartin' to the doors and windows, like he was sure somethin' was after him.

"Now, accordin' to the story he told me, he'd drove straight on up to the lake from my place that afternoon with no trouble at all. There's a big alpine meadow down past the south end of the lake and he'd unpacked the new snowmobile and spent a good two hours raisin' hell with it."

Hapwell cast Rick a meaningful glance and tapped his pipe against the stones of the fireplace. "Now, bein' a man who knows these mountains enough to respect 'em, he'd had the good sense to get back to his truck before dark and load up the snowmobile. The sun hadn't been down more than a half hour before he started back down here to Silver Peak. He was about halfway down the mountain, just comin' around that big hairpin below the long grade, when he seen the girl standin' in the road."

Rick felt the hairs on the back of his arms tingle as Hapwell turned his gaze from the fire and stared at him with faded blue eyes.

"Young she was, and pretty with long blond hair tangled around her face in the wind. Just popped up in his headlights outta nowhere, like a rabbit," Hapwell went on. "Young Jeff Fisher said he hit his brakes and damn near went over the cliff tryin' to miss her—"

"Come on," Rick interrupted. "What is this?"

Phylis's hand squeezed his and she shook her head again. Hapwell's cracked voice droned on.

"Thought he *had* hit her for a minute, then he looked back and realized she was still standin' there in the road. 'Course he run back down to see if she was okay . . . that's when he noticed she didn't have no shoes. Nothin on her, but a flimsy little nightgown of some sort. He said she seemed kind of confused."

"Come on, dammit, this isn't funny." Rick got to his feet and glared down at the old man. Phylis was watching him closely.

"Okay, when did you two cook up this little story?" he demanded.

Phylis shook her head. "Rick, I first heard this story three years ago when Hap was in his cups one night. I can introduce you to at least three other people who were there at the time."

"What are you trying to tell me?" Rick asked.

Hapwell sipped his whiskey and shook his head. "Just a story," he said. "You want to hear it or not?"

Rick dropped back onto the sofa and took a healthy swallow from his own glass of whiskey, then nodded in resignation. "Go ahead."

"I won't trouble you with all the details," said Hapwell. "The short version is that the girl talked Jeff Fisher into turning his rig around on the road—don't ask me how he managed that, 'cause I don't know—and driving her back up to the old Raynor place. He didn't say so, but I suspect he might've tried a little hanky-panky with her, but she was cold as ice. Anyway, he dropped her off by them big gates and started back down to town. Got about as far as the lake-road junction when he started to worry about her, so he turned around and went straight back up to the Lodge. Poked around for a while, but the place was all locked up and dark, so he figured she'd got inside and gone to bed."

"And?" Rick was listening intently now, not really doubting the old man's story, but not sure what it proved, other than the fact that coincidences happen.

The old-timer shrugged and refilled his cold pipe. "And nothin'," he said. "Wasn't nobody there. Young Jeff turned his pickup around and headed back down the mountain again."

"I don't get it," said Rick. "You told me this guy showed up half-crazy and hysterical at your place. What for?"

"Because," said Hapwell, tucking the pipe into his pocket, "halfway back down the mountain road, on the exact same curve where he stopped to pick up the girl the first time, he saw her again, standin' there just like before."

Rick stared at him. "What?"

Hapwell nodded. "Said he hit his brakes to miss her, but the pickup skidded and he hit her this time, except he didn't hit nothin' solid. He claimed the truck went right through her like she wasn't really there at all, except he felt this cold chill go through him, just like somebody had stuck an icicle in his guts."

"That's completely insane," Rick declared, slamming his glass down onto the table.

Hapwell nodded again, unperturbed. "That's

what the docs down to the state hospital said, too. They held a big court hearing and all, and they decided young Jeff Fisher was crazier than a shit-house rat. Last I heard they still had the poor bugger locked up in diapers and one of them straitjackets." He drained off the rest of his glass and stood to throw another log onto the grate.

"Do you expect me to believe that?" Rick demanded.

Hapwell shrugged. "Don't make no difference to me what you believe. Just figured you ought to know is all. Y'see, I seen that apparition myself in seventy-eight, me 'n two friends of mine. We was on our way back to town one night after doin' some huntin' up this way, and there she was, standin' in the middle of that exact same curve, big as life. Feller that was drivin' the truck we was in hit the brakes—"

"I suppose you went right through her, too." Rick's voice was dripping with sarcasm.

"Nope," said Hapwell, reaching over to poke at the fire with an iron rod from the hearth. "We missed her by a good couple of feet at least." He turned back to look Rick in the eye. "Feller drivin' couldn't stop the truck, though. We went right over the cliff, five hundred feet down. We must've rolled twenty, thirty times afore we stopped. My pal Tall Hudson—he was the feller drivin'—was killed outright. Tommy Whitehorse lasted for fifteen minutes or so before he bled out. Me, I couldn't help much with two busted legs." His gaze shifted back to the flames again. "'Course none of that's in the official record 'cause I never told none of it to the state patrol or the sheriff.

Didn't want to end up in no straitjacket like young Jeff Fisher."

"Jesus, Hap, I'm sorry!" Rick shook his head helplessly. "But whoever you saw that night couldn't have been same the girl I picked up. I talked to her. Christ, she was wearing my jacket when I left her. Ghosts don't go around borrowing people's clothes, do they?"

Hapwell shrugged. "Never said nothin' about no ghosts," he grunted. "Just said people can get some funny ideas in their heads up here." He got up and clumped away into the recesses of the bungalow.

Rick waited until he heard the bathroom door close, then turned to Phylis. "You haven't said much. Do you think I was hallucinating?"

She shook her head. "Of course not, but as I told you in town last night, this place has a . . . reputation. The girl I told you about who killed herself. Her name was Sara Raynor. Her father built the Lodge."

"I see," said Rick, suddenly angry. "And I suppose the girl I picked up is supposed to be her wandering spirit. No chance she could have been a niece or a cousin or some other member of the family just up here for the weekend to look over the old family homestead."

She looked hurt. "Rick, we just thought you should know."

Rick's shoulder was beginning to throb and he was suddenly bone weary. "Look," he said, "you're both very nice people and I genuinely appreciate you driving all the way up here on that bad road to help me out. I think you know I've had a bad time lately and I'm the first one to admit I've been pretty stupid about not recognizing the dangers of this wilderness." He paused to take Phylis's hand and squeeze it. "I'll even admit that I might be prone to go a little crazy from time to time, but I don't think I've seen any ghosts." He smiled at her. "And if I did, my first instinct would probably be to take a picture and get an interview." The smile broadened into a grin. "I hear the *National Enquirer* is paying big bucks for proof of paranormal phenomena."

"We really weren't trying to alarm you," she began.

"I didn't think you were," he assured her. "I just don't happen to believe in ghosts." He squeezed her arm gently. "Now, you said this big storm is coming in the next two days. Well, I am taking that warning very seriously. I will tune in to the weather every few hours, and if it looks like it's going to get bad enough to trap me here, I'll come down to Silver Peak and take you up on your offer of that spare room." He hesitated, searching her eyes. "If the offer's still good, that is."

"It's good," she said, and he surprised both himself and her by leaning over to brush his lips lightly against hers. She stood, pressing herself urgently against him, and he felt himself beginning to stir in response to the warm contours of her body. Hapwell harrumphed in the background and Rick pulled away, embarrassed.

"Thanks," he said huskily.

"I'll put fresh sheets on the bed tomorrow," she breathed.

A blast of cold air swept into the cabin and they

turned to see Hapwell standing impatiently at the door, motioning to Rick. "C'mon out here," he said gruffly. "I got something for you."

"You go ahead, I'll get my things," said Phylis, ducking into the kitchen.

A cold wind was blowing across the lake as the old-timer led Rick around to the back of a battered Chevy pickup. Hapwell opened a large wooden tool carrier and handed him a scarred plastic box. "Know what this is?"

Rick squinted at the box in the light from the bungalow's windows. A thin chrome antenna sprouted from its top. "Sure, an old portable CB radio, isn't it?"

"She's old, but she works just fine. Now she doesn't have a lot of power, but if you get yourself to the head of the canyon up by that road junction and point her down the hill, I'll pick up your signal. I got me a fifty-watt base station set up in the back of the store."

Rick whistled softly. "Fifty watts, is that much power legal for a CB?"

"Hell no, it ain't legal"—the old man cackled— "but it sure as hell works. Now, you get yourself in any trouble, you give me a holler. Otherwise I'm gonna expect to see your tail down in town by tomorrow night."

"I'll think about it," said Rick.

"You think real hard," said Hapwell. He climbed into the old Chevy and the motor ground to life. "I ain't of no particular mind to freeze my butt off runnin' no rescue party up here."

"Okay," said Rick, "and thanks. I really appreciate all your trouble."

"Ain't doin' none of this for you," the old man grunted.

Rick shook his head. "I don't understand."

The bungalow door opened and Phylis appeared carrying the insulated cooler she'd used to transport the food. Hapwell lowered his voice and pointed his bewhiskered chin in her direction. "Lady's awful sweet on you for some unaccountable reason," he growled in a tone that signified he was withholding judgment on Rick's suitability as a fit companion for the likes of Phylis Rand.

Rick smiled. "I like her pretty well myself."

"Phylis is the finest woman I ever knowed," Hapwell added. "If I was twenty years younger, I'd just whip your dumb ass for the hell of it and make off with her myself. As it is, she wants to fuss and worry over you." He shrugged. "There ain't nothin' I wouldn't do for Phil."

"I can see that," said Rick.

"What can you see?" Phylis dropped the cooler into the back of the truck and came up beside him.

"That we're all going to be very good friends," said Rick, squeezing her shoulder and planting another warm kiss on her soft lips.

"Come on." Hapwell revved his engine impatiently. "I want to get back down that damned mountain road sometime before hell freezes over."

Rick held the door open and Phylis climbed into the truck. She rolled down the window and leaned out to look into his eyes. "I believe there are certain . . . forces . . . at work that we don't understand," she said quietly.

He nodded, uncertain how to respond without offending her or the old man any more than he already had.

Phylis smiled. "You don't have to say anything," she said, raising her eyes to the star-studded black vault above the towering silhouettes of the forest. "Just be careful up here. For me."

He reached for her hand, brushing his fingers against the soft skin as the pickup's engine revved and Hapwell backed swiftly away through the trees.

CHAPTER 14

Thought Streams

RICK stood on the balcony, staring out across the black waters of Spirit Lake. The combined effects of the whiskey he had consumed earlier and the pain pills he had just taken had created a soft jumble of thoughts in his head. The faint lavender scent of Phylis's perfume lingered about him, the warm, pliant contours of her body still warm against his chest and thighs.

His eyes strained into the darkness, attempting to see ... something, anything that would validate what had happened to him the previous night and confirm that the living, breathing creature who called herself Sara had not really been a figment of his imagination. Her image came flooding back to him now, tangled golden hair blowing about pale shoulders, the thin fabric of her gown nearly invisible against the contours of her high breasts. He closed his eyes, trying to see Phylis's face instead. Saw only Sara, smiling at him in the dim lights of the Jeep's dashboard, examining the compact disc as if it were a strange new piece of futuristic technology.

No, dammit!

She was real, the niece or cousin of the dead Sara Raynor perhaps, or of some other family member who had once lived in the old lodge: someone who had had her photograph taken on the lake with Jimmy's brother or uncle, or whoever the dark-haired young man in the boat was, or had been. Even in its muddled state his naturally cynical reporter's mind could accept no other explanation.

"Dammit!" He shouted the word to the dark, empty sky and watched in sudden wonder as a shooting star flashed across the horizon.

He shook his head at the strange occurrence. He needed to sleep, prayed he would not have one of the black, suffocating dreams from which he would awaken screaming.

Forces . . . we don't understand . . . Phylis's words echoed in his head as he stepped back inside and wearily closed the sliding-glass balcony door.

The bright light in the sky had arced into the trees behind the Lodge, momentarily disappearing into a thick stand of ponderosa. Sara, who had been standing on the dock for what seemed like hours, had turned to watch its descent across the lake. Now her eyes followed a gently pulsing orb that floated through the forest, casting a golden glow onto the dark trunks of the trees. Fascinated by the strange object, she willed herself forward, slipping silently among the trees until she found herself in a small clearing whose floor was deeply carpeted in pine needles. The glow slowly subsided, revealing the same beautiful young woman in the bright yellow rain slicker she had seen in Rick's dark dream.

"Hello, Sara." The apparition smiled.

"Who are you?" Sara breathed.

"I am a spirit much like yourself," the girl answered in slightly accented English.

Sara gazed at the beautiful creature, uncertain whether to reply. Although the bright light about the girl had dimmed considerably, Sara noted that she was still surrounded by a soft golden aura that cast a subtle light onto the pine needles beneath her feet. "Are you an angel?" Sara finally stammered.

The golden girl's laughter tinkled through the clearing and she shook her head. "Nothing so grand as that," she replied. "I am simply a messenger who has come to guide you." She paused and drew closer to enfold Sara's hand in her warm grasp. "Do you know what has happened to you?"

Sara nodded and felt as though she might begin to cry. "I'm . . . dead," she murmured.

"Yes, but not yet gone on to your destiny," said the girl. "Do you know why?"

Sara bowed her head. "Something I did. Something very bad," Sara lamented. "I think . . . I killed myself."

"Yourself and another as well." The girl frowned. "You don't remember." It was a statement of fact, not a question.

Sara shook her head. "I—I've tried."

"That is why you have been left to wander this earthly plane," said the girl. "The thing you did must be clear in your mind before you can be allowed to go on. Only then may your fate be decided."

Something cold gripped Sara's heart. "Will I go to hell?" she cried.

The girl in the yellow slicker shook her head. "The hell you envision does not exist." She smiled. "There is only light and darkness and, between those, levels of happiness and misery." The smile darkened and her soft voice filled with foreboding. "But there are many terrible things that can happen to a spirit that is touched with darkness as yours has been, Sara. Things that could bring you to eternal misery and even destruction."

Sara said nothing, but stood trying to assess for herself what had happened to her, tried—as she had many times before—to remember the precise chain of events that had led to her present state. In her mind a swirling curtain of darkness blocked the horrible vision of what she had done . . . something involving Harold Raynor . . . and Ted. She felt a warm hand upon her cheek, the touch infusing her mind with giddy lightness.

"Do not try to remember," said the golden creature. "The memories will come on their own when you are ready to accept them." She smiled again. "And do not despair, for you are mostly a creature of light and goodness, and thus may be saved despite those memories. Otherwise I would not have been sent to seek your assistance."

Sara stared at her, dumbfounded.

"You have touched another spirit," said the girl

in the yellow slicker, "a spirit in great peril of spreading a blanket of evil and darkness throughout the world of the living."

"I don't understand," Sara murmured.

The visitor's aura visibly brightened and she pointed toward the lights of the bungalow at the far end of the lake. "Him," she said. "I have come to seek your help in freeing him from the clutches of the powerful demon that stalks him."

Sara nodded, shuddering at the remembrance of the cold, grasping presence she had encountered upon entering Rick's nightmare. "I . . . felt . . . the thing reaching for him in his sleep."

"It comes for him in his dreams," said the girl. "It feeds upon the dark side of his spirit, reminding him of the things he has done in life. He is very weak now, and though his spirit fights against the dark creature, each dream brings it closer to its goal of controlling him, of using his power and his influence among the living for its own ends. It must be prevented from this."

Sara was astonished. "But what can I do?" she asked.

The golden creature smiled, the aura flickering about her like fire. "The light of your compassion for Rick has already thwarted the demon once, allowing his spirit to rest," she said. "Perhaps if you gave him an even brighter dream, it would block the dark thoughts that prey upon his mind until his injured spirit has healed."

Sara shook her head sadly. "I would do anything I could," she said, "but I'm not even sure he can see me anymore."

The girl in the yellow slicker took her hand. "He

will see you again," she promised, "and you will be more beautiful and warm and alive than any woman he has ever known."

"Told you he wouldn't buy a damn word of it," Hapwell grunted. He guided the ancient Chevy onto the mountain road, grinding the balky transmission into a lower gear. "Feller like that's used to dealing in hard facts. He ain't gonna swallow no half-baked ghost story from some boozy old man."

Phylis sat on the torn plastic seat watching the road ahead unwind in the yellow beams of the truck's anemic headlights. "I'm not so sure," she said. "He knows he saw something he can't explain. If he's as good a reporter as they say, he's going to work it over in his mind until he comes to the same conclusion that you did. The girl he found on the road is the ghost of Sara Raynor."

Hapwell snorted something unintelligible and crammed a wad of rough-cut tobacco into his jaw. "Trouble is," he said, "if that's Sara Raynor's ghost, what's she doin' walkin' this old road fifteen miles from the house she killed herself in? I heard plenty of ghost stories in my time, but the spooks in the stories always stay put in the place where they died."

Phylis shook her head. It didn't make sense to her either. She actually knew something about ghosts, having been forced to take an interest in the subject soon after she'd bought the Silver Peak Saloon—which was popularly rumored to be haunted by the ghost of an evil desperado who had died in a gunfight downstairs, as well as by the spirit of a sinister "woman in red," who was said to roam the hotel's upper floors.

Phylis had dismissed the silly stories out of hand until late one afternoon during the restoration of the building. She had been standing in the street trying to decide on a new paint scheme for the sign above the main saloon entrance when she had happened to glance up to a third-floor window. The face of a pretty young girl in a bright red dress was looking sadly back at her from behind the glass.

Horrified that someone's child had somehow gotten into the still-condemned portion of the building, which was then a maze of rotten floorboards and exposed nails, and nearly as concerned for her insurance liability as for the child's welfare, she had raced up the narrow staircase behind the short hall that now served as the saloon's unofficial wintertime entrance and, after being forced to open the locked door with her passkey, had burst into Room 312 prepared to scold the trespassing child harshly. But she had found only an empty room, its once luxurious wallpaper slowly peeling in the fading sunlight. A thorough search of both the third and second floors had turned up nothing whatsoever and she had gone back downstairs half an hour later, convinced that her eyes had been playing tricks on her.

Phylis told no one else of the incident and had, in fact, put it completely out of her mind until two weeks later when she had sent a pair of workmen up to the third floor to begin stripping rotted carpet from the corridors, and left the building to take care of some business in Carson City. She'd returned three hours later to find the workmen's tools and lunch pails scattered about the third-floor corridor, minus their owners.

A long search had finally turned up one of the men at the bar of another saloon, where he shakily informed her that he and his companion had opened the door to Room 312, intending to store the old carpet there temporarily, and had been greeted by the sight of a girl in a red dress sitting at the window. One of the men had spoken to the girl, who had turned to smile wistfully at them, and then slowly vanished before their eyes.

The workman in the bar had politely declined Phylis's offer to return to work at double his previous wage, asking only that his and his friend's tools and lunch pails be set on the sidewalk in front of the Silver Peak.

The story had spread through town like wildfire, and unable to lure any of the local craftsmen to work, she had ordered some serious books on supernatural phenomena, intent on debunking the myth that her building was haunted. To her surprise, her research had turned up a long list of famous structures and places that were reputed to be haunted, nearly always by the spirits of persons who had died tragically, or under stressful circumstances, in or near those places. Not a single authoritative source, she learned to her dismay, had been able to disprove the existence of ghosts.

The only cheerful note provided by her books was an assurance that virtually all of the class of spirits known as "household ghosts" were harmless. Some, she discovered, were even friendly, as the girl in red appeared to be.

Buoyed by her discovery, Phylis had changed tactics, setting out to prove that if the Silver Peak were indeed haunted, its spirits posed no danger to big strong workmen. A bit of additional research in the county courthouse had disclosed that one Samuel Briscoe, a greenhorn prospector from Liverpool, England, had indeed lost his life at the bar of the Silver Peak Saloon on the night of June 5, 1877, when the Colt .44 revolver he had purchased that very day accidentally discharged as he was showing it to a friend.

Phylis had selected a spot on the bar directly below a suspicious bullet-sized hole in the saloon's tin ceiling and installed a small plaque paying tribute to the many brave pioneers who had come to Silver Peak in search of their fortunes, citing the unfortunate death of one Samuel Briscoe of Liverpool on this very spot as proof of the dangers faced by the brave adventurers. "Sam's place" quickly became the favorite seat at the bar.

Scratch one evil desperado.

The case of the woman in red had been harder to track down. Nothing in county law-enforcement records mentioned the death of a woman in the Silver Peak Hotel, by violent or other means. Ultimately a local historian had provided the answer, dropping by one afternoon to place a Xerox of a tattered newspaper article on the bar. The article, from an issue of the *Silver Peak Prospector* dated May 1863, told the sad story of ten-year-old Susie Parker, the daughter of a prominent local businessman.

Little Susie, "known to her friends and teachers as a sweet-tempered child," had been crossing the street in front of the Silver Peak on her way to a birthday party when she was struck down by a runaway freight wagon. According to the article, "The poor child was rushed to a vacant room in the nearby hotel and a doctor summoned. Alas, little Susie expired of her grievous injuries before medical aid could arrive. A weeping Miss Rachel Hopkins, seamstress, of this city, related that the child's pretty white party dress was soaked red with her blood."

Phylis had wept for poor little Susie Parker after reading the article, and her plans for the renovation of the upper floors now included redecorating Room 312 in cheerful new wallpaper—something for a little girl.

" . . . I said, I wouldn't buy it if I was him," Hapwell hollered, taking his eyes from the road to look across at Phylis. "It don't make sense."

She looked back at him and shook her head. "I don't buy it either," she said. "That's why I think I'm going to do a little research on Sara Raynor."

Hapwell grinned. "Figured it'd come to that sooner or later," he said. "If you was able to figure them two spooks from the 1800's, 1976 oughta be like slidin' on ice bare naked."

Phylis smiled. "I hope you're right, but I've just got one question for you."

He looked at her, his cheek bulging with tobacco. "Tell you anything I can," he said.

"Do you make up all those awful sayings as you go along, or do you think them up beforehand?"

The old-timer rolled down his window and spit

into the cold wind. "Didn't your mama never teach you no respect for your elders, girlie?" he growled.

"As a matter of fact, no." She laughed. The pickup's worn shocks clattered over a rough patch on the poorly maintained roadway and an uneasy silence settled over the darkened cab. Phylis leaned forward in her seat, straining to see ahead through the muddy windshield as they neared the treacherous curve where Rick Masterson claimed to have discovered Sara Raynor standing in the snow.

The Seduction

T H E horror show.

Rick was crouched in the dust beside the battered *kombi*—the familiar African term for the minivan the network had rented to haul him and his equipment. The surging crowd of exuberant black youths in the open field surrounding the Soweto soccer stadium was wheeling about in confusion now, their peaceful demonstration of moments before shattered by the sounds of screams and the stink of a petrol bomb that had exploded somewhere at the fringes of the crowd.

The white security-forces officer commanding the column of nervous troops watching from armored personnel carriers parked along the verge of the unpaved road said something to his sergeant, and Rick tapped Denys, his cameraman, on the shoulder. "Catch the troops," he whispered. "I think there's gonna be trouble."

Denys, a cheerful "coloured"—the nationalist

government's special designation for persons of mixed blood—shook his head and turned to grin at the jittery reporter. "Don't worry, baas, the soldiers won't shoot." He gestured to the ten thousand angry people on the field. "That crowd would tear them apart and they know it."

He pointed to a dirty smudge of black smoke rising in the direction of the screams. "Something's up over there. Want me to see if I can get in close for a shot?"

"Looks pretty dangerous," Rick said, hesitating. He'd been here three days now and had yet to capture on tape any of the violence that had been sweeping the townships since the government had declared its latest state of emergency. He wanted footage. Wanted it bad.

"You want to give it a try?" he asked.

Denys patted his camera, a fifty-thousand-dollar Sony Betacam bearing the network logo in bold colors. "No problem, baas, the whole point of these demonstrations is to let the news cameras show the world how they're suffering." He smiled engagingly. "Of course it would probably be better if you keep your pale puss right here."

"Okay," said Rick, glad he hadn't even had to talk the eager young cameraman into going for the footage, "but it's your call . . . if you're sure," he added without much enthusiasm. "And stop calling me baas, my name is Rick."

"Right, Rick." Denys grinned again and took off at a trot toward the predominantly Zulu crowd.

"Hey you, Masterson," shouted the white officer from the nearest APC. "Are you daft? Don't let that man go in there, those Kaffirs will kill him."

"Fuck you, Botha! The world wants to see what you and your pals are doing down here." Rick grinned. The officer's already florid face reddened in undisguised rage as the brash American reporter turned back to watch the field. The front ranks of the demonstrators opened to swallow Denys. The crowd surged briefly as a group of boys carrying the cowhide shields and spears of Zulu warriors suddenly broke into an impromptu dance for the camera. A ululating scream split the air, and an older group of ragged black men appeared, shoving their way through the mob beyond the dancers. Something bright flashed in the sun.

"My God!" The white officer's exclamation was drowned in the crowd's collective wail as the youthful dancers were shoved aside and people began to scatter in all directions. More metal glinted over the sea of black heads, and Rick caught a glimpse of a gleaming *panga* suspended above and behind Denys. The polished blade descended in a blurred arc, and the cameraman was tumbling on the ground, his legs doing a curious little dance in the parched red dust.

"What's happening?" Rick was shouting at the officer over the clatter of the soldiers' rifle bolts being slammed home. The officer did not answer and an unseen hand suddenly grabbed Rick from behind and jerked him into the shelter of the *kombi* as the Armored Personnel Carriers roared out onto the field with soldiers firing into the air from their open hatches.

"We've got to get out of here," screamed Rick's white driver, a down-on-his-luck safari guide who had turned his extensive knowledge of the country and its indigenous populations to the lucrative business of leading foreign news crews into the no-mans-land of the black townships, slamming the *kombi* into gear and cutting a tight circle on the narrow road. He stalled the engine halfway through the turn and the small van lurched to a halt in a ditch facing the mob. "Dammit!" The driver's fingers fumbled with the ignition switch, urging the tiny engine back to life.

"Wait! What about Denys?" Rick heard his own voice echoing in his ears.

"Forget him, mate!" The panicked driver pointed a finger to the center of the field, where a crumpled figure lay writhing in an orange ball of flames. "Your little stunt's done for him." A sudden gust of wind blew the cloud of greasy smoke toward the van and Rick choked on the stink of burned flesh. The maddened crowd of young black students suddenly changed direction again, sprinting back toward the safety of the stadium and leaving the solitary figure burning on the empty field.

Regaining his composure now that the immediate danger was past, the driver got the engine going and carefully pulled the *kombi* back onto the road. Turning to look at Rick, he gestured with his thumb toward the unspeakable thing on the ground fifty yards away. "I'm afraid to chance rolling this lot out there and getting stuck again." He smirked at the reporter's discomfiture. "You want to trot out and see if you can salvage your Betacam?"

Rick swallowed hard and nodded. Although he felt sick about Denys, he realized that there might just be fifteen or twenty seconds of usable footage in the camera's onboard cassette. Rationalizing his action with the thought that the brave camera-man's final footage should not have been shot in vain, he climbed out of the van and ran toward the column of black smoke that had been Denys. The camera was lying on the ground a few feet away from the twisted remains; he bent to pick it up, surprised to find it undamaged.

A shadow fell across him and he forced himself to look up. The wind had shifted again, enveloping him in thick clouds of roiling smoke. Grabbing the camera by its handle, he stood, momentarily blinded. Then, eyes squeezed shut against the noxious vapor and clasping a hand across his mouth, he stumbled forward and was hit by a blast of icy air that stopped him in his tracks. He opened his burning eyes and stared into a black void.

The familiar thing with the glowing red eyes stared back at him.

Rick let the precious camera fall to the ground and tried to run. His legs refused to move as the horrible thing snatched him up like a rag doll, lifting him with glistening black claws to the level of its burning eyes. A pair of hideously slimed lips formed in the absolute void of darkness below the eyes, curling into a sardonic grin over angled rows of decaying black teeth. A crimson tongue slithered toward him and the reek of sulfur assailed his nostrils as the thing noisily inhaled and he felt the breath being sucked from his lungs in a warm, steamy jet. Rick Masterson struggled to scream as a paralyzing wall of freezing darkness fell over his body and the stink of death filled the fetid air.

In the last moment before he lost consciousness he felt himself bathed in warm yellow light. A soft, pale hand grasped his, pulling him gently away from the horrible glowing eyes.

The hideous thing in the blackness blinked myopically, its slimed skin erupting in spreading blisters as the bright refractions of light touched it. It screamed its rage and pain as Rick was torn from its grasping claws.

Rick gasped, filling his lungs with clean, precious air. Music was playing, an old Moody Blues album he distantly remembered from high school. He opened his eyes to see the firelight flickering softly against the walls of the bungalow, felt the comforting support of the sofa cushions beneath him.

Sara hovered over him, a crystal goblet of ruby-colored liquid shimmering in her hand. Her pale features were radiant with color and he was suddenly aware of the redness of her full lips and the warm glow of the perfect skin beneath the thick fall of glossy hair about her shoulders. She knelt before him on the carpet, her eyes filled with concern.

"I had a terrible dream," he began.

Sara nodded, offering him the glass.

"What is it?" he asked, accepting the warm crystal from her hands and sipping the blood-red liquid within. It was perfect, a smooth fiery blend of textures that numbed his mouth and slid like molten lava down his throat. Bursts of intense light exploded behind his forehead and he felt suddenly light-headed.

She smiled, looking past him to the soft bloom of golden light hovering just beyond the balcony doors across the room. "It is only wine," she replied in a soft musical voice. She took the glass from his hands and held it to the hearth. Shattered beams of firelight sparkled crimson through the faceted bowl. "Isn't it beautiful?" she asked, raising the goblet to her own mouth.

"Beautiful," Rick repeated. He was terribly confused now, trying to recall more of where he had just been. Someplace horrible. Soweto, he thought. That day with Denys . . . Of course he had been dreaming. A cool hand slipped about his neck and he looked at the beautiful creature kneeling on the floor before him. She raised the glass to his lips again. More of the fiery liquid exploded within him and he felt an incredible erection growing in his jeans. He giggled, suddenly remembering something he had heard.

"They said you were a ghost."

Sara smiled and moved closer to him, her lips just tantalizingly out of his reach.

"Dance with me," she said, rising gracefully to her feet and pulling him up by his hand.

To his surprise, the stiffness in his knee was gone and he melted into her arms as the haunting, erotic strains of "Nights in White Satin" filled the room. He looked up from Sara's encircling arm to see an old-fashioned portable record turntable spinning on the dining table, thinking it strange he'd never noticed it until now.

"Happy, darling?"

Sara was smiling at him, her golden hair filled with glowing firelight, the sparkling goblet held high in her free hand. He nodded and she raised the delicious wine to his lips once more.

"What is this?" he asked again, drinking deeply and feeling the fire spreading down his spine.

She smiled mischievously. "A magical potion that will make you fall in love." The slender straps supporting the shoulders of her flimsy gown dissolved before his eyes and the thin material floated to the floor like mist.

Rick blinked and pulled away from her to see his own clothes falling away in tattered shreds that hung drifting in the air like smoke. A soft hand slid down his back, caressing the cleft at the top of his buttocks.

"Am I dreaming all of this, too?" he asked in a voice slightly touched with panic.

The hand pressed insistently forward and he felt naked flesh burning against his own. He closed his eyes as warm lips touched his and his mouth fell open to the insistent probings of a hot velvety tongue. Soft hips moved rhythmically against his own and he was sure that he was going to climax. But he did not, and still the magic fire continued to rage through his body.

He forced his eyes open and saw that the room was slowly tumbling about him, and his hand reached out to touch her breast. An indescribable sensation shot through his lower body and he lowered his gaze to see a silken leg sliding up over his hip.

The probing hand touched him in a lower place, its relentless fingers setting off shock waves of neural energy that exploded against the backdrop of colored lights already floating in his brain, and he felt his own hand dropping to explore the delightful warmth of her. She moaned in his arms and he gazed into her wide, dark eyes as she guided him inside her.

She sighed. "You mustn't leave me, Rick."

"No!" He could not imagine leaving.

Her lips fastened on his and she arched her back to engulf him. New waves of sensation swept over him and he threw his head back, gasping as his body began to shudder in uncontrollable spasms.

"I think I'm going to die," he whispered.

Sara moaned and clasped him even tighter as she felt the long shudders traveling through his body, transmitting their energy to hers. She kept her eyes shut tightly, afraid of breaking the fragile spell that held them as one for this brief moment in time. This bonding that was, she knew, critical to their mutual survival.

Sara understood so much more now, about her attraction to this man, about his flawed spirit—flawed as she herself was flawed—and about the deadly shadow that hung over his life, the shadow of the monstrous demon whose clever plan drew Rick's wounded spirit farther and farther into a dark underworld of human misery and destruction, a world he was meant to inhabit forever, his will and his talents as a public figure, respected by millions, ultimately turned to the demon's own evil purposes. Only by blocking these visions could Sara hope to foil the dark monster's plan. In so doing, she might save her own wounded spirit as well.

Her thoughts scattered in a burst of shining light as the human flesh she had been allowed temporarily to reclaim succumbed to the demands of his vibrant living body, and she threw her head back and shouted her joy to the stars shining down on them from the cold velvet sky beyond the skylights.

Very soon, the bright spirit had promised, Sara would remember all, and in remembering she would be given the opportunity to redeem the vile acts that had committed her to this purgatory of endless wandering. She would be redeemed by saving Rick from the evil thing that had claimed him. First, however, she must make Rick Masterson hers. Completely.

The bright spirit had warned that her efforts might end in her own destruction as well as Rick's. Sara did not care.

She had been waiting far too long.

The great demon, an immensely complex and intelligent creature composed of hideous layers of cold and shadow, lurked in the dark recesses of the bungalow's beamed ceiling. It had been watching the panting lovers with growing rage. The creature had taken many souls over the ages, picking and choosing with extraordinary care from among the brightest and best this miserable planet had to offer. It selected only those like Rick Masterson, whose truly dark thoughts and deeds were exceeded only by their potential to light their world.

The demon took great pride in its selections, disdaining the easy catches—the casual murderers, tyrants, and destroyers—in favor of these, the most difficult prey of all. Its patience was unlimited, for though its prey must be forewarned of its coming, they could never be allowed to guess its true intention, lest they purge the evil from their souls before it was too late. Such transformations could occur in the span of a heartbeat, a single thought rendering decades of patient stalking useless.

It had selected this one a very long time ago by human standards, recognizing in him the capacity for limitless evil, taking a proprietary pride in his growing cynicism and disregard for his fellow humans, aiding whenever possible in his elevation to the heights of his profession by cleverly bargaining with others of its kind. Masterson's career had benefited from the demon's manipulations many times. A strategic suicide here, a bloody slaying there. Events that had always put him in the right place at the right time, ensuring that his considerable talents were never overlooked by his superiors. The demon had even fomented a small war early in his career as an aspiring broadcast journalist, knowing he would be the first on hand to cover it.

The great demon had a large investment in Rick Masterson, an investment that spoke as much of its pride in delivering the choicest souls to the gates of hell as to the inordinate efforts it had expended in drawing him into its web. It knew full well that his ultimate corruption could deliver thousands of lesser souls to perdition and it was enraged by the interference of the bright spirit that had unaccountably intervened to protect him.

That the agent of its enemies had stooped to the

pathetic expedient of enlisting the pale banished spirit with whom Masterson was even now grunting and rutting only served to fortify the demon's resolve to have the man's soul for itself. It tempered its rage with the knowledge that the prize it had selected was well worth the battle, and it was not dejected. There were still many, many forces it could enlist to its aid.

The demon smiled in its cloak of blackness and withdrew into the night sky above the still, black lake to make its plans. It had never yet failed in the hunt and it did not intend to begin by losing Rick Masterson. It knew precisely where to find what it needed.

Awakenings

P H Y L I S Rand sat bolt upright in her brass bed, awakened by a sudden chill despite the fact that air in the cozy bedroom was warm. She glanced at the luminous hands of the clock on the bedside table. It was nearly 5:00 A.M. and she had been dreaming.

Phylis flushed deeply, remembering the erotic dream she had been having about Rick Masterson before something had intervened to jar her awake. Annoyed, she snuggled back under the covers and laid her head on the down pillows, hoping to recreate the magic of the dream. She tried to conjure up Rick's face again, but something dark and ominous clouded the image.

Another chill passed through her body and she opened her eyes, intending to turn up the electric blanket. It occurred to her that perhaps she had opened the window earlier in the day in order to air the room, then forgotten to close it.

Climbing from the bed, she hurriedly crossed to the casement overlooking the street in front of the hotel. She found the window securely shut and looked out at the clear, starry sky, wondering if Rick was sleeping well. That was when the spark of yellow light flickering in Hapwell's vacant lot across the street caught her eye.

Janet McMurty was crouched in the frozen dust before the twisted wreck of Mike Gomez's red Camaro, her watery blue eyes fixed on the guttering flame of the fat beeswax candle she had affixed to the hood. She moaned at the wave of dark sensations assaulting her brain, rocking back and forth on her heels and clasping her dirty hands over her gaunt breasts.

"Janet, what in God's name are you doing?"

Janet turned to see Phylis standing behind her, a heavy robe clutched tightly to her throat against the cold. "Demons," she moaned, reaching out to touch the crumpled fender of the car. "A lesser one here." She sobbed, a thick rope of mucus dribbling onto her upper lip. "It took two young lives, cold and uncaring. . . ."

"All right," Phylis said tightly. Janet's nonsensical meanderings were getting to be too much even for her and she was anxious to get back to bed. She leaned over and pulled the frail woman to her feet. "Let's go inside now."

Janet allowed herself to be led away from the pathetic remains of the Camaro and onto the sidewalk. "It's true, Phylis," she moaned, planting her feet firmly on the worn boards of the walk and refusing to move any further. She rolled her eyes toward the brooding shadow of the mountain behind the town. "Another demon stalks the forest and the dark places up there. It is a greater creature than the one that killed the two in the car . . . much greater. It's up there now. Waiting . . . stalking."

Phylis's eyes involuntarily followed the other's gaze to the distant mountaintop. A towering column of black cloud swirled above the snowcapped peak, blotting out the stars, and she wondered if the big storm was moving in earlier than predicted.

"It uses people." Phylis turned to see Janet still staring up at the mountain, her voice verging on hysteria. "People and spirits, dark and light," Janet babbled, "the living and the dead . . . uses them to get its own way." She turned to look pleadingly at Phylis. "It wants the man, Phylis."

Phylis frowned. "What man?"

Janet shuddered, her thin body racked with a sudden chill. "Him," she said, pointing to the mountain. "Him with the dark aura . . ."

Pain.

Rick groaned. The throbbing knives in his knee and shoulder were minor irritants compared with the way his head felt. His mouth tasted as though something had died in it. He opened his eyes, surprised to find himself lying fully clothed on the sofa before the cold fireplace.

"Oh God!"

He forced himself up to a sitting position, squinting against the white glare of sunshine pouring into the room through the skylights. He stood shakily, looking around the room, and last night came flooding back to him. He limped to the pine table where the old-fashioned record player had been. The table contained the collection of cardboard grocery boxes brought by Phylis and Hapwell. Nothing more.

"Just dreaming," he mumbled, staggering into the kitchen and locating a thermos filled with the remains of last night's coffee. He poured a cup and crossed to the balcony door to sip the tepid liquid. Outside, the lake sparkled blue beneath an even bluer sky.

The dream had seemed so real.

"Sure." He laughed, remembering how his clothes had disintegrated and floated away, the blood-red wine that Sara had given him, the record player that was no longer there. He opened the glass door and stepped onto the thin crust of snow still adhering to the balcony floor. Oblivious to the chill wind whipping at the thin fabric of his plaid shirt, he stared at the harsh glare from the windows of the big house hidden away among the trees at the far end of the lake.

"Yes," said Phylis, "I understand completely." She was talking into the phone behind the bar, nodding in response to the voice on the other end of the scratchy line and scribbling notes on the back of an order pad.

Hapwell, his beard speckled with remnants of the toast and scrambled eggs he had been eating, got up from his table near the slots and stood watching her from the other side of the bar.

"Yes, thank you very much . . . Yes, me, too . . . I will." She hung up and examined her notes, underlining one or two points she had written on the pad.

"What you up to?" Hapwell demanded.

Phylis looked up in surprise. "Oh, good morning, Hap. When did you get here?"

"Dammit, woman, I been sittin' over there eatin' breakfast for the last twenty minutes. Who you been jawin' with all this time?"

"Paris," she said mysteriously. "God, twenty minutes? Was I really on that long?"

"Forty," said Denny the bartender, arriving to fill Hapwell's cup. "Glad I ain't gonna get your phone bill this month."

"Paris, France," Hapwell mused. "Cousin of mine got the clap over there in forty-six." His blue eyes narrowed suspiciously. "Didn't know you knowed any frogs."

Phylis sighed at Hap's outrageous view of the world and held out a cup to Denny. The bartender filled it and walked away to tend to a couple of cowboys who were eating steak and eggs at the far end of the bar. "I don't know anyone in France," she said to the old-timer. "I was talking to Rick's friend Jimmy Randall. He's over there on temporary assignment."

"Randall, that the kid whose old man holds the lease on the bungalow up to the lake?"

Phylis nodded. "The network located him for me." She hesitated. "I told them I was a friend of Rick's."

"Well, ain't you?"

She flushed, remembering the hot, longing touch

of Rick's lips against hers, the brief, urgent press of his body—and her dream, in which everything that she had been feeling at the bungalow had proceeded to its logical conclusion. "I suppose I am," she finally said. "Anyway, I remembered what Rick said about the pictures of someone he thought might be Jimmy's brother and Sara Raynor." She paused to sip her coffee.

"Well, you gonna tell me what he said, or you waitin' for my arteries to finish hardenin'?"

Phylis looked down the bar to be certain they weren't being overheard, then leaned forward on her elbows. "I'm not sure where to begin," she said. "I thought this Jimmy could answer a couple of simple questions." She looked down at her notes and shook her head. "Instead I seem to have opened up a whole new can of worms. In the first place, the guy in the picture wasn't Jimmy's brother. Jimmy was an only child. He said I must mean his uncle Ted. Ted Steele was his mother's younger brother. Jimmy worshiped him. Ted was like a big brother to Jimmy until he was lost."

"Whoa," said Hapwell, "you just lost me."

"I told you it was complicated," said Phylis. "You see, Uncle Ted disappeared without a trace in"—she bent to examine her notes—"December of 1976."

"The same year and month the Raynor girl died."

"Yes, but apparently that was just coincidental. Ted was twenty-two at the time, newly graduated from Princeton and a junior partner in his father's San Francisco brokerage firm. One Friday night, just before Christmas, he got into his car and drove away from his apartment in Berkeley and was never seen again. They never even found his car, which was unusual in itself, because it was a new Corvette and the police told the family that high-profile cars like Corvettes almost always turn up somewhere right away."

Hapwell slurped his coffee and made a sound approximating a low whistle. "That sure as hell does rank right up there as plenty strange. What about this Ted's connection with the Raynor girl?"

Phylis shrugged helplessly. "None that Jimmy knew of. Ted only visited the lake once, when Jimmy was about ten. The only girl he remembers seeing Ted with was visiting another family at the lake. Jimmy said she was pretty and he thinks Ted mentioned that she was from Detroit."

"That's it?"

Phylis nodded.

"So, you're dead-ended then?"

"Not exactly," she said. "Something else happened last night—actually this morning. Something very strange. It's given me another idea about Sara Raynor's ghost."

"Uh-oh," said Hapwell. "Do I want to hear this?"

"I don't know," said Phylis. "Do you?"

Sara blinked.

She was standing before the dusty mirror in her father's study, staring at her own image in the cold morning light. A deep flush rose in her cheeks as she remembered the previous night and the things she had done with Rick. She had never seduced a man before, never even made love to anyone except . . . Ted. His image suddenly came flooding back to her and she remembered something. It was nearly Christmas and they had planned to meet, here at the lake.

Sara closed her eyes, trying to remember more of what had happened. Ted was driving up from Berkeley in the new Corvette, the one his parents had given him for graduation. It had been snowing and she had stood at the French doors for hours, watching the enormous white flakes drop silently into the black waters of the lake, searching for the headlights of his car on the road.

Sara had deliberately chosen the Lodge for their weekend, even though she knew Ted had feared and despised the place ever since her father had threatened to kill him that August morning when she had leaped out of the sailboat and thrown herself in front of his rifle, spoiling his aim as her mysterious lover had sailed away into the morning mist, and threatening to kill herself if Raynor tried to pursue him.

Afterward it had taken her weeks to find Ted in New Jersey, and still maintaining the illusion that she was her Detroit friend, Susan, whom Harold Raynor had mistaken for his daughter in the weak morning light, Sara had convinced Ted to see her again. Then they had begun meeting secretly, she sneaking away from school for weekend visits to a nonexistent aunt in Manhattan, traveling for hours by air to wait nervously in empty hotel rooms for the "casual" dates they shared in the city. There had been three such dates before they had made love again, Ted taking her back to a friend's Park Avenue apartment for an entire delicious weekend of sex, takeout Chinese food, and old TV movies. Sara had never been so gloriously happy in her life.

The following year Ted had graduated from Princeton and moved to Berkeley to take courses in sculpture and design while he figured out some way to gently talk his family out of their obsession with his apprenticeship in the family brokerage firm. It was a move that had coincided perfectly with Sara's transfer in the fall from St. Claire's to the University of California at Berkeley, where Harold Raynor had reluctantly allowed her to take a small apartment. She and Ted had spent the next several months seeing each other on a regular basis, although his increasingly busy schedule at Steele Brothers combined with his growing suspicions about her reluctance to meet his family, or to allow him to pick her up at the apartment, had begun to cast a definite pall on their relationship.

Sara had asked Ted to meet her at the lake just before Christmas with the promise of a weekend of cross-country skiing and lovemaking before the massive fireplace. According to the lie she had constructed, the romantic weekend had been the idea of her friend Sara, who was spending the holiday with her volatile father at his chalet in Switzerland, a lie, she consoled herself, that was at least partly true—Sara Raynor had indeed planned the weekend and Harold Raynor had already left for Europe on business and was expecting his daughter to join him there in time for Christmas Eve. Sara, however, had no intention of using the Swissair tickets that had arrived by messenger from the Raynor Corporation that morning.

When Ted Steele arrived at the Lodge, Sara had planned on telling him the awful truth, that she was the daughter of one of the country's richest and most hated men. She thought there was a small chance that he would not believe her, and so she had chosen the Lodge because it was filled with incontrovertible proof of her identity. Afterward she planned to throw herself on his mercy, begging him not to hate her for who she was and praying he would still love her despite the tangled web of lies she had told him. If there was a God in heaven, she had convinced herself, he would have her anyway. She could get a job and work to support them both, leaving him free to leave his hated apprenticeship at Steele Brothers and pursue his art.

Sara looked away from the mirror as a cloud passed before the sun, extinguishing the light filtering in through the dirty windows. She felt a hot, choking sensation in her throat as she remembered Ted's long-delayed arrival at the lodge in the snow-covered Corvette, which without chains had barely made it up the treacherous mountain road. She had already started a roaring fire in the study and they had fallen onto the long sofa by the light of the leaping flames, making passionate love as the sky outside had grown progressively darker and the snow had piled up knee-high beyond the French doors.

Later, as they snuggled naked beneath one of the priceless Navajo blankets that dotted the heavy oak furniture, they had shared cold sandwiches and wine from the small store of food she had brought along for the weekend, and she had haltingly blurted out her story, afraid to look directly into his eyes for fear of how he might react.

When she was at last finished, Ted had gazed silently into the fire for a very long time while Sara huddled miserably beneath the blanket, listening to the snapping of the logs in the fireplace and sorry she had had the horrible idea of telling the truth. Why couldn't she have left things as they were? At least then she would have had him for however long it had taken him to discover her secret on his own.

Many moments had passed before she felt his soft touch on her arm and looked up into his shining eyes to see him smiling at her.

"Honey, that's wonderful," he had said.

Sara had stared at him, not quite comprehending. She had played out many possible reactions in her mind, but this was not one of them. "You mean you don't mind?"

"Mind?" He had grinned, squeezing her to him. "What's to mind? My old man will be in seventh heaven. He's been trying to get close to your father for years. Learning that Harold Raynor's son-in-law-to-be is also the junior partner at Steele Brothers is going to be the best Christmas present the old goat ever had."

"But your art!" she stammered.

Ted had shrugged boyishly and something small and fragile had broken inside of her. "Art? Honey, you can *buy* art. I've learned an awful lot at the brokerage in the past few months and now I realize that art doesn't mean a damn thing. Hell, I love art.

But I want to do something important, to change the world."

"But you will," she had protested.

He had smiled then, his perfectly aligned teeth flashing in the firelight. "Damn right," he said, "but not with art. Money. Money and power. That's how you change the world."

The room was growing darker.

Sara peered at her fading image in the mirror, certain she could see a tear running down her cheek. She extended her hand toward the dusty glass, anxious to confirm its solidity, her own reality. Ghostly fingers disappeared into the dimly shining surface. The wind rattled through the eaves, mocking her.

She turned and glided silently across the room to the cold hearth, wanting to remember more, but afraid now. Desperately afraid.

"Tell me, you little son of a bitch!"

Sheriff Bull Ryan stood swaying over the frightened burglary suspect. The boy, a slender redhead of about sixteen, was huddled in the corner of a cement cell in the basement of the Silver Peak Courthouse. One cheek was swollen purple below a painfully sliced eyebrow and several fragments of the kid's front teeth already speckled the floor along with bright drops of his blood.

"Dunno nuthin', honest!" The kid whimpered like an injured animal and scrabbled for the shelter of a rusting iron bunk.

Ryan artfully snatched at the kid's ankle, dragging him into the harsh glare of the naked bulb that swayed overhead, filling the cell with nightmarish shadows. "You little fucker!" he screamed. "You know plenty and you're going to tell me or I'll break every bone in your goddam scrawny body." He straddled the cowering boy and slapped the blood-slicked blackjack against his palm with a wet, cracking sound that echoed off the filth-encrusted walls. "Now I'm gonna ask you just one more time—where did you get them stereo speakers we found in the trunk of that piece of shit car of yours?"

The kid shook his bloodied head. "I already told you, I bought 'em from a guy down in Carson."

Ryan nodded. "A guy in a brown van in a 7-Eleven parking lot off Highway fifty, right?"

The kid cringed and nodded.

"Well," said Ryan, setting his jaw and raising the blackjack high overhead, "you can't say I didn't give you fair warning, you little asshole."

The kid screamed, curling himself into a fetal position and squeezing his eyes shut against the bone-crushing force of yet another blow. Long seconds passed and he squinted up into the light to see Ryan's arm frozen in midswing. The fat sheriff's eyes were open and staring fixedly at some distant point beyond the shadowed wall of the cell.

The kid trembled in an agony of anticipation as Ryan stood like that for several more seconds. Finally a low guttural rumbling issued from the sheriff's throat and his jaw fell slack. A silvery strand of drool splashed onto the kid's face and he squeezed his eyes shut again as a loud metallic clang echoed through the jail corridor. The kid opened his one good eye and looked up to find himself alone. Ryan's booted footsteps clumped away in the distance, the hollow sound echoing back down through the long, underground corridor.

CHAPTER 17

Heaven

J A N and Harv Spencer were parked at the edge of a scenic overlook five miles to the south of Silver Peak, a mountainous vantage point from which they could survey the stark majesty of the entire eastern Sierra range. Their impulsive decision to detour through the historic Silver Peak mining region had been made during the couple's leisurely drive back to Southern California following their weekend wedding in one of Reno's innumerable roadside chapels. The decision to marry had been equally impulsive, and both husband and wife were now nervously wondering how their respective families, hers in Baltimore, his back in Ohio, were going to take the news. Jan, a petite brunette with a flashing smile and a model's leggy good looks, was certain that her mother, who had always envisioned her only daughter marrying a prosperous doctor in a huge church wedding, was going to stroke out when she met her slightly rumpled new son-in-law.

Harv, a husky electronics engineer with a computer nerd's shaggy beard and a heart of gold, carefully perched his petite bride on a massive boulder fronting an unspoiled vista of craggy mountaintops and backed off to fiddle with the new video camera he had purchased especially for the trip. "Okay, babe, try to look happy," he teased, raising the camera to his eye and pressing the record button.

Jan stuck her tongue out and made a funny face for the camera. "Ladies and gentlemen, here we are in the middle of beautiful nowhere," she chirped, indicating the surrounding mountains with a grandiose sweep of her arms. "We've been married for almost eighteen hours now, and as you can see, life is just an endless round of glittering parties and theater openings."

"Hey," said Harv, lowering the camera and looking hurt. "I thought you were the one who wanted to take this detour. We could've spent another night in the hotel."

"Come here, you big ape," she demanded, jumping up from the rock and throwing her arms around his neck. "Haven't you known me long enough by now to be able to tell when I'm teasing you?"

Harv blushed and she stood on her tiptoes to plant a tender kiss on his nose. "There's no place I'd rather be than right here in the middle of nowhere with you, you lovely old teddy bear," she whispered, nibbling on his earlobe.

"You sure?" he breathed, still uncertain what had drawn this incredibly beautiful and talented woman to him. Jan was an actress and a successful model, and he had fallen helplessly in love with her from the first moment she had leaned over his computer console at the aerospace lab where he was employed as senior systems analyst, enveloping him in a breathtaking aura that smelled vaguely of lilac. She had come there on a fashion shoot that was to feature the lab's giant radio telescope and had ended up wanting to know how everything worked.

Harv had escorted her around the lab for the rest of the afternoon, trying lamely to explain the complexities of radio astronomy in language that a non-Ph.D. would understand and looking for all the world like an unkempt, lovesick puppy. He hadn't dreamed of asking her for a date, though he had desperately wanted to, and had lain awake that night thinking of her, imagining he could still smell her perfume on the hand she had squeezed before taking her leave.

He was on the verge of falling into a lilac-scented sleep when the phone had rung and her voice had cheerily asked if he would like to meet her at an all-night coffee shop in The Valley for pancakes and coffee. She had claimed she hadn't been able to sleep either. They had ended up talking until dawn and had been nearly inseparable ever since. This weekend's wedding had been the outgrowth of a lively weeks-long discussion concerning the impossibility of two transplanted Californians staging a satisfactory ceremony for two big families— one Italian and one Jewish—living in the Midwest and on the East Coast.

"If you're still not sure about how I feel, I could show you again," she teased, hooking a thumb under her bulky fisherman's sweater. "I saw a picnic table right over there."

Harv looked around in sudden panic, surveying the small overlook and trying to decide if she was serious. "Uh, honey, maybe we better wait until we find a motel," he stammered.

"Spoilsport." She pouted, slipping her arms around his neck and pressing her lips against his.

Harv closed his eyes and sighed as her tongue slipped into his mouth, probing and delicious.

Neither of the young lovers noticed the black-and-white sheriff's patrol unit roll silently into the scenic overlook and glide to a stop behind their rented minivan.

Bull Ryan sat behind the wheel of the black-and-white Bronco, his hands clenching and unclenching the thick rubberized plastic. His beady pupils had shrunk to black pinpoints, giving his eyes a zombielike appearance, and his usually florid face had taken on the color of dead ashes. He twitched and his flabby jowls spasmed.

"Them?" he droned, swinging his massive head around to face the embracing lovers.

The elemental curled in his brain sent a violent surge of pain shooting down Ryan's spine and he responded with a jerky nod.

"Murder them," Ryan groaned. "Yes. It is good to murder them." He reached for the door handle, then yanked his bloody hand away as though he had touched molten metal. The big head nodded jerkily a second time and a rough parody of Ryan's gravelly voice rumbled up out of the depths of his

wattled throat. "Yes. I will rape the filthy whore of
a woman first, then I will smash the man's brains
on the stones and burn the vehicle." A strand of
greenish phlegm glistened at the corner of his
mouth as his lips curled back to reveal his stained
yellow teeth. "The whore has it coming," he
growled.

"They both have it coming."

The newlyweds broke off their kiss at the sound
of a car door opening behind them and Harv
squinted amiably at the massive figure silhouetted
before the patrol unit in the bright afternoon sunlight.

"Oh hi, Officer." Harv grinned sheepishly and let
his hand slip into Jan's.

"It's perfectly okay, Officer." Jan laughed, flashing her gold ring at the slowly advancing figure.
"We're a hundred-percent legal."

The dark thing inside Ryan's brain smiled its
hideous smile, confident now that the host would
unquestioningly obey its most depraved command. Still, it must be absolutely certain. A thrill of
delicious anticipation coursed through it as it
wondered what orders the great demon would
have for it after it had proved itself by ordering
the host to brutally murder the first humans it
encountered on the road.

The superior creature had approached the elemental in the midst of its host's cruelly satisfying
workday, promising the thing an everlasting feast
of ripe, rotting souls if only it would grant one
small favor. The lesser creature was at once

immensely honored and profoundly terrified. Only rarely in its long existence had it encountered a creature of the greater demon's magnificence and power, never been addressed by one so mighty. It swelled with pride at having been so chosen, inserting itself more firmly into the core of the host's being. It must perform this test of its control over the human perfectly. Never might another such opportunity come its way. Should it fail, however, it knew the superior creature's retribution would be swift and terrible.

"Is something wrong, Officer?" Harv was frowning at the silent policeman, staring nervously at the heavy revolver in his hand.

Rick had spent the entire morning setting up a portable darkroom in the bungalow's unused guest bathroom, burying himself in the familiar smells of photographic chemicals and paper in an attempt to clear his mind of the disturbing images with which he had awakened. After the equipment was arranged to his satisfaction, he had ducked into the kitchen for a quick lunch of soup and sandwiches, then returned to the darkroom to process the photos taken the day before.

Now, as he waited alone in the darkened space while the film rolls steeped in the tanks of developer, the riddle of Sara Raynor returned to him. His mind replayed the strange erotic dream of the night before and he knew that sheriff or no sheriff, he must return to the abandoned lodge at the far end of the lake to settle the question of the girl on the mountain road.

* * *

The sun was lowering and piles of towering cumulus were stacking against the western edge of the Sierras by the time Rick stepped out of the darkroom and glanced through the balcony doors to the opposite end of the lake. He checked his Rolex and was surprised to see that it was already just after four in the afternoon. Feeling slightly guilty at having reneged on his promise to Phylis, he hurried to turn on the bungalow's console radio to listen to the latest weather report. The air filled with the nasal tones of a pubescent Reno disc jockey who promised that another weather update would be broadcast in an hour, then slipped smoothly into a speech extolling the virtues of Springsteen's latest album. Rick shrugged and snapped off the radio, reasoning that the promised storm had not yet materialized and making a mental note to tune in again later.

"It's so cold," Janet moaned. She clasped her skinny arms about her chest and rocked back and forth in the straight-backed chair that Phylis had placed, according to Janet's precise instructions, in the empty hotel room above the saloon. Gobs of yellow beeswax spluttered from the six fat hexing candles set about on the rotting floorboards, the smell mingling unpleasantly with the musty odor of the room.

"Can you see anything?" Phylis whispered without much conviction. She had been watching for nearly two hours now as Janet, perched in the hard chair, sipped Wild Turkey from the bottle they had brought up from the bar and worked frantically at the mass of corded macramé in her lap with her long, knobby fingers.

Phylis had been feeling very foolish for some minutes and was on the verge of calling off the whole ridiculous exercise she had reluctantly let the other woman talk her into, convinced now that the séance was simply Janet's way of ensuring herself a warm spot and a supply of free booze for the afternoon.

Although she felt sorry for Janet—whose tie-dyed granny gowns and blue-tinted wire spectacles recalled her origins as the last remaining member of the Starlost Cooperative, a long-defunct hippie commune that had flourished briefly beside an abandoned strip mine outside of Silver Peak at the height of the Age of Aquarius, Phylis was convinced that Janet's psychic qualifications were, at best, the highly overrated product of Silver Peak's imaginative folklore.

As the locals told it, Janet had, until just a few years ago, regularly haunted the wooden sidewalks of Silver Peak with baskets of the organically grown herbs she bartered for the price of a double shot of cheap whiskey. When herbs were not in season, it was widely rumored, Janet had not been above inviting the local menfolk up to the commune's last decaying log cabin—where she lived amid a sea of psychedelic eight-track tapes and an undetermined number of cats—for a demonstration of the hippie practice of free love followed by a scalding dip in a murky volcanic hot spring that had been ingeniously diverted to heat the cabin.

Those few souls either brave enough or drunk enough to take Janet up on her offers had come away remembering only the stifling heat of the place and the intense odor that generations of rampant cat breeding had conspired to produce.

Janet had long claimed to be a gifted psychic, a claim the citizens of Silver Peak had laughingly dismissed until the day three winters previously when a planeload of skiers bound for the pricey resorts of nearby Lake Tahoe had disappeared into the mountains in the midst of a roaring blizzard.

Late that same night, Janet had been sitting in the Bloody Miner Saloon when the news of the tragic crash and the massive search operation then being organized had come over the television set behind the bar. Cocking her head to the drunken miner who had unaccountably been staking her to drinks all night, she had blearily reported that the downed plane was nowhere near the area where the search was being concentrated. Rather, she insisted, it was located in a stand of pines less than three miles from Silver Peak, and three of the passengers, including the teenage daughter of a prominent Arizona politician, were still alive, although seriously injured.

His curiosity aroused, and the prospects of accompanying Janet back to the stifling confines of her "cathouse" seeming less attractive by the minute, the tipsy miner had piled her into his surplus army Jeep and driven to the specified crash site via a treacherous, snow-covered fire road— "just to have a look," as he later told the *Enquirer*. To the miner's everlasting astonishment, the broken outlines of an aircraft fuselage had appeared through the trees and a faint cry for help warbled above the howling wind almost immediately upon his and Janet's arrival.

Within hours Janet's picture had been flashed to news agencies around the world and her reputation had been born. The grateful politician, whose daughter had miraculously survived the crash and been rushed to Reno for emergency surgery, had purchased a gleaming new mobile home for Janet; it now stood in a clearing beside the decrepit log cabin, which still housed most of the cats. Janet, meanwhile, had written a rambling book on psychic phenomena that reportedly did well in New Age outlets, and she was in occasional demand for public-access talk shows and private consultations. The latter she always dispensed without charge, claiming that to accept money would be a violation of her psychic gift bordering on sacrilege.

Phylis watched ruefully as the dregs of the Wild Turkey disappeared down Janet's gullet and the little woman turned to her with shining eyes. "I feel as if I'm very close now," she whispered. "Very close."

"Well, Janet," said Phylis, getting to her feet and wondering if there was some way to keep Hapwell from learning about the embarrassing incident, "I don't think it's working out very well, so why don't we just go downstairs and call it a day."

Janet stared at her like a disappointed child. "But Phylis," she whined, "I thought you wanted me to contact the spirit of Sara Raynor."

Phylis smiled and she wondered how could she

have been so gullible as to believe this pathetic alcoholic could actually summon up ghosts, armed only with a bottle of booze and a few candles. "Maybe some other time, Janet," she said gently. "It doesn't seem like the spirits are going to show—" She broke off in midsentence as the temperature in the old hotel room suddenly plummeted and Janet's head snapped around to face the candles.

"Evil," Janet groaned. Her breath was coming out of her flaring nostrils in white puffs, and crystals of frost rimmed the blue glasses teetering upon her bulbous nose. "Dark and evil!"

Phylis shivered beneath her heavy sweater, uncertain as to exactly what was happening, but unable to imagine that the skinny woman on the chair was capable of pulling off such trickery. A thick gray mist was beginning to form above the floor, the freezing vapor scattering the candlelight into weird dancing patterns on the stained wallpaper of Room 312. "Sara Raynor," she asked in a tremulous voice, "is she here?"

Janet's eyes rolled back into her head and the veined lids fluttered shut as her thin lips stretched back to expose a surprisingly beautiful set of teeth. "Suffering," she moaned. "So much suffering."

"Who?" Phylis demanded. "Who is suffering?"

"Them!" Janet screamed. "The young couple."

Phylis was puzzled. To her knowledge there was no story about the ghosts of a young couple in Silver Peak. She had only brought the psychic here to see if the spirit of the young girl Rick had encountered on the mountain road could be summoned to explain her appearances.

"What young couple?" she asked, frustrated.

"Them!" Janet repeated the word again, the emotion in her reedy voice conveying a sense of abject horror. She writhed suddenly in her chair, her head snapping back and forth so violently that Phylis was becoming concerned for her safety.

Phylis tried to keep her voice calm as she reached out to touch the agitated psychic, hoping to distance her from whatever long-ago event she was seeing. "When did these people live, Janet? What year?"

Janet's eyes popped open, bulging in horror, and she stared at Phylis. "Now," she screamed, "they live now!" Her thin body was racked by a fit of sobbing and she suddenly rolled off the chair and fell to the floor with a resounding thump. "Oh God," she wailed, "he's murdering them."

Phylis was on her knees beside the wretched woman. She turned her over on her back and peered into her wildly contorted face.

"Who, Janet? Who's murdering them?"

Janet's head shook slowly from side to side, her graying shoulder-length hair tumbling loose against the warped floorboards. "The dark thing," she whimpered.

BOOM, BOOM, BOOM!

The deafening pounding shook the room with such violence that Phylis's head whipped around in terror. Sweet Christ, what had she unleashed here?

BOOM, BOOM, BOOM!

The sound reverberated through the walls again, its force rattling the wavy glass in the window frames. Phylis got her arms under Janet's bony shoulders and managed to pull the hysterical psychic to a sitting position.

"Janet, get up. I'm taking you downstairs!"

"The pain!" Janet screamed, doubling over and clutching her abdomen in sudden agony.

SKREEEEEEEK!

Phylis let go of the struggling woman and whirled to face the room's only door. It swung open on ancient hinges to reveal a dim figure in the unlit corridor beyond.

"Jesus God! What in the hell is goin' on in here, woman?"

"Hap!" Phylis sagged with relief and she turned her attention back to Janet, who had by now fallen into a whimpering stupor.

Hapwell stepped into the room and stopped dead in his tracks. The faded blue eyes took in at a glance the candles sputtering in the heavy mist. "Kee-ripes," he exclaimed, "it's cold enough to freeze the balls off a brass monkey."

"Help me get her out of here," Phylis cried, ignoring his remark and grabbing Janet's arms to drag her toward the door.

"What happened?" he asked, taking hold of the psychic's ankles over her worn Indian moccasins.

Phylis shook her head. "I'm not sure. She said she was going to try to contact Sara Raynor to see if she could learn more about the danger that Rick is in. She went into some kind of trance, then the temperature dropped and she saw something. Whatever it was drove her straight over the edge. She had just gone into this fit when you started pounding on the door."

They moved out into the corridor and set Janet down on the bare floorboards to get a better grip on her. Hapwell looked back at the freezing room and turned to stare into Phylis's eyes. "I never pounded on no door," he said with a slight quaver in his voice, "But your friend's in danger sure enough. I come up here lookin' to tell you there's a big mother of a snowstorm blowin' up over the mountains. Couple more hours and Masterson's gonna be snowed in up there on that lake just like Sara Raynor was."

The black-and-white patrol unit sat in a small copse of aspens half a mile from the Silver Peak road. Inside, Sheriff Bull Ryan, his khaki uniform ripped and soaked with blood, his florid face a cross-hatching of vivid red scratches, lay stretched across the front seat, snoring loudly.

The dark thing in Ryan's mind was ecstatic. The test of the host had gone better than it could ever have imagined, the hulking sheriff having drawn the death agonies of the young married couple at the roadside overlook to an exquisite crescendo of pain and emotional torture that had lasted for hours.

Although it hadn't occurred to the elemental beforehand, the ritual slaughter it had initiated at the great demon's urging had brought with it a sweet windfall. Huge chunks of Ryan's rotting soul had begun putrefying into a rich, stinking stew even as the fat lawman was still forcing his obscene, grunting bulk onto the bloodied and screaming woman, having just smashed the man's brains to a jellied pulp on the cold gray stones of a Forest Service walkway, and touched the flame of his brightly colored plastic cigar lighter to the gasoline-drenched handkerchief he had wicked into the van's fuel tank.

Looking up from its gory task of choreographing the insane ritual, the thing had unexpectedly found itself awash in the deliciously rancid broth of Ryan's dying soul.

Afterward it had ordered the stupefied sheriff to drive up this lonely dirt road, where, after placing him into a deep coma, it had gorged on his rotted essence, the feast more than replenishing the energy it had expended in directing his mad slaughter of the helpless newlyweds. Now, bloated to the point of drowsiness, the elemental curled in the dark hollow of the host's diseased cranium and waited eagerly for the greater demon's call, serenely secure in the knowledge that it would never know hunger again.

Trespasses

R I C K brought the Jeep to a stop in the circular drive before the Lodge and stepped out onto the fresh layer of snow that had fallen in the past hour. More dirty black clouds were piling up in the darkening sky beyond the roof of the building and the flurrying snow was already whipping up into miniature tornadoes that whirled across the stubbled expanse of unkept lawn and piled into small drifts at the base of the log walls.

He glanced down at his watch, estimating that perhaps another half hour of weak daylight remained before the early winter darkness settled over the lake. He had allotted himself that much time to explore the rambling house for some clue as to the identity of the girl he had found on the road. After that, he planned on driving directly down to Silver Peak, unwilling to chance the weather any longer. He had managed to pick up a Carson City station on the bungalow's radio and had learned that a severe winter storm warning was now in full effect for the surrounding mountains. Most of his essentials were already stowed in the back of the Jeep and he was looking forward to spending a few days in the old hotel as Phylis's guest.

A grin creased his features and he reached back into the Jeep for the heavy flashlight that Hapwell had tucked in among the cartons of groceries. "Better safe than sorry," he reminded himself as he shut the door and started up the snowy walk to the shadowed entranceway of the Lodge. A deeper chill settled over him as he stepped into the darkness beneath the eaves and he felt a sudden overwhelming urge to forget the whole damn thing and return to the warmth of the Cherokee's powerful heater. An image of Phylis's smiling face flashed through his mind and he imagined himself cutting into a rare steak at one of the tables in the cozy confines of the Silver Peak's dining area, touching her soft hand across the checkered tablecloth, and reading the promise of things to come in her eyes.

"First things first," he chided himself as he trudged through the carpet of dead pine needles to the Lodge's front door. The vividness of the previous night's dream still had him rattled and he knew he would not sleep again—in Phylis's bed or anywhere else—until he had proved to himself that the strange girl he had met on the road was just another ordinary human being like himself and not . . . something else. If such proof existed within the Lodge, then he could rationalize last night's events as no more than an erotic fantasy prompted by his remembrance of the girl. If not . . .

He dismissed the alternative from his mind. Of course she was real. He had touched her, talked to her.

This time the heavy front door was securely bolted and he cursed himself for not remembering Ryan's promise to lock the place up before he left. Backtracking along the covered walkway, he stepped off the porch at the end of the house, twisting his knee painfully in an ankle-deep drift of snow. "Shit!" he yelled, stopping to fumble a couple of pain pills from his pocket and swallowing them dry before limping into a thick stand of brooding pine trees beside a long, blank wall leading toward the back of the house. A fresh onslaught of wind-driven snow stung his cheeks and eyes and he clicked the flashlight on to compensate for the gloom beneath the trees.

Sara lay on her back atop the yellowing lace of the canopied bed that had been hers in life. Her eyes were tightly shut and she wondered, as she often did at such moments, whether she was really dead at all. Perhaps she had dreamed the whole horrible thing.

She opened her eyes to look at the familiar row of delicate pink roses bordering the pale yellow wallpaper at the foot of the bed. Had they really faded with the passage of time, or was it an illusion created by the dim light filtering through the broad mullioned window across the room? The ballerina lamp on the white bedside table was only inches from her hand. She had only to reach out and turn it on.

"No!" Her refusal to confirm or deny the state of her existence by the simple expedient of touching the lamp came out as a soft whimper. She shut her eyes tightly, unable to bear the thought of watching her ghostly hand slip through the porcelain figurine at the base of the lamp. She would far rather lie here in the dark, listening to the snowflakes striking the window, and pretending.

The snowflakes! Ted's face suddenly imprinted itself on her consciousness and she saw him standing before the French doors in the study. He was staring out into the hazy curtains of a driving snowstorm. It had been snowing for more than three days and he was still angry. He turned to face her and his eyes were full of unspoken accusations.

"Dammit, Sara, when is it going to stop?"

She had been sitting huddled on the sofa before the dying fire, studiously ignoring him. They had consumed the last of the food that morning and there were only enough logs in the woodbox to last another day at most. She had not answered Ted for the simple reason that she had no idea when it would stop snowing. Although she had never spent a winter at the Lodge, she had heard the locals tell of whole weeks when the snow never stopped falling, the thick white drifts piling up so high that only the tops of the tallest pines showed above them. More than at her ignorance of the weather, however, she was furious with Ted for having betrayed their love by so gleefully planning to take advantage of her name to enhance his family's flagging fortunes. It was, she realized the moment she had seen his eyes light up at the mention of the Raynor name, the real reason she had carried on her ridiculous masquerade with Susan and Tammy for all those years. Sara wanted to be loved for herself alone, not for Harold Raynor's money.

"Dammit, Sara." Ted's voice had taken on a note of hysteria. "We have got to get out of here." He sank into a chair beside the hearth, defeated. "We'll starve to death."

"Oh Ted, stop being so dramatic," she had snapped. "By this time Daddy has probably noticed that I'm not in Switzerland. I'm sure he'll come helicoptering in with the cavalry at any minute. After all," she added sarcastically, "you did say you were dying to meet him."

"Very funny," he spat. "And suppose he doesn't figure out where you've gone. Suppose he doesn't come up here looking for you, what then?"

Sara shrugged. "Well, you could always get up off your soft, crybaby butt and go out and chop some more firewood before the trees are completely covered and we freeze to death."

"Oh, very good. And then what are we supposed to do for food?"

"Well," she replied thoughtfully, "Daddy insisted I learn to handle guns when I was a little girl. I could always take one of his hunting rifles and go out and shoot Bambi and Thumper. Then you could roast their little bodies over the fire and I could make mittens and earmuffs out of their fur." She giggled. "We'd be a regular little wilderness family."

"I say we try to drive out," he said, ignoring her sarcasm and staring into the fire. "There's an old

Jeep in one of the outbuildings. If I can get it started, we could probably make it to the mountain road without much trouble. The radio says it's not snowing nearly as hard down at the lower elevations."

"Wonderful," said Sara. "And suppose we get stuck halfway between here and the 'lower elevations'? What are we supposed to do then?"

"Dammit," he yelled, "I'm trying to come up with something practical here!"

"As long as it doesn't involve doing any real work," she interjected nastily.

Ted jumped to his feet then, his fists clenched in fury, and for a moment she had thought he was going to strangle her. "Aw, fuck it," he finally said. "You just sit here and wait for your daddy. I'm going to go get that Jeep started."

"It won't start," she had screamed after him. "It hasn't been started for years. Besides, it doesn't even have a heater."

The door had slammed behind him and she buried her face in her hands, wishing she had never been born.

Sara opened her eyes again, listening to the sounds of the growing storm outside. She was certain she heard footsteps among the trees. She rose and drifted to the window, peering down into the dark thicket of trunks below the swaying branches. Fat puffs of snow swirled before her eyes, obscuring her view of the forest. She watched for a moment longer, wondering when the bright spirit would return to take her to Rick again.

*   *   *

The path through the trees was blocked by a line of outbuildings connected by stout chain-link fences.

Rick stood in the deepening snow, playing his light across the locked gate of a section of fence that stretched from the blank wall of the house to a shed the size of a double garage. He was not surprised that a millionaire's estate should be provided with such security measures; however, he still had to get around, or over, the damned thing if he was going to get into the house. Looping his fingers into the wire mesh of the tall fence, he experimentally pulled himself up a few feet. A year ago he wouldn't even have considered this an obstacle. Now a searing jolt of pain shot through his shoulder, joining the fiery chorus already raging in his knee.

"Damn!" He winced, dropping to the ground with a heavy thud and biting his lip against the pain. He leaned panting against the wire, waiting for the agony in his shoulder to subside and playing the flashlight down along the length of the fence, looking for an opening. The panes of a small window at the front of the shed on his side of the fence glittered in the beam.

"Bingo!"

Crossing to the window, he peered in through the dirty glass, able to make out only the outlines of a large, shrouded object beyond a cobwebbed worktable. The window itself was striped with the silvery tape of an old-fashioned electrical alarm system, which he seriously doubted was in working order, even if there had been anyone around to respond. Reversing the heavy flashlight in his hand, Rick smashed out the window, reached inside, and unlatched it.

Sara started at the distinctive tinkle of breaking glass somewhere in the darkness beneath her window. The first thought that entered her mind was that someone else had arrived to burglarize the Lodge, an increasingly common occurrence in recent years. "Maybe I should go down and scare the shit out of them," she mused aloud, remembering how she had startled the fat sheriff the day before. Curiosity propelled her to the window and she looked out to glimpse a flash of light beside the nearest outbuilding. Fear clutched at her throat as she realized that she had never entered that particular building since . . . that day.

She wrinkled her brow, trying to remember what was inside the building, but nothing came. Whatever it was, she knew it must be horrible. A thing she had blocked out of her mind for all time.

The air inside the outbuilding was cold and stale, as though it had been sealed off for a long, long time. Flashing his light across the gloomy interior of the single large room, Rick guessed that the building had originally sheltered the estate's working vehicles and machinery. Beyond the cluttered worktable, onto which he had gingerly clambered from the open window, the considerable floor space was taken up by old lawn mowers, parts of a disassembled tractor, and several unidentifiable pieces of smaller equipment.

Between these rusting artifacts and a long, low object covered in a dusty tarp, a narrow aisle led to a metal garage-type door.

Rick lowered himself to the floor and made his way to the stout metal door, hoping that it could be opened from the inside. Flashing the light along the dull painted finish, he spotted a pitted chrome twist handle connected to rods at opposite edges of the door. Whether the old latch was frozen with rust or locked from the outside, it refused to budge when he twisted the handle.

"Damn!"

Glancing back through the gloom to the lone window by which he had entered the building, he could see the last faint traces of daylight vanishing from the open area beyond the trees. Fat flakes of snow were now swirling in through the shattered glass and he knew he should abandon this foolish illegal search and head down the mountain before the oncoming storm made him a prisoner as Hap and Phylis had warned.

He turned to retrace his path through the shed and something clattered loudly at his feet. Flashing the light down onto the dusty floor, he saw an iron crowbar protruding from the tarpaulin covering the long object. Perhaps if he could quickly force the jammed door latch, there would still be time for a quick look around the house.

He stooped to pick up the rusting crowbar and saw the glitter of bright metal beneath the tarp. Getting to his feet, he jerked the tarp free of the covered object, revealing the long sleek shape of an old wooden speedboat. The ancient Chris-Craft, its waxed and varnished mahogany decks gleaming like new beneath the flashlight's beam, sat upon a chrome-wheeled trailer.

All four of the trailer tires were flat, their rubber cracked and rotted with age. Inside, the boat's elegantly stitched upholstery was similarly deteriorated, and patches of the red leather covering the seats had split to reveal wads of dusty cotton batting beneath. Rick examined the interior of the powerful craft, obviously designed as a rich man's toy, amazed that anyone would have simply left such a valuable boat here to rot in the unheated shed. Something skittered in the shadows beyond the range of his vision and he turned the light into the boat's front cockpit in time to see a small gray mouse disappear into a gap in the split leather. Shaking his head at the insult to the beautiful machine, he hefted the iron bar and walked around to the rear of the boat to attack the door. Then something else caught his eye.

On the other side of the shed, hidden by the speedboat, a tattered tarpaulin shrouded a second large form. His curiosity as to what other valuables the former owner of the Lodge may have left to deteriorate in the cold shed aroused, Rick stepped boldly to the new object, grabbed the corner of the cover, and pulled.

A thick cloud of dust exploded into the musty air, the dancing motes swirling into his eyes and causing him to cough violently. When the fit had subsided, he aimed the light at the abandoned object beneath the tarp and his eyes widened. "Now, why in the hell would anybody in their right mind leave this here?" he muttered. He ran his hands along the glassy flanks of the forest-green

Corvette, leaning into the cockpit and turning the flashlight onto the cluster of fogged dashboard instruments behind the steering wheel. The Corvette's odometer showed that the car had been driven less than a thousand miles before being abandoned here. He flipped open the glove compartment, revealing a small packet of yellowing papers. The 1976 registration showed the car's owner to be one Theodore Steele of Berkeley, California. Rick shrugged. The name meant nothing to him. Replacing the papers where he had found them, he turned and retrieved the crowbar from the car's detachable roof, determined now to force the shed door open and explore the Lodge, storm or no storm. There was something very strange about the Raynor house and he was going to get to the bottom of it.

CHAPTER 19

Schemes

"OH, goddammit, I do not believe this!"

Phylis stood with Hapwell in the beams of the Chevy's headlights, regarding the jumble of rocks and snow covering the road where it curved out around a bulge in the canyon wall just ahead. The position of the slide combined with the bulk of the mountainside to block their view. The road might be clear for the rest of the way to the lake or the whole damn thing might have slid into the deep canyon below.

Hapwell shrugged and spat a steaming wad of tobacco juice at the newly formed barrier. "Ain't exactly no big surprise," he ventured. "This old road slides a dozen times every winter."

"*After* snowstorms," Phylis said, stepping closer and examining the fresh fall of earth, which was still only lightly dusted with snow, "not two hours into them."

"Does look a little peculiar," Hapwell allowed,

striding forward to pick up a chunk of rock and shining the powerful beam of his battery lantern up the steep slope. "Could've been a small earthquake, I reckon."

"Well, it doesn't matter what caused it," said Phylis. "The question is how we're going to get up there now."

"We ain't," said Hapwell. "Not without horses or snowshoes anyway."

Phylis turned on her heel and started back toward the pickup. "We'd better hurry, then."

"What, tonight?"

"Well, of course tonight," she said, climbing into the cab of the idling truck. "That friend of yours over in Lawton has packhorses, doesn't he? Maybe he'll let us borrow a couple. We could be back here in less than two hours."

"What in the hell for?" Hapwell yelled, stumping back to the Chevy and climbing in beside her. "I ain't even had no damn supper yet. Besides," he grumped, "that Masterson feller's got enough supplies up there to keep him goin' till spring. Don't tell me you're so lovesick you can't at least wait till mornin' to see him."

Phylis lowered her eyes and nodded sheepishly. "I think I am, Hap," she unexpectedly confessed. "I really do." She raised her gaze to meet his and her voice took on a tone of harder resolve. "But that's not why we've got to get to him tonight." She gestured out through the window to the drifting road beyond the rock slide. "Something is very wrong up there. Rick is in mortal danger. I'm absolutely certain of it."

Hapwell grunted, letting out the clutch and starting

the painstaking process of inching the Chevy back down the slippery road. "You been listenin' to that goddamn crazy woman is all," he said.

"Hap," she said angrily, "you were in that room and felt the cold. Don't tell me you think that was normal."

The old man cast her a sidelong glance. "What else did she tell ya after you got her outta that trance she was in?" he asked noncommittally.

"She said," Phylis replied with more calm than she actually felt, "that there was a black veil hanging over the lake. Something so dark and frightening she couldn't see through it. She'd never experienced anything like it before and it scared the hell out of her." She paused, remembering the torrent of nearly unintelligible warnings that had come flooding from Janet as soon as she had taken her down to the bar, having snapped her out of her trance by pouring whiskey through her bloodless and trembling lips while Hap had gone to fetch blankets. "Janet thinks there's some terrible demonic presence hovering over Rick, something that follows him everywhere he goes, waiting for an opportunity to take him."

Hap ground the Chevy's transmission into second and the old truck lurched forward, wheels spinning against the slick road surface. "How the hell did she come up with all that?"

"I told her all about him," Phylis replied, "everything I know, that is. Janet thinks Rick was supposed to have died in that explosion in Yugoslavia, but that the demon let him live so it could use him to ensnare other souls here on earth." She hesitated again, once more reviewing the psychic's outrageous theory in her own mind. "She thinks something prevented the demon from taking Rick the day he was injured and that now it may be using Sara Raynor's ghost to draw him back into its trap."

Hapwell snorted and spat out the window. "Is that all?" He laughed. "No wonder they call her Janet from Another Planet."

"I believe her, Hap. At least I think I do. You saw her in the old hotel room. She was terrified half out of her mind by whatever she saw up there."

"Well, maybe it's a carload of crap," said the old man. He halted the Chevy at a wide spot in the road, then backed to the cliff edge until its tailgate was hanging out over the edge of a yawning chasm, shifted gears again and popped the clutch. The old truck shuddered and the wheels caught traction as it completed the turn and headed back down the mountain. "On the other hand," he reflected, "if anybody else'd told me what happened to me 'n Tall 'n Tommy up here, I reckon I would've called that a load of crap, too." He nodded to himself and gradually increased the speed of the pickup. "Suppose it won't hurt to come back up and save that fool city boy of yours from gettin' snowed in, anyway. In the meantime," he added, "ain't nothin' says this half-assed rescue expedition can't at least wait till I get me somethin' to eat, is there?"

Bull Ryan stared straight ahead at the glare of his own headlights bouncing off the increasingly thick flurries of wind-driven snow that batted softly against the Bronco's splattered windshield and clumped together at the edges of the decreasing space being cleared by the straining wipers. The patrol unit skidded against the sharp turn he was entering and he automatically corrected with a touch of acceleration, reaching blindly for the lever between the seats and shifting the vehicle into full-time four-wheel drive.

The back and shoulders of the sheriff's blood-stained khaki uniform shirt were soaked through from the snow that had collected on him as he clambered up from the roadway a few minutes earlier to set the explosive charge that had brought half the mountainside down onto the road behind the Bronco, but he seemed not to notice the trickles of freezing water now running down his back to pool in the deep cleft between his buttocks. The small portion of his brain that was still functioning more or less normally wondered idly what had possessed him to steal the dynamite from the isolated mining site outside of Silver Peak and cause the avalanche that would, for all practical purposes, maroon him up at Spirit Lake without food or supplies. Something dark and cold slid across his mind and he shrugged, certain that he must have had a good reason for what he had done. His pupils shrank to pinpoints and he peered into the glare of the last long upgrade on the steep road, searching for the faded sign that marked the junction of the lake road.

The sky had gone completely black and the snow was piling up in soft sculptured drifts that threw sparkling highlights back from the beam of Rick's flashlight as he stepped out of the sheltering woods beside the Lodge. Freezing gusts of snow-filled wind off the lake slapped at the fabric of his corduroys and he quickly crossed the open space to the edge of the back patio and played the light over the rattling French doors leading into the Lodge's main room.

The rising wind had torn Ryan's hastily contrived beer-carton patch free of the broken pane and it now lay just inside the frosted doors. Rick played the light into the inky shadows of the empty room. A moldering moose head glared back at him through glassy eyes as he reached through the broken windowpane and let himself in.

Sara lay on the crumbling lace coverlet, moaning softly to herself. The glow of the bright spirit's presence flickered ominously against the faded wallpaper as the girl in the yellow slicker glided closer to the bed.

"Sara," the strobing figure whispered, "do you understand what you must do?"

Sara opened her eyes and looked at the bright apparition. The pink roses on her wall shone through the girl's midriff, creating the illusion of a cheap hologram she had once seen in a London novelty shop. The yellow slicker gleamed with a sudden surge of brightness and the roses all but vanished.

"Do you understand what you must do?" the bright spirit demanded.

A sob welled up in Sara's throat and she nodded. "Yes, but why? You said I was to help him."

The spirit's demeanor softened and she flashed Sara a reassuring smile. "You must do as I ask only if all else fails," she said. "If it becomes necessary, you will be helping him in the only way that he can be helped."

"But the demon?" Sara's voice was a soft tremor.

"The demon is his enemy, Sara, his and mine and yours. The dark forces at its command will be powerless to touch Rick if you follow all of my instructions exactly," the girl in the yellow slicker whispered. "You do want to help Rick, don't you, Sara?"

Sara sat up and realized that her own spirit had once again been clothed in flesh. She sighed with relief as she felt her weight sinking onto the yellowing lace covering the bed.

"That's better, isn't it?" The girl in the yellow slicker laughed.

Sara nodded, running her fingertips over the soft warm skin of her arms. "When will he come?" she asked.

The spirit laughed again. "He is already here," she said, her image beginning to fade. "Prepare yourself for him, Sara, and do as I have instructed."

The glow surrounding the girl in the yellow slicker had dimmed to a wisp of golden mist against the pale roses.

"Wait!" Sara called. "You said I would remember the things I had done."

"You shall," whispered a voice as faint as the beating of the snowflakes against the window. "You shall remember all."

"But when?" Sara pleaded.

"When it is time." The voice sighed, vanishing

into the brushing of the pines against the eaves. "Hurry now and prepare yourself for the man . . . and you shall be redeemed. And be on your guard, Sara, for as flesh, you, too, are vulnerable to the demon."

Sara sat gazing at the spot on the wall where the bright spirit had hovered. The fire of life tingled in her limbs and she felt the clammy touch of the crumbling lace against her skin. Swinging her feet onto the soft carpet, she stood and turned toward the door. The sounds of a man's footsteps clearly echoed from a distant part of the Lodge.

Rick stood at the desk in the study, thumbing through the yellowing scrapbook by the glow of the flashlight beam. He had scanned the voluminous accounts of Harold Raynor's career and conquests, ending with the final article that told of the tycoon's strange disappearance in a sudden winter storm at his summer residence. Rick closed the book in frustration, having learned little more than that Raynor had been as ruthless in his business dealings as he had in tracking and killing the numerous animals whose heads now graced the walls of his trophy room. He had hoped to learn something about Raynor's family, and particularly about the daughter— his only child—who was alleged to have committed suicide in this house, but there was no mention of Sara in the old clippings.

He rifled quickly through the desk's other contents, discovering nothing more than carefully detailed ledgers of household accounts and a few meaningless business documents, and was about to turn his attention to the bookshelves across the room when a sound from another part of the Lodge caught his attention. Flashing his light beyond the cold fireplace, he made out the entrance to a corridor in the direction from which the sound had come. He crossed the room and peered into the blackness of a long passageway.

"Hello?" he called. "Is anybody here?"

The faint, haunting strains of familiar music resounded against the heavily paneled walls from somewhere in the darkness above.

The great demon waited in shadow at the foot of a steep stairway at the end of the dark corridor. It trembled with delicious anticipation at the sound of Rick Masterson's voice, pressing itself tight against the clammy wood of a swollen door leading to an unused room, waiting for its prey to pass. The feeble beam of the man's light slid irritatingly across its nether parts and it shuddered uncomfortably in the glare, resisting the urge to lurch away from the damnable illumination. It had waited much too long for this useful creature to drop into its clutches to betray its presence now, and it forced itself to ignore the hot discomfort as the light moved on to the stairway and the man stopped to peer up the creaky steps into the darkness of the second floor.

The great demon watched in satisfaction as Rick Masterson cocked his ear to the amplified strains of the soft music from the floor above, grudgingly according its bright enemy a measure of respect for the brilliantly conceived, albeit pitifully transparent, plan by which it hoped to deny it the victory of turning the man's tainted soul to its own purposes. Its enemy had been clever indeed, recruiting the confused spirit who inhabited this miserable region to its cause with promises of instant redemption for transgressions which, rightly, should have caused her to wander here for decades or centuries longer.

Clever indeed, its hated enemy, having even attempted to send a living seer into its domain. But not nearly as clever as itself. Not by a long measure. It grinned maliciously, displaying the same slobbering contortion of its deformed features that it had allowed the crazed seer to glimpse for the briefest of instants. A hollow chuckle of glee rose in its rotting chest as it savored the recollection of how the mere sight of its splendid hideousness had sent the bumbling human psychic into spasms of terror. By now the elemental it had recruited from the forest should have destroyed the meddling woman who had set the seer upon it. Soon the crude elemental would be arriving, encased within the body of the fat policeman to rid the demon of the last serious obstacle to its conquest of Rick Masterson's soul.

The prey was moving again and the demon returned its full attention to him, attuning its senses to his measured ascent of the long, narrow flight of stairs, one cautious step at a time. Its grin broadened as it visualized how the hated forces of light that fought perpetually against it and all its kind would react to its perfect thwarting of their plan.

Forces of Darkness

R i c k stood at the top of the narrow staircase that had brought him to the upper floor of the Lodge. Ahead stretched a long, thickly carpeted corridor along which were arrayed the guest rooms and private quarters of Harold Raynor's domain. He played the dimming beam of the flashlight along the dull expanse of a richly paneled wall, revealing a dusty gallery of European prints glorifying the hunt; legions of spaniels and setters clutching the limp bodies of deceased game birds at the booted feet of bored aristocrats.

At the far end of the corridor the light picked out a tall mirror grotesquely framed amid a tangle of deer antlers. Beside the stand a spill of warm yellow candlelight flickered beneath the sill of a hardwood door decorated in an exquisitely carved relief of twining wildflowers. The music Rick had heard from the foot of the stairs echoed loudly along the paneled walls, the unmistakable tones of

John Lennon's "Imagine" lightening the otherwise bleak atmosphere of the dank, forbidding passage.

"Hello?" Rick listened for some reply to his call. The music scratched to an abrupt halt as someone snatched an old-fashioned stylus across the grooves of the record. A deep silence, broken only by the faraway sound of the storm blowing against the lodge's weathered shingles, descended over the passage.

"Sara?" Rick flashed his light on the distant door, reluctant to advance farther into the Lodge's private regions without an invitation from whoever was occupying the room at the end of the hall. Something dark and cold brushed against his shoulder from the rear and he whirled back to face the stairs. The flashlight beam was absorbed in inky shadow at the edge of the stairwell and he felt the hairs rising on his arms, certain that someone was lurking in the dark.

"Hello?" The darkness on the stairs seemed to coalesce into a solid mass, welling up from the first floor like a pool of brackish, foul-smelling water to envelop the shaft of illumination pouring from the flashlight lens. Rick took an awkward step backward, then turned and retreated hurriedly along the faded blue carpet. Something felt terribly wrong here, but he couldn't assign a name to it. He paused halfway down the corridor to examine the flashlight, uncertain as to what had just happened in the stairwell. The beam, although marginally dimmer than he remembered when he had first switched it on, seemed perfectly normal.

A sudden burst of static crackled down the corridor and Rick turned toward the door again as the plaintive lament of Harry Nillson's "Without You" boomed along the dark passage. The old song, another moody favorite from high-school days, unexpectedly filled his head with half-formed visions of Sylvia Tucker, the breathtakingly beautiful sophomore for whom he would willingly have died when he was fifteen, and his fears of the moment before forgotten, he limped toward the flower-bedecked door, determined to discover who was in the house. As he approached the pool of candlelight flowing from beneath the door, something clicked over in his mind and he was enveloped in a peaceful aura, convinced that he had nothing to fear from this house and that all the answers he sought lay just beyond the threshold.

"Giddup, ya blasted son of a whore!" Hapwell nudged the spavined gray mare along, tickling its protruding ribs with the heels of his worn boots and peering out into the stinging blast of the howling norther through the narrow gap between his battered hat and the thick muffler he'd wound three turns 'round his face, Arab fashion. The gentle, experienced nag beneath him plodded dutifully through the deepening drifts that were forming along the sheltered inner verge of the road, her big hooves plopping softly against the padded tarmac as she climbed the last steep grade up the mountain to Spirit Lake. Hapwell turned in his saddle to look back at the dappled packhorse following immediately behind, and winked at Phylis, bringing up the rear of the small procession on a pretty brown quarter horse named Daisy.

"Oughta hit the junction any time now," he shouted above the scream of the wind. "Bet ya wish ya'd stayed home by your stove now, don't ya?"

Phylis shook her head and pointed ahead to a dark object that loomed through a momentary gap in the thick curtains of snow whipping up out of the canyon. Hapwell turned to follow her gaze and clucked into the gray's ear, indicating to Phylis with a hand signal that he was moving ahead to investigate. He switched on the powerful battery lantern he'd hung from the butt of the old Winchester rifle slung in a tooled case alongside his saddle, the light surrounding him in a blazing aura of flying snowflakes.

Phylis kept her eye on the glowing bubble of light as the old man's silhouette faded into the storm. She marveled again at Hapwell's easy skill in handling not one but two horses on the treacherous road, shifting uncomfortably in her own saddle and trying to calculate how long they had been riding. Although her increasingly tender backside screamed that it had been several hours, her common sense told her it had probably been more like forty-five minutes to an hour at the most.

She and Hapwell had been headed down the last desolate stretch of mountain road to Silver Peak when they had encountered the two local ranchers from the county's volunteer mounted search and rescue team. The grumbling pair had been trailering their horses up the mountain toward Spirit Lake, searching for Sheriff Ryan, who, it seemed, had gone missing. The sheriff's office, the ranchers had reported, had been trying frantically to contact him for several hours—ever since a burned-out minivan had been discovered on a scenic overlook a few miles south of town.

A full-scale search-and-rescue effort had been launched by a concerned deputy when it had begun snowing and Ryan had still not called in on his radio. It was feared now that his vehicle had broken down on one of the isolated back country roads that crisscrossed the mountains, and the two volunteer ranchers had been assigned to check out the rugged Spirit Lake area.

Hapwell, a founding member of the Silver Peak Search and Rescue Team, had had no trouble in convincing the grumbling ranchers to let him take over the cold and thankless task of searching the lake for the despised sheriff. Phylis had sweetened the deal by sending the men back to the Silver Peak Saloon along with a hastily scrawled note instructing Denny to give them both steak dinners with all the trimmings, on the house. After the ranchers had departed, the two of them had started up the mountain with the intention of making for Rick's bungalow, then circling the lake road in his Jeep to look for Ryan before heading back down to Silver Peak. Although the old-timer had ostensibly taken over the search for Ryan, Phylis knew that Hapwell considered it highly unlikely that the slothful sheriff would have driven all the way to the lake in the face of an approaching storm. She was secretly relieved that Hap shared her alarm over Rick's welfare, although he still stubbornly insisted that his concern resulted from Rick's failure to come down from the mountain or to report in on the CB unit and not from Janet's supernatural histrionics.

The old man's lantern shone brightly just ahead now, indicating to Phylis that he had stopped. She urged the quarter horse forward with little clucking sounds, riding off the grade and onto a flat expanse of ground just fifty yards short of the junction between the lake and mountain roads. Hapwell stood on top of the dark object she had spotted earlier, and as her visibility improved she saw that it was Ryan's black-and-white patrol unit. The four-wheeler was overturned on its side twenty feet from the pavement; she could see Hapwell shining his lantern through the open window on the driver's side.

"My God, what happened to it?" she called.

The old-timer rose to look at her and spat casually over the side of the upended vehicle. "Goddamn fool must've tried to take a shortcut across to the lake road," he growled, pointing to a faint set of tire tracks leading from the mountain road to the spot where the patrol unit now lay on its side. "Must've been in a damn big hurry, too, from the look of it. Hit that big rock right there with his front wheel and it flipped him ass over tin cup, pretty as you please."

Phylis craned her neck, trying to see in through the Bronco's ice-glazed rear window. "Is he still in there?" she asked tremulously.

Hapwell shook his head and dropped to his rump on the side of the vehicle, then jumped lightly to the ground.

"Nope, reckon he took off lookin' for shelter." He crouched beside the Bronco and pointed to a line of broken footprints continuing off in the same direction in which the vehicle had been traveling before the accident.

Phylis wrinkled her brow beneath the knitted cap she'd pulled down over her ears. "But why would he have gone that way?" she asked. "I didn't think there was anything up at that end of the lake at all."

"Nothin' but the old Raynor Place," Hapwell agreed. He crammed a fresh chaw of Mail Pouch tobacco into his cheek and chewed contemplatively for a long moment. "Best I can figure is he must've knocked himself on the head in the accident and now he's wanderin' around lost out there somewheres."

Phylis shivered, remembering the many times the loudmouthed sheriff had come into the Silver Peak Saloon, rousting her regular customers for no particular reason and making obnoxious remarks about "getting together" with her. If she could have selected anyone in town she'd like to see lost in a blizzard, Ryan, with his swaggering arrogance and lewd suggestions, would certainly have been at the top of her list. Still, she reflected, no one deserved to freeze to death, not even Bull Ryan.

"What do you think we should we do?" she asked, guiltily thinking more about seeing Rick than finding the fat sheriff. Without waiting for an answer, she suggested, "Maybe we should still go on to the bungalow and get Rick's Jeep. I'm sure he'd be glad to help us look for Ryan."

Hapwell remained in his crouch, still contemplating the faint line of footprints leading away from the Bronco. "I reckon we better not take the gamble," he reluctantly allowed. "Them prints is gonna be gone before long, and unless Ryan took to the road up ahead, we're gonna need the horses to find him in this country, before it's too late." He jerked his head back toward the overturned vehicle. "The damn fool idiot even left his coat in there."

"Oh," said Phylis, trying to hide her disappointment. She tried to conjure up a sympathetic image of Bull Ryan freezing to death in the lonely woods. The sheriff's beady-eyed leer flashed through her mind instead. "How long do you think he can survive out in this cold without proper clothing?" she asked.

Hapwell shrugged, got to his feet, and levered himself onto the gray's back with a nimbleness that defied his seventy-plus years. "Not very damn long," he grunted, urging the horses into a brisk walk. "Not only ain't he got no coat, but the front seat of that Bronco's smeared with blood. Lots of it. I reckon old Bull Ryan has done gone and got himself in a world of shit."

Sheriff Bull Ryan was at that moment trotting through the knee-high drifts of snow gathered along the lake's northern shore, huffing along at a pace that threatened at any second to explode his flabby heart within the heaving cavity of his chest. Ryan's chin was crusted with a congealed mask of freezing drool and the thin mountain air wheezed in and out of his abused lungs like a leaking bellows. Two high spots of color marked his pallid cheeks and his eyes stared unblinking into the shrieking storm.

The elemental controlling Ryan was profoundly worried.

Despite its cozy nook deep within the sheriff's mind, the thing knew that it had failed the magnificent demon, failed to destroy the human creatures who had meddled with the superior being's prey.

Things had begun going wrong with the badly timed explosion on the mountain road, the explosion that was supposed to have swept the interfering humans and their puny vehicle into the canyon, where they would have been buried beneath tons of rock and earth, perhaps never to be discovered again.

Instead of burying the two intruders, however, the avalanche had thundered down the mountainside minutes before the arrival of its intended victims, allowing them ample time to stop and gawk. Fortunately they didn't seem to realize that the slide was intended for them. The thing had watched and listened from the cluster of high boulders where Ryan was hidden as they had turned back toward the town. Then, in a hurried attempt to move its host to the abandoned human habitation by the lake for the larger and more important portion of its mission—the destruction of the pale female spirit who was somehow being employed by the great demon's enemies—the dark thing had seriously miscalculated again, forcing the fat sheriff to take the foolhardy risk of turning his speeding vehicle cross-country in an attempt to save a few meaningless seconds of time.

Now the elemental was seriously compounding the danger to itself and its mission by gambling on the host's ability to function at all. It knew full well it was driving the overweight man well beyond his physical limits in a frantic attempt to salvage the situation—and its own continued existence.

The thing shuddered miserably within its dark cocoon, envisioning the unimaginable consequences of further disappointing the great demon, which even now must be waiting impatiently in the human habitation beyond the thick forest into which the exhausted host had just plunged.

It was rudely jarred out of its worried reflections as the host suddenly grunted and stumbled facedown into a drift-covered pile of rocks.

The sub-creature in Ryan's brain shrieked in its rage and frustration, extending claw-tipped tendrils into a delicate bundle of nerve fibers, driving searing bolts of pain into the huge man's vitals. Ryan gagged and screamed under its brutal ministrations. Great steaming lungfuls of foul air belched from his heaving lungs and his bloated face turned purple as the thing prodded and tortured him, expending vast quantities of its precious energy reserves to get him back onto his feet. The fat sheriff screamed and twitched in mindless agony, flopping across the snowy forest floor like a beached walrus until he at last impaled himself on a jagged spur of pine protruding from the base of a tree that had been felled by lightning in a storm the previous summer.

The thing in the sheriff's brain momentarily withdrew into itself to assess the damage to its host organism. Ryan's twitching abruptly stopped and his bulging eyes rolled down to the bloody shaft of wood protruding from the soft folds of unhealthy flab beneath his now useless left arm. His fleshy lips contorted into a mad grimace and he bawled like a gut-shot bear, his low, shrieking moan reverberating above the wind that was now bending the tops of the tallest trees nearly double.

"Did you just hear something?" Hapwell had halted at the edge of a windswept meadow fringed by thick stands of forest and was raising his hand for silence.

Phylis guided her horse up beside him and listened to the shriek of the wind through the trees. After a moment she shook her head. "No. What did it sound like?"

Hapwell listened a moment longer, then shook his head and returned his gaze to the snowfield.

The old man had dismounted some minutes earlier, handing over the reins of the two horses to Phylis and trudging along ahead with his lantern close to the ground in an attempt to keep up with the quickly vanishing tracks in the snow. "Looks like he's heading for the old Raynor place for sure," he said, pointing toward the dark outline of trees at the opposite edge of the meadow.

"How much further is it?" asked Phylis. Her fingertips were beginning to go numb inside her fleece-lined gloves and the pain in her thighs and back had long ago settled into a steady ache that no amount of shifting could relieve.

"I make it less than a mile now," he replied. "A damn hard mile," he added.

CHAPTER 21

The Wanting

S A R A was beautiful.

Stretched full length on the lace-covered canopied bed and illuminated by the flickering glow of the hundreds of candles spread across the floor and atop every piece of furniture, her perfect form and features reminded Rick of nothing so much as a sepia print of the Sleeping Beauty.

Minutes before, he had softly approached the flowered doorway of her room, captivated by the feeling of desperate longing expressed in the music. Raising his hand to knock and seeing the door slightly ajar, he had touched the white porcelain knob and it had swung open to reveal the scene he was now observing.

The record playing on the portable turntable came to an end, another dropping down the metal spindle to take its place. Carole King's "So Far Away" started to play as Rick moved through the candles to the bed and looked down upon the sleeping girl. Her eyes fluttered beneath the delicate veil of their nearly transparent lids and a slight flush of color played about her cheeks.

"Sara." His voice was a whisper below the achingly pure tones of the heartfelt old song.

Sara's breast rose and fell beneath the sheer fabric of her pink party gown. A slight frown formed beneath the heavy golden tresses framing her forehead and the slightest suggestion of a pout played at the corners of her full red lips.

"Well, at least you're no ghost," Rick whispered, relieved that he had not, after all, only imagined this beautiful creature. He leaned forward to call her name again and, almost as an afterthought, placed a gentle kiss upon her inviting lips.

"Hey, Sara, wake up. It's me," he whispered.

Sara's eyes opened and she looked up at him as though discovering an uninvited male visitor here in her bedroom were the most natural thing in the world. "Rick." She smiled, raising herself up on her elbows and looking around at the sea of flickering candles. "I guess I must have fallen asleep."

"I'm sorry to have stumbled in on you like this," he said, suddenly embarrassed. "I thought the place was empty—I mean, everyone said . . ."

"Hush," she said, placing an icy finger to his lips.

"You're cold," he exclaimed, pulling back in alarm.

Sara's smile broadened and she swung her bare feet onto the floor and stood before him. "It's nothing," she lied. "The storms often make it cold at this time of year."

"But the rest of the house," he stammered, half turning in the direction of the open door. "I mean there's not even a fire downstairs. There's a big storm coming. Do you have enough food to stay up here?"

Sara stared at him. Ted's angry face suddenly flashed before her and she remembered something else. There was no food in the house and the fire had gone out. Ted had driven away in the old Jeep, vowing to send help after she had refused to join him. A wave of panic swept over her. She must find him and stop him before—damn! She couldn't remember.

"Sara?" Rick was looking at her strangely now.

She blinked and focused on his earnest features, tried to remember what she was supposed to do. The crystal wine decanter she had taken from her father's study winked at her from among the candles clustered on the bedside table and she grasped it and held it up to the light. "Let's have some wine," she whispered, raising it to his lips.

He laughed. "What, no glass tonight?"

Sara looked crestfallen, casting her eyes hopelessly about the room in search of the absent goblet. "I . . . don't know what happened to it," she finally admitted.

Rick took the sparkling decanter from her hand and raised it to his lips. "Oh well, when in Rome . . ." He smiled. "Cheers."

Sara watched closely as he took a deep draft of the crimson liquid, closing his eyes and shuddering as it burned down his throat.

"Christ, that's good," he exclaimed, looking at her and holding out the elegant container in offering.

Instead of taking the decanter, she moved closer to him, pressing her body against his as the bright spirit had suggested and touching her own lips to the glittering crystal rim. He looked at her, breathing in sharply at the unexpected electricity generated by her touch, then tilted the container up for her until the liquid ran into her mouth, double streams of ruby-colored wine running out at the sides of her lips and splashing soundlessly onto the filmy material of her gown.

A sudden image of Phylis filled his brain and he pulled away. "Sara, there's something I have to tell you," he whispered hoarsely. "About what happened the other night . . ."

Sara pressed the rim of the decanter to his lips again, and he drank deeply of the delicious wine, wondering how the pain pills he had taken earlier would react with the strong alcohol.

"Drink," she whispered. "For me, Rick."

"What?" Rick's field of vision suddenly wavered like an interrupted TV signal and he stood swaying unsteadily before her. The rows of candles slowly dissolved into a blurred collage of giggling, wraith-like creatures composed entirely of light and shadow. "That's pretty weird." He giggled. His knees suddenly collapsed beneath him and he toppled forward onto her. Sara guided him onto the bed and perched on the lace coverlet, staring at him.

"Rick," she whispered, glancing worriedly around the room. The candlelight was dimming as dark shadows slipped beneath the door, welling up about them like black ink, staining the flowered paper on the wall. Her voice was tinged with panic as she touched her lips to his ear. "You have to love me, Rick. Only me."

There was no answer, and as the shadows continued to fall she reached beneath the tattered pillows and withdrew the long, gleaming blade the bright spirit had told her would be waiting there.

Sara stared at the sacrificial blade for a long moment, mesmerized by the peculiar way the dimming candlelight played along its wickedly razored edges. The shadows were coming closer, dark tendrils moving in to touch the lace coverlet, creeping up to caress Rick's body. Sara shuddered, taking his face in her free hand. "Rick," she pleaded, "please wake up."

A bolder tendril slipped up over the foot of the bed, forming into a glistening claw. Sara screamed, and taking Rick's warm hand in her own icy one, she touched the curved blade to the soft white skin at his wrist, tracing a thin red line across the vulnerable flesh. The skin parted soundlessly before the steel and a single drop of his blood, ruby bright and glistening in the dancing yellow light, welled up.

"No!" she screamed, raising her eyes defiantly to the stained ceiling and shaking her head violently. "I do not want to do this." Something tore at her throat and an aching sob bubbled from her lips. "I can't," she wailed. The curved blade clattered to the floor as she raised the crystal decanter to her lips and drained the remainder of its contents in a single long swallow.

"Someone please help me," Sara whimpered, curling up on the bed and placing her cheek protectively against the warm flesh of Rick's throat.

The great demon in the shadows threw back its scaly head and howled with glee, a deep, booming sound that rumbled through the empty lodge, carrying with it the obscene surge of joy it felt at seeing its enemies' carefully laid plan crushed beneath the clawed stumps of its beautifully deformed feet. The delicious irony of the pathetic whimpering spirit having so readily failed the creatures of light, just as she had failed in her own miserable life, was almost too much for it to bear.

Never mind that the bumbling sub-creature it had recruited from the forest had failed to intercept and destroy the meddlesome humans who had reached into its world in a clumsy attempt to alter events they were incapable of comprehending. Never mind that the stupid elemental had also managed not to arrive at the abandoned human habitation in time to destroy the place before its weeping ghost had again been made flesh. The great, cunning creature knew now that it would win, regardless of those setbacks. That it had, in effect, already won. Sara Raynor's fatal weakness had maneuvered its sleeping prey into precisely the situation the demon required in order to complete its conquest of his stubborn soul.

Many times before this the demon had entered Rick Masterson's sleeping mind, relentlessly probing the human's fevered subconscious in order to torment him with horrifying visions from his own dark past, visions that Masterson perceived as horrifying dreams. Each new vision had been more terrifying to the man than the one before. And each had been precisely calculated to convince him of the utter desolation of his soul, and of the futility of hope. But on each previous occasion, just as the demon had been on the verge of realizing its goal by capturing the man's spirit and turning it to its own convoluted uses, its hateful enemy had interceded, shielding the man from his own sense of despair, beaming its damnable light, and awakening him an instant before the demon could complete its conquest.

The demon slid like quicksilver across the ceiling now, shielding itself against the burning points of candlelight that sparkled across the room below—yet another feeble ploy of its enemies to keep it away from the man. Sliding down the wall alongside the canopied bed, the great slimy creature regarded Rick Masterson through the irritating glare of the candles.

It smiled again despite the pain the light was causing to its hypersensitive receptors. The human lay helpless on the bed, breathing shallowly in the deep sleep the creature of the light had initiated so the ghostly creature at his side could seduce him. It was a sleep from which they would be powerless to awaken him while the clever demon finally accomplished its evil work.

Ignoring the weeping creature of cold flesh on the bed beside the man, it began to spin its great dark web about him. There would be no escape for Rick Masterson this time.

Silken strands of purest ebony spun out into the air from pulsating organs on its leathery, wart-encrusted abdomen, floating down through the freezing air to form the tough, feather-light sac in which it would imprison the man's soul. The web grew quickly, spreading and enveloping the human and his ghostly companion, and the candlelight about them gradually dimmed until it became nothing more than a faint phosphorescent glow against the faded wallpaper.

Now at last it would have its way.

Rick Masterson would have his dream, but it would be a far different dream from the one its enemies had planned for him.

Demon's Dream

F I R E L I G H T, warm and lovely.

Rick lay on his back atop a brightly colored Indian blanket spread on the floor before the Lodge's massive stone fireplace, the silken weight of Sara's glistening thighs pressed tantalizingly against his hips. He moaned softly, stirring within her, and raised his eyes to scrutinize her lovely face. Light from the leaping flames blazed golden in her hair, the thick sweep of it falling across her pale shoulders, curling down about her breasts, and casting her features in shadow.

Outside, the snow was still falling, thick cottony clumps thumping softly against the panes of the French doors. Rick craned his neck back to peer out at the black expanse of sky beyond the doors and saw the drifts creeping steadily above the lower squares of the frost-encrusted glass.

Sara began to move above him with rhythmic urgency, her breath coming in short, startled pants, and he felt his body responding automatically. Reaching out to touch her, he ran his hands along the soft contours of her hips, slid his fingers up and over her heaving rib cage, and cupped her strangely cold breasts in his palms. A distant warning registered somewhere at the back of his mind and he raised one hand to touch her shining hair, pushing the heavy mass of it aside to reveal her face and to ask why she was still so cold.

Sara recoiled from his touch, jerking her head away and thrusting her hips down onto him with renewed force before he could look at her face. His back arched in autonomic response to the cold, violent pressure of her unexpected movement and he squeezed his eyes shut as icy legs tightened about his freezing loins. He struggled in sudden panic and she moaned above him, her breath a jet of frosty steam in the firelight, then threw herself onto his chest with an urgent, sobbing sigh, her pale arms pinning him to the blanket with surprising strength. Tears welling up in his eyes, Rick surrendered to her, thrusting deep into her freezing essence as a long, shuddering orgasm swept through him. A vision of Phylis, warm and smiling, swam in his brain, and he was filled with a profound sense of loss, longing for what might have been.

"See it?" Hapwell was pointing through the trees to a speck of light that alternately appeared and vanished amid the curtains of blowing snow.

Phylis leaned close enough to be heard above the storm, her lips nearly touching the frosted fabric of his muffler. "What is it?" she yelled.

"Dunno," was the shouted reply.

They had been slogging through the woods on foot for some minutes, having lost Ryan's trail halfway across the frozen meadow at the north end of the lake and frustrated by the horses' growing reluctance to step blindly through the treacherous drifts. Making it across the meadow, they had staked the frightened animals in the dubious shelter of the tree. Now, as the storm raged about them, horizontal sheets of thick snow driving off the black waters of the lake with increasing force, their own survival had suddenly taken precedence over the search for the sheriff. Hapwell had been leading them toward the Raynor place when he spotted the strange light flickering through the trees ahead. Whatever its source, it appeared to be moving, always managing to stay just a bit ahead of them.

Phylis squinted into the distance again, trying to catch another glimpse of the elusive spark. "Maybe it's him," she ventured.

Hapwell scowled and buried his head into the wind. If Ryan had stumbled into this howling wilderness without a coat, he doubted that he would have had the sense to remember a flashlight. Concerned now for the woman's safety, Hap was intent only on reaching the Lodge with its big fireplace and stout log walls. If Ryan had somehow managed to make it there, well and good. Otherwise they would just have to wait out the storm before continuing the search. He turned to look back across the lake toward the bungalows, wishing now they'd made for the safety of Rick's place when they'd had the chance. "All them supplies," he muttered.

"What?" Phylis was shouting to be heard.

"I said we ought to be almost there," he yelled.

A violent gust of wind rattled the panes of the French doors and Rick turned to look, imagining the sound of obscene laughter and the sight of degenerate eyes staring through the smudged glass. A glimmer of light flashed beyond the panes and a voice called faintly above the storm. Rick struggled against the weight of the girl again, attempting to rise to his elbows for a better look at the strange activity outside.

"Don't look," Sara whispered. Her breath was cold and stale in his ear and he suddenly wanted her off of him. He pushed up with all his strength and she rolled aside, curling before the fire in a miserable heap. "Please, Rick," she sobbed without looking at him, "you mustn't look. It's what the demon wants you to do."

"What in the hell are you talking about?" he demanded, climbing to his feet and searching for his clothes.

The girl did not answer immediately. Keeping her face hidden from him, she stared into the fire. "The demon," she said. "This is part of its plan."

"Oh Christ, Sara, if that really is your name," Rick exploded angrily. "Don't start that supernatural shit with me again. I've had all I can take. There aren't any demons and there aren't any ghosts. You're just a spoiled rich kid with a nice ass and a flair for the dramatic, and I'm a poor slob who's been having wet dreams about you. Now we've fucked each other and it's all over. Get it?"

Sara's naked shoulders trembled with her sobs. The clammy dampness of her frigid touch still clung unpleasantly to Rick's skin and he turned away from her. The taste of the wine he had consumed rose sickly sweet in his throat, making him feel slightly nauseated, and he wondered what in the hell he'd been doing with this girl half his age. After all, he was trying to straighten out his life, not screw it up any worse. Besides, he realized, he desperately wanted to see Phylis, had wanted nothing else since their kiss the night before. He wondered how he was going to explain his arrival in Silver Peak with the strange girl, shrugged off the thought. First he had to get to Silver Peak.

He found his jeans and sweatshirt strewn across a sofa and quickly pulled them on, then crossed to the French doors to peer out into the howling blizzard.

"Jesus," he exclaimed, surveying the deep, undulating drifts that covered the patio. "It's snowing like a son of a bitch out there. I think we'd better get the hell out of here while we still can. Get your clothes on. My Jeep's out front."

He turned to look at the girl and saw her wide-eyed expression of horror. Her face was drawn and dead white and flecks of foam speckled her bloodless lips.

"Sara, what is it?" Alarmed by her deathlike pallor, Rick stepped toward her.

"He's come back," she whimpered. She raised an arm so slender it reminded him of photos he had seen of death-camp survivors, and pointed to something behind him. "I remember now. He comes back here."

Rick looked at her, puzzled. "What are you talking about? Who comes back?"

Sara suddenly shrieked and buried her face in her hands, cringing against the stones of the fireplace. A latch rattled behind him and Rick whirled to see the French doors flung open. A snow-encrusted figure stood swaying in the open doorway, reflections of the dim kerosene lantern he carried glittering like burning coals in his bloodshot eyes. The apparition whipped the dark floppy hat from his head and swept the room with an imperious glance. Rick recognized the cruel face instantly, a face he had last seen on the front page of a yellowing newspaper on the study's cluttered desk.

"Oh God!" Rick moaned and stumbled away from the open doors as Harold Raynor's stony gaze settled upon the trembling girl by the fireplace.

"You've caused me a great deal of trouble, Sara." Raynor's flat accusation echoed through the dark study.

"Wait a minute," Rick stammered, stepping forward. "Will somebody please explain to me what in the hell is going on here?"

Ignoring Rick's presence, Raynor strode through him as though he did not exist. Rick screamed in horror as the rotting essence of the industrialist's long-dead soul passed through his flesh, steeping him in its obscene vapor. Rick staggered backward, gagging at the stench, and fell to his knees. His stomach heaved and he vomited onto the pine needles scattered about the floor.

"Daddy, how did you get here?" Sara's question rang against the cold walls. Rick clutched his heaving stomach and turned to see Raynor standing over the frightened girl.

"I used my ingenuity," shouted the apparition. He raised an accusing finger and pointed it at her. "You've placed us in an extremely dangerous predicament, Sara," he said. "I have personally faced great danger as a direct result of your defiance. None of it would have been necessary had you obeyed my orders."

"I'm sorry," she murmured.

"Henceforth, you'll do exactly as I say." Raynor's voice dropped to a tone of matter-of-fact command. He glared down at the naked girl and pursed his lips resolutely. "Now cover your nakedness and help me with the supplies, daughter."

Sara gazed at him and an obedient smile lit her shrunken features. "Yes, Daddy. I've been so hungry. There hasn't been any food for days."

"Well, we'll soon fix that," said Raynor. "You must never forget that we Raynors are survivors. Always." He turned and walked away, leaving Sara still trembling beside the hearth.

"Sara?" Rick's voice seemed lost in the depths of the huge room and he realized that she could no longer see or hear him. She was playing out some long-ago event with Harold Raynor, an event that had resulted in both their deaths. He watched in fascination as the girl stood and began mechanically dressing herself in jeans and a sweater he had not seen before. There was a clatter at the double doors and another blast of wind-driven snow swirled into the study. Rick turned to see Harold Raynor drag a heavy bundle in from the snow and drop it onto the carpet with a loud thump.

"Your young friend made it as far as the second curve on the Silver Peak road before the brakes on that old Jeep gave out." Raynor laughed, prodding at the bundle with the toe of an expensive Italian climbing boot. "Fortunately the damn thing exploded and I managed to spot the fire before the snowfall buried it entirely." His flat eyes gleamed in the firelight and a thin smile flickered across his lips. "Otherwise," he said, "I might have starved to death on the walk up here." He withdrew a gleaming, ivory-handled buck knife from the pocket of his expensive parka and knelt over the bundle.

Sara stared at him, uncomprehending. "Ted? But Ted didn't have any supplies with him when he left here, Daddy. The summer staff took everything away when they closed the lodge." She hesitated, then asked in a tremulous voice, "Where is Ted, Daddy? Is he all right?"

The buck knife flashed in the firelight as Raynor slit the cords securing the bloody cloth-wrapped bundle he had dragged in from outside. "He dressed out to better than seventy pounds," he said, turning to smile up at her. "More than enough fresh meat to keep us going until help arrives." He unfolded the bloody nylon of a ski jacket, exposing half a dozen chunks of charred purplish meat.

Sara's scream shattered the night. Raynor looked up at her, mildly irritated. "For God's sake, Sara, get hold of yourself. It's not as if I killed the boy myself. He was already frozen nearly solid by the time I found him." He shook his head, fussing with the clumps of meat, arranging them in an orderly line on the floorboards.

"You've absolutely no idea how difficult it is to butcher a burned and frozen carcass in the field," he complained, "not to mention the task of packing all this weight nearly nine miles through deep snow. Naturally I consumed some along the way, but still there should be plenty."

"Daddy?" Sara's voice was a soft whisper.

Raynor looked up from his sorting to see the girl raising the heavy Belgian deer rifle she had lifted from a tall cabinet cleverly secreted behind the paneling beside the fireplace.

"Sara, put that gun down immediately!" Harold Raynor commanded.

Sara's first shot blew off the top of his head, scattering his brains across the stone facade of the fireplace with a rapid series of wet slapping noises. The gore was still dripping slowly down the stones as her second and third shots blew a ragged, fist-sized hole in the spot where Harold Raynor's black heart had been. Shots five through nine turned all that remained of his cruel face to a seething purple jelly flecked with glistening shards of yellow bone.

A deathly black void descended over the room and Rick Masterson felt himself being sucked into a sightless whirlpool of malevolent energy that filled his eyes and ears and lungs, choking off all sensation except the deep rumble of the demon's laugh.

"Rick!"

Something warm slapped his face and he struggled up out of the black void to see Phylis looking down at him, her eyes filled with concern. Hapwell's grizzled face floated above her shoulder and he was sure he was still dreaming.

"Phylis?"

She smiled back reassuringly and he raised his head to find himself lying on a coverlet of crumbling lace atop a dusty canopied bed. Hapwell's battery lantern sat on the paint-peeling bedside table, filling the room with harsh white light.

"Thank God," Rick breathed, pulling himself to a sitting position and taking Phylis into his arms. The gentle scent of her perfume reached his nostrils, driving out the stench of the dimly remembered nightmare, and the soft swell of her breast was warm against his chest. "How in the name of God did you ever find me here?" he asked, pulling away to look at her.

"It's a very long story," said Phylis.

"Better question would be what in the damned hell you're doin' here in the first place," snorted Hapwell, surveying the decaying room with obvious distaste.

Rick shook his head. "I just came up to take a look around," he said. "I was trying to learn something about Sara Raynor." He touched the bed cover, remembering how he had found her in his dream. "I'm not exactly sure what happened."

"Well, I'll tell ya one thing that's happened," said the old man. "Ya damn near got yourself stuck up here for the winter. Thought you was gonna come down at the first sign of a storm."

"Oh shit, the storm. Is the road still open?"

Hapwell shook his head. "Hope you like horses," he grunted, " 'cause that's the only way outta here now." He crossed to the window and squinted out into the darkness. "That is, if the poor buggers ain't froze to death out there. If we ain't damn quick about it, it's gonna be too late for horses. On your feet now. We gotta make tracks."

"Sure, whatever you say," said Rick. He got unsteadily to his feet and stood swaying dizzily before them.

"Rick, are you sure you're all right?" Phylis took his arm and slipped her shoulder beneath it.

"Yeah." Rick nodded, embarrassed. His head was spinning as though he'd been drugged.

"Come on, then," Hapwell ordered, "we got a long, cold walk to a long, cold ride." The old man lifted the lantern from the table and led the way to the long upstairs corridor.

"Did you find what you were looking for here?" Phylis asked as they walked toward the stairwell.

Rick nodded grimly. "Don't tell Hap," he confessed, "but I have just had a close encounter with the ghost of Sara Raynor."

Phylis's eyes widened. "You've got to tell me all about it," she whispered. "I've been trying to figure out why she haunts the mountain road. What could she be waiting for out there?"

"I think she's been unconsciously going out there to try to prevent something from happening," he replied. "Something, unfortunately, that already happened a long time ago and that she felt she was responsible for. I think it was the reason she took her own life and that of—"

A shrill, gurgling scream filled the air and the couple looked up to see Hapwell standing frozen at the head of the stairs. The old man backed slowly away, the glare of his lantern revealing the massive, lurching figure of Bull Ryan, which was just emerging zombielike from the black pit of the stairwell.

Ryan screamed again, his blood-soaked body lurching up the steps like a grotesque marionette. The sheriff's eyes gleamed red in their swollen sockets and his hair was a tangle of wet spikes. One arm flopped uselessly at his side, the ripped sinews of his shoulder gleaming whitely through his shirt. The other arm was raised across his chest, the blood-blackened hand clutching a double-bladed ax.

The monster halted at the topmost step and its lolling head snapped around, the red eyes fixing Hapwell in their gaze. "Murder him!" it droned in a macabre parody of Ryan's voice, and then it lurched toward the old man, uttering unintelligible squeals of pain with each clumsy step it took.

"Hold on now, Sheriff," said Hapwell, glancing quickly over his shoulder to confirm that Rick and Phylis were still behind him. "You've had a rough time of it, but it's over now. Why don't you drop that thing and let us take care of you." Hapwell reached slowly for the flap of his jacket. "Got me a bottle of good whiskey right here," he added. "Just the thing to warm you up."

Ryan's tortured face melted into a pitiful approximation of its usual appearance and the sheriff's swollen tongue snaked out to touch his cracked lips. "W-whiskey?" he muttered.

"Sure." Hapwell smiled, producing a flask and extending his arm. "The good stuff. Help yourself."

Ryan leaned toward him and his huge body

shuddered in agony. "No!" he screamed. "Murder!"

The ax swung at Hapwell in a shining blur of bright metal and the old man half turned and staggered, falling heavily against the paneled wall. Rick and Phylis stared in horror at the jet of arterial blood spewing from Hapwell's severed wrist. The bloody ax gleamed above Ryan's head and the sheriff screamed and swung again, the force of the swing nearly cleaving the old man from shoulder to sternum.

Ryan stood surveying his work for a long moment, then placed a booted foot on Hapwell's chest and jerked the ax free with a sickening sucking noise. The big head ratcheted around and Ryan's insane gaze focused on Rick and Phylis. "Murder the bitch?" he queried the thing inside his brain. Something unseen jolted his body and a slobbering grin split his colorless face.

"Run!" Rick screamed, snapping out of his horrified trance. He shoved Phylis back down the corridor ahead of him, praying they could reach the heavy door of Sara's bedroom ahead of the madman. Phylis's foot snagged a section of loose carpet and she tumbled to the floor. Rick fell heavily on top of her, great jagged bolts of pain shooting through his injured shoulder. Ignoring the agony, he flipped onto his back as Ryan clumped to a stop above him. The sheriff slobbered above them, a heavily booted foot lashing out to connect with Rick's ribs. Rick rolled aside in agony and heard Phylis's scream and saw the flash of metal in the glare of Hapwell's lantern, which lay upturned on the floor beside the old man's body. He kicked out desperately, aiming for Ryan's legs as the ax described a gleaming downward arc. A loud, sickening thump exploded beside him and something warm and wet splashed onto his face. He turned his head to see Phylis's vacant eyes staring at him. The bloody ax was buried deep in her chest.

"Cunt had it comin'," Ryan muttered. The hulking sheriff towered over Rick, staring dully at Phylis's body. He emitted an earsplitting screech, clawing at his chest with his workable hand. His eyelids fluttered wildly, his eyes rolling back in his head, and he teetered forward, crashing to the floor with a bone-crushing thud.

Stunned, Rick rolled away from the carnage and crawled cautiously to Ryan's side. The sheriff's black, lolling tongue and staring eyes left no doubt that he, too, was dead.

Using the wall for support, Rick clambered to his feet and limped painfully toward the stairwell, his only thought now to make his way out of the cursed house and into the Jeep parked outside in the drive. With luck he could make it to the bungalow, barricade himself inside against the coming of . . . of what?

He fixed his gaze on the lantern at Hapwell's feet. Something dark and viscous rolled down the corridor from the stairwell, enveloping the light in a wave of pure blackness. Rick stared into the void and screamed. A pair of fiery eyes glared back at him from the shadows above the stairs and something freezing grabbed him, diamond-hard claws digging into the tender muscles of his injured shoulder. He shrieked in pain, trying to hang on to consciousness as he felt himself being dragged down the stairs and through the Lodge. Rick's eyes bulged as he saw Sara's emaciated figure by the fireplace. She seemed frozen in time, still leaning over the remains of Harold Raynor's ruined body. Then he was swept through the open French doors and out into the howling blizzard. The black waters of the lake fell away beneath him as he was lifted higher and higher, toward the scudding storm clouds that blotted out the tops of the surrounding mountains. He drew in a lungful of freezing air and screamed again. Something glimmered at the edge of the diminishing lakeshore and he saw the bungalow, set like a Christmas miniature among the pine trees far below. Golden light blazed from its windows, hard geometric shafts of it reaching out to illuminate his writhing body. Something he could not see howled in the darkness above and he felt the sudden blessed relief of the cruel claws loosening their grip on his tortured flesh. A vast silhouette swept away overhead and was lost among the black clouds.

Rick Masterson's mind snapped as he fell toward the hard, spiked tops of the trees a thousand feet below.

CHAPTER 23

Sacrifice

T H E horror show.

Rick Masterson came awake screaming, the muscles of his neck corded into gnarled ropes, his throat raw with the unrelenting terror of what he had just experienced. He could not stop screaming. The high, frantic sound of his voice reverberated off of walls he could not see, echoing and redoubling in intensity until he thought his eardrums must shatter. Still he could not stop. He felt his heart pounding in his chest, threatening to burst. He prayed for death. Anything to stop the horrible mad screaming.

Something wet splashed into his mouth, dribbling into his throat and gagging him. The world went silent and his eyes flew open, bulging in terror. Sara, radiant in her pink party dress, sat worriedly watching him from the far end of the pine dining table. Firelight flickered softly behind her, the sounds and smells of crackling pine logs lending a clean, cheery atmosphere to the bungalow's main room. Rick's eyes darted wildly about the familiar room. He was sitting at the opposite end of the pine dining table, bathed in a glare of unnaturally bright illumination from a huge candelabra in the middle of the table. The wetness touched his mouth again and he looked down to see the frosted goblet of clear water raised to his lips by his own hand.

"What in the hell is happening?" he croaked.

The girl in the yellow slicker appeared from the kitchen. She was carrying a tray holding three steaming china cups. "The demon," she said, smiling and placing the tray on the table. "It nearly had you this time." She placed one of the cups in Rick's hand and he looked at it suspiciously.

"What is this?"

"Coffee," she replied. She took a seat at the center of the table opposite the flaring candelabra, passed another cup to Sara, and took the third for herself.

"Have I gone insane?" Rick asked seriously.

The girl in the yellow slicker shook her head and sipped carefully. "No, Rick," she replied. "But very soon you will believe that you have. The demon is extremely powerful and it wants you very badly."

"Why?" he demanded. "Why does it want me?"

She shook her head sadly. "It wishes to use your influence to sway other spirits among the living."

"My influence?" He laughed and swallowed a mouthful of scalding coffee. "I thought it wanted to kill me." He jumped to his feet, panicked by a sudden thought. "Phylis and Hapwell, are they . . . ?"

"Perfectly safe, so far," she reassured him.

"What do you mean, so far?"

"The creature that pursues you has used your past—dark memories buried in your subconscious—

to make you despair of finding anything good in the world. Until tonight."

Rick stared at her. "The dreams . . ."

"More than dreams, Rick," said the girl, "the disintegration of your soul."

"Oh Christ!" Rick buried his head in his hands, remembering. "All the things I've done! The shitty, awful things . . ."

"Tonight it changed its tactics," she continued, ignoring his grief. "Until now it has been content to replay events from your past." She hesitated, sipping her coffee and looking at Sara. "Tonight it showed you a glimpse of the future."

"Phylis?" he gasped, leaping to his feet. "And Hapwell? You mean Ryan is going to murder them?"

"The demon is a master of lies," the girl said carefully. "But yes, it is very possible that you could be responsible for their deaths." She hesitated. "It is even possible that you yourself might kill them."

"That is insane," said Rick. He glanced guiltily at Sara, who sat quietly, and his voice dropped to a whisper. "I love Phylis," he said.

The girl in the yellow slicker did not reply and he inclined his head toward Sara. "What about her?" he asked. "How does she fit into all of this?" Sara cast her eyes down into her cup and said nothing.

"Sara's destiny was to wander this earthly region until her mind had accepted the deed that resulted in her having taken her own life. She felt responsible for the deaths of her lover and her father when, in truth, she was largely blameless." The girl smiled and extended a slender hand to caress Sara's hair. "Sara has remembered what happened, and because she has helped in our struggle to rescue you from the demon, she has been redeemed. Now she is free to move on to another level of light."

"I still want to help you, Rick," said Sara. "If you'll let me."

"Help me?" Rick laughed bitterly. "How? By fucking me again?"

Sara lowered her eyes as the girl in the yellow slicker opened her blue flight bag and withdrew Harold Raynor's buck knife. "This may be the only way," she said, raising it into the light.

Rick stared at the wicked-looking blade, entranced by the reflections of firelight swirling down its length to the intricately carved ivory handle. After a moment he tore his eyes away and shook his head. "I don't get it," he said.

"The demon preys only on the living," the girl in the yellow slicker whispered. "Once you have passed over, it can no longer touch you."

"You want me to kill myself?" Rick was incredulous. "No fucking way, lady."

"It may be the only way," she said again. "You must believe me. The demon is extremely powerful, its darkness greater than all the light we have thus far been able to bring to bear against it. The lives of your friends may depend upon it not taking you."

"I thought it was supposed to be sacrilege to kill yourself," he muttered angrily.

The girl in the yellow slicker shook her head sadly. "This is not what we would prefer," she said, "but it may be a greater sacrilege to allow a soul, even one's own, to fall victim to the forces of darkness, if it can be prevented. You are weak, Rick. Vulnerable."

Sara moved closer to him, taking his hand in hers. He stared at her, realizing that her touch was once again warm. Gone was the deathlike chill that had permeated her flesh. Gone, too, was the emaciated pallor he had witnessed during her confrontation with Harold Raynor. "I'll help you, Rick," she said. "But only if you want me to. You have to say it's all right."

A sudden gust of wind rattled the windows of the bungalow and the girl in the yellow slicker glanced out at the black sky in alarm. "You must hurry, Rick," she prodded. "The demon will not wait much longer." She hesitated, then leaned closer. "You must think of Phylis," she said. "Already it is plotting its next attack."

She held out the blade. Rick stared at the bright metal, feeling suddenly dizzy. Slapping her hand away, he jumped to his feet and strode angrily to the glass doors of the balcony, gazing out into the howling void beyond. The girl's voice was a hypnotic drone behind him. "It has no pity, Rick. It will stop at nothing. I fear your damaged spirit is not strong enough to fight it."

The glass of the balcony door seemed to dissolve and Phylis's image suddenly wavered before his eyes. She was naked, tied down on a rough bench in a cavernous place of leaping shadows. Burning red eyes leered at her from high up in the darkness and Bull Ryan's hulking form materialized above her. Phylis screamed soundlessly, her body writhing in a frantic attempt to twist away from the bloody sheriff. A trail of slime glistened between her breasts as his obscene fingers slid slowly down her torso.

"Stop it!" Rick screamed, shutting his eyes to block out the awful vision. It continued to play across the blank screen of his eyelids, Ryan's filthy hand slipping onto the soft, white skin of Phylis's stomach.

"It's all right, Rick," Sara crooned, and he felt the cold, unyielding touch of the knife in his hand. "Just say yes, and it will all be over."

"No!" he screamed, clutching the knife and leaping at the hideous apparition beyond the doorway. "No!"

Something sharp and jagged sliced into his flesh and he felt a flood of warmth filling his hand as his arm went numb. He opened his eyes to stare into Sara's loving eyes. The smiling face of the girl in the yellow slicker hovered behind the girl in the pink party dress. A golden aura flowed from her beatific features. "I'm sorry, Rick." She smiled. "I have failed you." The light beaming from her body crackled across the space separating her from Sara, filling her golden hair with flecks of dancing fire that swirled and lifted it above her shoulders. The girl in the yellow slicker floated slowly up toward an even brighter halo of light, light that seemed to be pouring in through the skylights in the ceiling.

Sara rose and drifted up to join the bright creature waiting in the light, turning back and smiling down on him. He felt himself growing weightless, looked back to see his own body slumped in the snow, Harold Raynor's knife clutched in his hand. A crimson pool was growing about him and he trembled as a scream of black rage echoed through the night.

Afterlife

R I C K Masterson swam up out of his night-mare. Somewhere high above him, elevator music was playing a fractured instrumental rendition of "Judy in the Sky." Cold white light was glaring against his eyelids. Voices were speaking in hushed tones.

"I think he's coming out of it now." A strangely accented masculine voice rattled in his ear and a shadow flickered above him, blocking out the light. He opened his eyes, blinking against the harsh glare of banked fluorescents set into a plastic grid at the center of a low, white ceiling. Phylis's face materialized before him and she smiled encouragingly. He felt the weight of her hand on his shoulder, saw worried faces hovering in the background.

"Where am I?" he croaked, the part of his mind that was sluggishly coming around admonishing him for just having uttered the grand cliché of all clichés.

His throat felt terribly parched and it hurt to speak.

"Hush," said Phylis, placing a straw between his lips. He sucked at the plastic automatically and freezing water bathed the raw membranes of his mouth. He spluttered, choking on the liquid, and raised his head to blink around at the small, brightly lit room. He saw that he was in a hospital bed. A plastic bag attached to a metal stand dripped clear fluid into a tube attached to his right arm.

When the coughing fit subsided, he tried to speak again. Phylis laid a finger upon his lips and shook her head. "You're in Room two-twenty at the Sierra Medical Center in Carson City," she said. "You've been here since last night."

A pleasant-looking Indian man with a curly black beard and an elaborately wrapped white turban leaned forward and smiled at him and Rick saw that he had a stethoscope around his neck. "This is Dr. Franjee, who, incidentally, saved your life." Phylis stepped away from the bed to allow Franjee a closer look at him.

The doctor nodded and reached for Rick's wrist. He took his pulse, then scribbled a note on a chart affixed to a metal clipboard. Hapwell stepped forward and scowled down at Rick.

"What happened?" Rick whispered.

"Damn near went and got yourself killed is what happened," the old-timer grumbled.

Rick shifted against the starched sheets in an abortive attempt to sit up. His vision blurred and a jolt of pain shot through his left arm. He fell back onto the sheets, rolling his eyes to stare at the offending limb. It was heavily bandaged from wrist to elbow.

"You will find for the next several hours that any sudden activity will make you feel light-headed," Franjee cautioned. "You have lost a great deal of blood."

"You was pale as a ghost when we found you," said Hapwell. "Another few minutes and you would've been a goner for sure."

Rick raised the bandaged arm, remembering Sara and the girl in the yellow slicker. "Oh Christ," he moaned, "why didn't you just let me die?"

Franjee cocked his head and frowned. He stepped forward, preparing to ask a question. Phylis and Hapwell exchanged a quick glance and she intercepted the physician. "It was just lucky we made it to your place when we did," she interjected, looking Rick directly in the eye, "or your fall might have been fatal."

Rick looked at her, puzzled.

"Don't see how a grown man can trip through a plate-glass window," Hapwell growled. "I expect you must've been drinkin'."

Franjee was now watching Rick's eyes with more than professional interest. The doctor seemed to relax as the reporter took Hapwell's cue and nodded agreement. "Guess maybe I did have a couple too many," he muttered.

"I am very glad to hear you say that, Mr. Masterson," said Franjee. "I must confess that when your friends arrived here with you, I was fairly certain from the nature of your wound that you had attempted suicide. Naturally that would have required me to notify the authorities and place you under psychiatric observation."

Franjee scribbled another note in his chart and

left the room after cautioning Phylis and Hapwell not to remain too long. The moment the door closed behind him, Phylis turned on Rick with fire in her eyes.

"Okay," she said, "we lied to keep you out of the loony bin, Mr. Masterson. Now suppose you return the favor by explaining how you came to be bleeding to death in the snow outside your bungalow."

"The window—" he began.

"Oh, the window was broken," she hissed, "but we found an eight-inch knife in your hand. What in the hell were you trying to do?"

Rick gazed at her flushed and beautiful face, wanting nothing so much as to be able to throw his arms around her and tell her how much he loved her. Instead, he turned his head away. How could he explain what he had experienced, convey to her that he must die or perhaps risk her life, and Hapwell's, too. "They . . . wanted me to kill myself," he said miserably.

Phylis leaned closer, the anger suddenly draining from her features. "Who, Rick? Who wanted you to kill yourself?"

He shook his head, grasping her arm with his good hand. "I wouldn't do it, Phylis." He looked at the bandages on his other arm, remembering. The memory of what had happened to him in the bungalow started a chain reaction in his mind and he struggled up to a half-sitting position despite the pain.

"Ryan?" he said. "The sheriff."

"Ryan is dead," said Hapwell. "We found him skewered on a length of pine a quarter mile from the old Raynor place. Probably gonna be there till spring." His eyes narrowed and he peered suspiciously at Rick. "How come you're askin' about him?"

"I saw him murder both of you in the Raynor house," said Rick.

"Okay, that's enough." Phylis stepped between the two men. "You were imagining things, Rick. You've been unconscious for hours. We'll discuss all of this after you've had some rest."

"We'll discuss it now, dammit!" he snapped. "I *was* at the Raynor house tonight, or last night, or whenever it was, and I *wasn't* hallucinating, not any more than Hapwell was the night he and his friends saw Sara Raynor on the road leading up to the lake." He raised the bandaged arm a few inches off the bed, moaning with the effort. "And I didn't do this to myself. Now sit down and listen to me if you want to live, because you're both in mortal danger."

There was a stunned silence in the room that lasted for several seconds as his friends simply stared at him. The moment was broken by Hapwell, who dragged a chair across the polished floor and straddled it.

"Go ahead and shoot, pilgrim," the old man drawled. "I just got a feelin' this is gonna be a story worth hearin'."

It took Rick nearly half an hour to tell his story, which he carefully edited to exclude the details of his erotic encounters with Sara, saying simply that she had been asked by the creature she referred to as the Bright Spirit to help block the dark nightmares inspired by the demon. When he was finished, Phylis and Hapwell sat looking at him for several more moments, the play of emotions across their faces indicating that they were both trying hard to believe his incredible tale.

Phylis finally reached across the sheets and placed her hand on his cheek. "Well, the damned demon can't have you," she said flatly. "I won't let it have you."

Rick sighed with relief, burying his face in her palm and kissing it. "Christ, what am I going to do?" he asked. He jerked his head upward at the sound of a chair scraping violently against the floor.

"I'll tell ya what *we're* gonna do," Hapwell growled. "*We're* gonna fight the bastard."

Rick looked at him, incredulous. The grizzled, bandy-legged little man was trembling with rage. "How?" he asked. "How do you fight something you can't even see?"

Hapwell stuck a pinch of rough-cut tobacco into his jaw and began to chew. "I've hunted near every kind of animal there is," he said, "including the two-legged kind. Way I figure it, if this thing has got a brain, then it can be lured and trapped and killed, same as anything else."

Phylis stared at him. "Hap, we're not talking about an animal here. This is not a physical being."

The old man folded his arms and spat contemptuously into a plastic-lined wastebasket. "Don't make no difference," he said, looking pointedly at Rick. "We already know what it wants, so that's our bait. All we got to do is figure out what'll kill it." He paused, squinting down at Rick's bandages and the IV line running into his arm. "How do you feel now?" he asked.

Rick twisted uncomfortably in the bed and grinned sheepishly. "Like I've been trampled by a herd of elephants."

"Good," he said, pinching off the clear plastic IV line and disconnecting it at the bag. He slipped an arm behind Rick's shoulders and raised him to a full sitting position. "Because the first thing we're going to do is get you out of this damned place before Doc Franjee changes his mind about putting you in a rubber room where the bogeyman can get to you. Think you can walk?"

Rick swung his feet over the side of the bed, suddenly aware that the short hospital gown he was wearing was *all* he was wearing. Phylis stared at his exposed crotch and grinned lewdly. "Well now, there's one good reason not to let the demon have you," she quipped.

"Hey, cut that out and find my clothes!" he yelped, pulling the sheet over his lap and blushing furiously.

The sky was still leaden and the last traces of daylight were fading as Hapwell and Phylis helped Rick into the cab of the old man's pickup. During the hour-long drive back toward Silver Peak, the two of them recounted the story of their search for Ryan and the discovery of his half-frozen corpse in the forest. Unable to move the body, and concerned with their own survival, they had made their way to the Raynor house with the intent of holing up there until the storm abated. Discovering Rick's Cherokee in the drive, they had searched the empty house, then drove to the bungalow where they had found him bleeding to death on the snow-covered balcony. Phylis had stopped the bleeding with a tourniquet while Hapwell had braved the storm in order to retrieve the horses. They had wrapped him in blankets and packed his unconscious body down to Silver Peak, where an ambulance had been summoned. By the time they'd gotten him to the hospital, according to Franjee, Rick had been within minutes of death. His life had been saved by a massive blood transfusion and fifty stitches to his badly lacerated arm.

"The only thing I want to know," Hapwell asked when the story was finished, "is how in the hell you got all the way back to the bungalow in that storm without your Jeep."

Rick squeezed his eyes shut. "I honestly don't know," he said, his head pounding. He had been straining to come up with some logical explanation for his seemingly miraculous transport from the Lodge since he had learned of it. "Maybe you should have let Franjee put me in that rubber room after all," he finally said. "Maybe I really am crazy and just dreamed up the whole thing."

Hapwell shook his head, unconvinced. "That still doesn't explain what your Jeep was doing at the old lodge." He reached into his coat pocket and withdrew Harold Raynor's ivory-handled buck knife, tossing it casually onto the Chevy's rattling dashboard. "And if you dreamed the whole thing, where did this come from?"

Rick reached out with his good hand to touch

the gleaming metal blade, which seemed to glow malevolently in the dim reflection of the dash lights.

"Don't you see?" said Phylis, placing her hand on his. "This proves you weren't dreaming. Somehow you were transported from the Raynor place back to the bungalow. Transported by some real physical force."

"Oh Christ!" he breathed.

Cheated.

Robbed of its victim.

Initially the great demon's rage had known no bounds. Screeching and bellowing in a frenzy of destruction, it had whirled above the black waters of the storm-tossed lake for hours, whipping the tortured surface into frothy torrents, of freezing spray, piling layer upon layer of ice onto the hated human habitation until, just before dawn, the Lodge had stood glittering like a glacier at the end of the lake. Squinting against the pain of the first gray light on the horizon, the demon had watched with grim satisfaction as a mighty groan echoed against the surrounding mountains. The massive redwood beam supporting the high roof finally splintered beneath the load and Harold Raynor's beloved lodge had collapsed in on itself like the rotten husk of a worm-eaten apple.

Its blinding anger somewhat abated by the destruction of the dwelling, the demon had lurched into a cave high on the side of a mountain overlooking the lake, filling the darkest recesses of the cavern with a wave of black hatred so pure and crystalline cold that it had shattered the peaceful hibernation of a large black bear, bursting the poor dumb creature's heart in a single instant of profound terror.

That had been a night and a day ago.

Now the demon lay in the cave, the black web of its essence still wrapped around the stiffening hulk of the bear's great body. Its reason had returned some hours ago and it had shunted aside its terrible anger and begun plotting how to recapture its prey.

It allowed itself a small smile, reflecting upon the stupidity of the blundering humans who had snatched Rick Masterson back from the Other Side just moments before the man's soul would have been lost forever. It had watched helplessly from the rafters of the bungalow as the intruders had ministered to Masterson; seen the man's spirit flickering as he hovered between life and death. Knowing intuitively that an attempt to take him then would have pushed the man irrevocably to his death, and permanently beyond its reach, it had raged out into the stormy night to vent its frustrations.

Calm had finally returned at some point during the long day in the cave, when it had become aware—through the unerring sense that permitted its kind to track their victims anywhere in the cosmos—that the man's physical being had passed its crisis. Deep within the convoluted recesses of its mind, it had seen the flame that was Rick Masterson's soul strengthen and grow steady, and it had known once again that it would have its prize.

Now, viscous strands of stinking black saliva

dripped from its jaws as its delicate olfactory sense reached from the cave and savored the delicious reek of the feast it had so long been denied. The scent of man's essence was growing stronger by the moment and it sensed that its victim was being returned from the distant place where the other humans had taken it. Its mind raced as it laid its new plans. It would have Rick Masterson's soul, yes. But now it would have more. Much more.

The demon would take Masterson in a manner so diabolical and horrible that his every waking moment until the demon delivered him to its hellish masters would be a living nightmare. For, once it had claimed his soul, it intended to have the reporter murder his friends. Slowly. Painfully.

Grinning at the perfection of the revenge it would wreak on those who had attempted to deny it its rightful prey, the thing released the desiccated carcass of the hapless bear and slipped out into the night.

Expanding into a dark cloudlike mass, the demon soared above the snow-covered trees and began to sing its ancient song, directing its voice down into the broad valley below the lake. The song, a seductive skein of clever lies and promises brilliantly interwoven with bits and pieces of unassailable truth and undeniable logic, skipped through the ether, sweet as the call of a nightingale, seeking the mind of one particular human, a human it had carefully probed and measured days earlier.

Hapwell slowed the truck, preparing to turn off the Carson highway and onto the two-lane blacktop leading up to the town of Silver Peak. The old vehicle slid around the turn and clattered onto the icy roadway, gathering speed in order to make it up the first of the steep grades. A narrow side road loomed in the glow of the Chevy's weak headlights. Hapwell flicked a switch beside the sagging sun visor and a spotlight mounted on top of the cab flared to life, flooding the landscape with bright illumination.

Phylis had been sitting on the worn plastic seat beside Rick for the last several minutes, eyes closed and humming softly to herself in the cozy warmth of the cab. Now her eyes suddenly opened and she peered out at the familiar landscape. "Turn off here," she ordered.

"Are you crazy?" Hapwell yelled. "If I slow down now, we'll never make it back up that hill to town." He squinted out at the bumpy track leading off into the sage. "Besides, I know where that damn road goes."

"Don't you see?" she argued. "It may be a way to save him. If we go back to town, the demon will be waiting. It has to know we rescued Rick. We've got to do something it's not expecting."

Hapwell slammed on the brakes and the Chevy lurched onto the bumpy, unplowed side road, its wheels spinning on the frozen surface. "What've you got in mind?" he grunted, straining to keep the wildly jouncing steering wheel under control.

"You said we could trap it," she answered. "Trap it and kill it, or at least hurt it badly enough to make it go away."

The old man goosed the Chevy over a steep rise and slammed on the brakes to keep from sliding into a massive boulder. He somehow got the vehicle under control again and glared at Phylis. "How you figure on doin' that?"

"Remember what Rick told us?" she said. "About the day all of this started. The explosion. Haven't you wondered why the demon didn't just take him then?" She bit her lip, thinking. "And since then, the dark dreams, broken by the Bright Spirit . . . Darkness and light, opposing forces. We can fight this thing—with the light."

Hapwell stared at her for a long moment and a chuckle escaped his whiskered lips. "Well, I'll be damned." He laughed. "Maybe you got something there after all. If we can get it down here."

"We can't do it alone," she said. "We'll have to have help." She peered out into the darkness beyond the reach of the probing spotlight. "Just pray that Janet's home," she said.

"And sober," Hapwell added.

Rick sat between the two of them, attempting to follow their conversation like a spectator at a high-speed tennis match. He was feeling dizzy again and he couldn't think of anything to say. The whole discussion was too ridiculous. You couldn't trap something that existed only in your mind, much less kill it.

Phylis leaned across to squeeze his hand, her perfume filling his nostrils. "Trust me," she assured him. "We'll beat this thing together." She looked into his eyes. "You do trust me, Rick?"

He smiled weakly and nodded, suddenly overcome by her beauty and the love in her voice. He couldn't remember the last time he had trusted anyone, except maybe Jimmy.

The Chevy rounded another curve and pulled to a stop in front of a large house trailer set up beside a log cabin. Rick watched through the windshield as Hapwell and Phylis went to the door and conferred with a pale woman in a granny gown. Three scruffy cats slipped out through the open doorway and disappeared beneath the trailer as the trio talked. Phylis was especially animated, gesturing and pointing into the foothills behind the trailer. Rick tried to smile as the pale woman in the trailer door peered at him and waved timidly. A crooked grin played at the corners of his lips as his eyelids drooped and he fought off an overwhelming desire simply to go to sleep.

CHAPTER 25

The Lure

T H E trailer's overheated living room reeked of cats.

Rick sat in a broken-down recliner looking into the rheumy eyes of Janet McMurty. He felt the woman's bony knees pressing against his and his stomach turned as she blew a cloud of acrid smoke into his face. They had been going at it for hours now—Janet asking him scores of probing questions about his life, his childhood, his views on the afterlife, continuously instructing him to keep his mind perfectly clear, to believe nothing that he saw or heard, trusting only in herself, and Phylis. He had groggily agreed, wishing for nothing more than a few precious minutes of sleep.

Meanwhile Hapwell had been in and out of the trailer half a dozen times, his hands covered with grease, to ask where some object or the other might be found. At some point, the old man had paused for a cup of coffee and he and Phylis had outlined the basic concept of their plan to Rick. He had reluctantly agreed that it might possibly work, even though a part of his fogged brain still refused to admit the hard physical reality of his predicament.

"Do you understand what we must do?" Janet asked for what seemed like the hundredth time.

He nodded weakly, squinting into the darkened room for a glimpse of Phylis or Hapwell. Janet took his chin in her rough, bony fingers and forced his gaze back to hers.

"They've gone on ahead," she said, "to finish the preparations." Without warning, her eyes rolled back into their sockets and her voice changed to a keening, dread-filled singsong. "It is coming for you now," she wailed, "a dark destructive presence, gliding like quicksilver down the mountainside, silent and cold and deadly—"

A choking little scream suddenly bubbled up out of her throat and a fierce shudder ran through her body. She shook herself out of the trance and stared at him in awe. "It wants you, Rick," she murmured. "My God, how it wants!"

"What if . . ." Rick began.

"What if?" She giggled, her mood suddenly and unaccountably brighter than he had seen it. "Sweet Jesus and Mother Mary, what if?"

"I mean," said Rick. "If . . . it doesn't work."

"If what doesn't work?" she demanded.

"The plan, goddammit!" he snapped. "What if the plan doesn't work?"

Janet blinked owlishly and emitted another long hysterical giggle. "Plan? What plan is that, Rick?"

"Hapwell and Phylis's plan," he snapped, suddenly angry. The woman was obviously demented.

Janet smiled, revealing the incongruously perfect set of white teeth behind her cracked lips, and took a deep drag from the yellowed cigarette dangling between her knobby fingers. "There *is* no plan, Rick," she said with frustrating logic. "You know that. We've already discussed that. There can't be a plan in your mind or it won't work." She held the cigarette out, offering it to him. The pungent reek of marijuana assaulted his nostrils.

"Shit," he said, shaking his head in disgust.

"I'm going to fix you a nice cup of herbal tea now," she said, patting him on the cheek and getting to her feet. She consulted a broken alarm clock on a battered end table. "It'll soon be time for us to go."

"Can you at least tell me *where* we're going," he huffed.

Janet shook her head and disappeared into the kitchen. "All you have to do right now is stay awake," she called cheerily. "We don't want that nasty old demon getting back into your head in your weakened condition, do we?" She began clanging pots together in the chipped porcelain sink, humming a tuneless melody and running water into a kettle.

Rick slumped back into the sprung recliner, struggling to keep his eyes open. The others had deliberately not told him any details of their scheme, fearful that the demon would read his thoughts and convincing him—at Janet's added urging—to go along with whatever plan they had concocted. He let his eyelids flutter closed. It was, he thought, a damn good thing he trusted Phylis. Hell, it was more than that. He loved her. . . .

* * *

The demon strode swiftly down the deep narrow canyon leading from the lake, waves of radiant energy from its dark passage reverberating off the steep walls, touching off a series of rumbling avalanches in its wake and scattering small terrified creatures before it. The smell of the prey was strong in its olfactories and its leathery chest swelled with the exhilaration of the hunt. Never before had it felt so magnificently powerful.

It paused at the terminus of the canyon, ascending to a tumbled outcropping of boulders and squinting in annoyance at the twinkling lights of the town below. Rotating its cunningly pointed ears, it tested the freezing air for sympathetic vibrations from the woman it had earlier assailed with its song. Its hideous face split into a triumphant grin as the seductive strains of its own dark melody drifted faintly back to it on the howling wind.

The humans' feeble trap was being set on a windswept defile far from the hateful lights of the town.

The trap that was, of course, fatally flawed.

Shrieking its joyful hunting cry into the raging storm, the mighty creature lumbered forward, its huge scaled claws crashing down to pulverize several car-sized boulders in its path.

CHAPTER 26

The Trap

T H E horror show.

Rick lay on the blood-soaked floor of the lodge's upper corridor. Phylis's lifeless body was stretched beside him, the double-bladed ax protruding from her chest. Sara and the girl in the yellow slicker stood watching helplessly from a cone of golden light as something black and cold and evil glided toward him, clawed hands reaching, eyes glowing red. Something roared in the distance, a powerful throbbing that shook the ground beneath him. Bitter tears burned his cheeks and he wished he had lived a better life, been more caring and forgiving and loving.

Too late for regrets. Much too late . . .

The roar grew louder.

He opened his eyes.

The noise was overpowering, a flat, blatting series of explosions echoing like machine-gun fire off dimly perceived walls of soaring gray stone.

Wind-driven flakes of snow whipped about his face and he turned his head to see a strange figure draped in a patterned shawl before the glow of a single flickering candle. Janet crouched before him, chanting, her eyes rolled back in her head, the gnarled, dirty fingers working in her lap. Her strident voice was nearly drowned out by the thundering sound filling the strange amphitheater.

Rick shook his head, trying to remember where he was. He vaguely recalled having drunk the vile tea that Janet had pressed insistently to his lips in a chipped and filthy ceramic mug. He had gagged on it, spilling half of the scalding liquid down his chest, then, leaning heavily upon the crazed woman, had allowed himself to be led outside into the storm. He had paused once to vomit into the snow before stumbling around to the back of the trailer, where an ancient Cadillac waited beneath a sagging lean-to.

He had laughed hysterically at the faded psychedelic colors emblazoned across the car's crumpled fenders and soaring tail fins, before falling—or being pushed—into the front seat.

Scowling impatiently, Janet had slammed the heavy door shut on him, then slipped behind the steering wheel and started the car. The monstrous vehicle had shuddered once, belching clouds of greasy smoke as the powerful engine rumbled to life. She had backed the car expertly away from the trailer, then guided it out onto a barely visible track leading up into the mountains.

Rick vaguely remembered clinging to the tattered leather door pull as the heavy car had lurched into the driving snow. The madwoman had been humming a nameless tune that lulled him into a deep, trancelike sleep.

Rick tried to sit up.

He discovered that he was bound hand and foot, unable to move beneath the faded flannel blanket that had been casually tossed over his body. Turning his head from side to side, he scanned his gloomy surroundings. He lay in the center of a vast, rocky floor, open to the sky and circumscribed by dark, ragged walls. Huge shapes of iron that might have been the remains of giant machines shadowed the walls surrounding the pit. Nearer to where he was tied, a gantry of blackened girders pointed crookedly to the sky.

Hapwell and Phylis stood beneath the skeletal construction. Both were gazing at him.

"Phylis," he yelled. "What are you doing?"

She turned away.

"Hapwell, for God's sake!"

The old man looked at him, then raised his eyes, squinting at something in the far distance. Rick turned his head, following the old man's gaze. Something black and monstrous was slipping down the farthest stone wall, blotting out the machinery, the boulders, and the floor as it advanced.

"Come to us," Janet screamed, her wispy hair flying in the arctic breeze that streamed ahead of the advancing blackness. She threw her shawl to the ground, exposing her grotesque naked body to the approaching specter. "Accept this unworthy sacrifice that we may be one with thine perfect darkness," she howled.

"No!" Rick screamed, straining at his bonds.

Coal-bright eyes burned into his soul from the suffocating black mass as the demon rose up and towered over him. A triumphant shriek of demonic laughter pealed through the air, dulling the roar that already filled the pit.

"Now!" He heard the single word screamed out above the din, turned his head to see Phylis reaching for a lever affixed to the side of a huge yellow machine.

The thing was hovering directly above him, its foul breath enveloping him in a noxious vapor that bespoke things long dead. Something moved at the limits of his peripheral vision and he slowly swung his head back to see Janet reaching down to her naked feet, lifting a rusty double-barrel shotgun to her shoulder.

"Do not interfere," she screamed, leveling the barrels not at the demon, but at Phylis.

"Janet!" Phylis screamed in horror as Hapwell pulled her clumsily to the ground.

"Fools!" Janet screeched. "Can't you see His magnificent perfection?" She stared up with adoring eyes at the hovering figure of the demon, then lowered the shotgun, training the rusty barrels on the crouching figures of Phylis and Hapwell. "His will cannot be denied." She smiled.

Rick heard himself screaming as the demon's triumphant laugh echoed through the quarry with redoubled intensity. Burning eyes glittered against the starless sky, and a dark, grasping claw descended toward his face. The last thing he saw as the cold blackness enveloped him was Janet McMurty. Eyes bulging behind her wire-rim glasses, flecks of spittle dripping onto her leathery breasts, she squeezed down on the shotgun's twin triggers and a searing bolt of fire exploded into the night. Janet's head vaporized in a pink cloud and the ruined shotgun, its smoking breech peeled back like a banana, clattered to the rocky floor.

The dark claw hovered uncertainly above Rick's face as Janet's body flopped wetly to the ground. In the distance, he was dimly aware of Phylis leaping to her feet and throwing her weight against the lever on the side of the huge yellow machine.

The massive diesel generator belched black smoke and the steady throb of its engine deepened to a deafening roar as the rocky quarry exploded in a burst of blinding quartz-hard light. All about the vast perimeter, bank upon bank of dazzling industrial lamps flared to life atop rusting iron towers.

The demon, a thing of absolute cold and darkness, screamed as sixty million candlepower of hot, unyielding light lanced into its essence, a burning hell of brightness that surrounded it on all sides. It whirled about madly on the stones, seeking to escape as it had once before, in the unexpected flare of the terrorist's phosphorous grenade that had prevented it from snatching its prey from a war-torn European alleyway.

Then, however, there had been the cool darkness of the deep, tunneled doorway to protect it from the deadly light. Here, in this barren open space of rocks and iron, there was no shelter. Hot wisps of oily vapor were rising from its scaled back and it realized that it was dying. Surely its enemies could not have been so clever.

Surely not.

The demon burst into flame, the hard cruel wind of the growing storm hurrying its destruction. Clouds of thick black smoke shot through with orange fire whipped away into the roiling clouds above the quarry.

Rick Masterson stared up into the blinding glare of the arc lights and saw the face of the girl in the yellow slicker smiling at him. Her soft voice rang inside his head, reducing the screams of the dying demon to a tiny background squeal. "I was very wrong about you, Rick. There is hope for you after all."

Her golden image slowly dissolved into the flaring illumination blotting out the darkling sky.

"An abandoned strip mine?" Rick adjusted his position against the pillows in the blessedly comfortable brass bed above the Silver Peak Saloon and allowed Phylis to prop another soft cushion behind him. "How did you ever come up with that?"

She laughed and pointed to Hapwell, who was tilted precariously against the wall in a straight-backed chair, sipping Jack Daniel's. "His idea," she said.

Hapwell shrugged. "Wasn't me come up with the idea of burnin' out the dark bogeyman with light," he said. "I just figured we oughta have *lots* of light and I remembered the company that run that old strip mine up behind Janet's place back in the fifties. At the time they bragged they'd laid in enough generators and arc lamps to light up Yankee Stadium ten times over." He laughed.

"Only trouble was gettin' 'em runnin' after all these years. Ended up ruinin' the battery out of my pickup," he added meaningfully.

"Well, you both scared the hell out of me," said Rick. "For a couple of minutes there I thought you'd both turned on me with all that sacrifice stuff."

"You can blame Janet for that," said Phylis. "She told us that since the demon could read your thoughts, she was afraid if you knew what we were planning, it would know, too. That's how she talked us into going along with the sacrifice ritual."

Rick stared at her. "You *knew* about that all along?"

She nodded. "The original plan was to lure the demon up to the quarry by letting it think she'd decided to turn you over to it. She'd seen the thing in a vision and she convinced me it was the only way."

"It weren't until she pulled that old blunderbuss on us that we realized she really planned on goin' through with it," Hap interjected. "It was just damn lucky for all of us that old Janet wasn't the world's tidiest person. I looked over that antique shotgun of hers afterward and found both barrels plugged up tighter than Dick's hatband."

Rick frowned. "Plugged? Plugged with what?"

Hapwell laughed and dug in his shirt pocket for a pinch of crumbly brownish fiber. "Best I can tell, it's marijuana. Real old marijuana. I figure she must've hid her a stash in there years ago and forgot all about it."

Rick smiled ruefully. "Well, they do say drugs are hazardous to your health." He yawned.

Phylis sat on the edge of the bed and placed her arm around him. "So, Mr. Masterson, I finally got you into my bed after all. What do you suggest we do now?"

Hapwell harrumphed noisily and got to his feet, stretching theatrically. "Well, guess I'd better get me some shut-eye. Gotta figure out something to tell old Eli the deputy in the mornin' so's he can go up to that mine and discover what's left of Janet without clapping us all in the crazy house."

He left, closing the door behind him, and Phylis looked meaningfully at Rick. "Well?"

"I don't know if I'm in shape to do much of anything at the moment," he confessed.

"That's okay." She smiled, reaching over to place her lips softly against his. "We've got plenty of time now. All the time in the world."

Epilogue

T H E dark sub-creature lay coiled in Ryan's frozen brain. Neither sleeping nor waking, it had fallen into a patient torpor that had lasted for as many days as it had taken for the heavy snowfall to bury the man's body completely. At first, it had waited fearfully for the return of the magnificent demon in whose service it had so miserably failed, resigning itself to being viciously and painfully destroyed.

Many more days passed and still it had lain quietly, trapped within its frozen host, suffering the gnawing hunger of the whole dark winter and reflecting on the many things it had learned from the great demon—the demon whose screams of agony had echoed through the world the day after Bull Ryan's physical being had ceased to function. As it waited, the dark thing pondered the significance of that scream, concluding at last that the demon's failure to return and destroy it could mean only one thing: the greater creature had itself been destroyed.

It finally smiled, realizing that its superior had been a creature like itself, larger and older perhaps, but no wiser or less vulnerable to the effects of its own greed and stupidity. That realization prompted the sub-creature to decide that it, too, might someday possess the strength and cunning to roam the world at will, feasting upon the choicest souls, one day perhaps even presenting itself at the gates of hell, bearing rich gifts for the dark minions of the nether regions. It would not, however, suffer itself to be destroyed. It would be even more clever and cunning than the old demon, which must have grown lazy and fat after centuries of uncontested superiority.

The thing in Ryan's brain had known deprivation, had learned to survive under the most hostile conditions. And it determined never again to allow itself to become complacent or overly eager

A sudden warm spell struck the mountains of the eastern Sierra in May. Patches of blue water began to appear on the frozen crust of Spirit Lake and the surrounding mountains resounded with the roar of spring avalanches. A few days later, Bull Ryan's twisted remains showed above the snow for the first time and the elemental began to stir, its depleted energy reserves fueled by the slowly seething juices of the decomposing body.

Although the hunger burned within it like a living thing, it resisted the urge to slip into the inviting warmth of any of the beasts that came to gnaw upon the carcass, knowing that other men would soon come in search of its rotting host, men who would carry it back to the dwelling places of humanity, which it now realized were the key to increasing its powers.

On the ninety-fifth day of its captivity, the dark thing heard the sound of snowmobiles entering the forest from the adjoining meadow at the north end of Spirit Lake.

The thing shivered in anticipation of the truly evil deeds it would do.

It coiled, preparing to spring.

MICHAEL O'ROURKE is a screenwriter and novelist who lives in Southern California with his wife Sally. This is his first novel for HarperPaperbacks.